THE SHINING ISLE

The Traveler Series
Book 2

Ly de Angeles

2nd edition (expanded) 2016
3rd edition Australasia 2019 (Ingram Spark)
First Printing, 2006, Llewellyn Worldwide, USA
ISBN 9780648502586

Editors– The Albion/Lestrange Family

Cover – Diogo Lando © 2013 www.diogolando.com/

Author – www.lydeangeles.com

ALSO BY DE ANGELES –

The Way of the Goddess, Prism/Unity, UK, 1987
The Way of Merlyn, Prism/Unity, UK, 1990
Witchcraft Theory and Practice, Llewellyn, USA, 2000
The Feast of Flesh and Spirit, Wildwood Gate, AUS, 2001
When I See the Wild God, Llewellyn Worldwide, USA, 2002
Pagan Visions for a Sustainable Future, Llewellyn, USA, 2004
The Quickening, Llewellyn Worldwide, USA, 2005
The Shining Isle, Llewellyn Worldwide, USA, 2006
Tarot Theory and Practice, Llewellyn Worldwide, USA, 2007
Magdalene, 2012
The Feast of Flesh and Spirit 2nd edition, 2013
Initiation | A Memoir, 2016
The Skellig | A Shapechanger Tale, 2017
Witch | For Those Who Are, 2018
Genesis | The Future, 2019
The Quickening (Australia) 2019

THE SHINING ISLE

Magical Realism

The Traveler Series
Book 2

Ly de Angeles

"You make a wasteland and call it peace!"
Calgacus, chieftain of the Caledon
Albion, circa 84CE

PART ONE

Samhain

CHAPTER ONE

HOLLY TREMENHERE WAS DESCENDED FROM an ancient line of tribal kings and queens but a couple of thousand years had eliminated all respect for such things except in secret places.

Fat lot of good it does me anyway, she mused as the ferry carved a wake through the lowering sea.

She stood as far up towards the prow as she could get, her back-pack acting as a pillow between her body and the steel railing. The big bag kept the bite of the fierce, salt laden autumn wind from sending her inside with the other passengers where she did not want to be.

She pulled her hat as far down over her ears as she could and adjusted her scarf—already stiff with brine—that was wound around the lower half of her face.

The important thing about that wind was that it almost blew the anxiety from her and it was also the cleanest thing she'd smelled in years.

She unconsciously felt for the small, soft leather pouch that she habitually wore on a long thong beneath her clothing. It had been her aunt's secret gift to her on her twelfth birthday and contained two copper pennies, three small, downy raven feathers tied together with red thread and one tiny white stone from the heart of the island towards which she was headed. She'd certainly ask her aunt about the meaning of the contents on this visit. No one else knew about it, not even Patrick; she'd been very careful about that.

She attempted to ignore the gnawing little rat-voice of guilt at having left him without telling him, but she'd lived with him long enough to know that he'd try to talk her out of it again, and she might just have given in again. Once upon a time she'd thought he'd be enough for her—that because he loved her she would at last forget how meaningless everything seemed. But living together had become intolerable: football, meals on time, beer at the pub, the movies occasionally, his mates, their wives or girlfriends who worried about what to wear, small talk or television, sex at bedtime. That and a nine-to-five job that varied little and required nothing but a pleasant manner dealing with the public.

No. Holly had to get to Mim.

FROM A DISTANCE THE ISLAND APPEARED to be a roiling mass of cloud, an illusion of earth and mountain, and she moaned a small sound of joy at the sight of it.

How long since she'd been here? She was twenty eight now and it'd been just before she and Patrick had moved in together. Five years? Six? Yeah, six, (how could she forget) because it had been the same year that her grandfather had died, her mother had remarried what's-his-name and moved to Bainbridge, and Holly landed the job on the front desk at HNC Insurance.

Dull. So dull. With the wind stinging her eyes and making them water she found herself skimming over the years looking for the sparks, knowing full well they weren't there, and working very hard at keeping the constriction out of her throat and ignoring the sneer of her personal inner demon.

THE FERRY ENTERED INTO THE MISTS of Inishrún at just past 3:30 in the afternoon – early enough for its return to the mainland before a predicted squall. It maneuvered between fishing boats, traditional curraghs and past a black-sailed Hooker before mooring alongside the low rock jetty with a thud of tires against stone.

Holly was the only non-islander to disembark and the moment her feet touched the land she felt it—a shudder, some kind of blessing, an inhuman yet pleasant touch—just like both times before. She shivered slightly with the sense of it, unwound the scarf from her face, shouldered her pack and walked along the wharf to the only shop along the foreshore, a little multi-purpose tourist mart selling everything from buckets and spades for the kiddies to cheap wine, handmade sandwiches and serious fishing equipment for the professional angler. It had never seen a decent trade, what with only one stone circle and one sacred well and no hotel or entertainment venue other than the pub and the community hall. The mainlanders who considered the two hour ferry trip worthwhile were few, and usually older folk, always on their way to somewhere more spiritually significant, and always in the summer months.

Holly walked at some distance behind the other six people who'd traveled with her: four women, their shopping bags bulging, their outdated overcoats buttoned up tight over thickset bodies; sensible shoes, floral patterned scarves tied around escaping wisps of hair, and two men, obviously brothers, wafting the smell of fish and whisky. There was something peculiar about them all that she couldn't quite work out until after they'd gone in their separate directions: all walked with straight backs and an uncommon grace.

Their curious sideways glances in her direction, as they'd moved through the unmanned turnstile, were understandable. Holly came in at just under a hundred and sixty three centimeters, was slender from regular early morning tai-bo classes, had thick, dark lustrous hair that presently escaped from where she'd shoved it under the rust colored hat and, with the exception of eyes that were a lighter shade of brown, resembled a younger version of her aunt.

She didn't think that they'd know her from her previous visit because, last time, she, her mother, her brother Steven, her sister Alice and Alice's new baby, had made the crossing on a privately hired launch. They'd all piled into the island's only taxi and gone straight to Aunt Mim's for a weekend yelling session. What she hadn't realized was that the driver had noted Holly's uncanny resemblance to their wise woman and had mentioned it to someone, who had mentioned it to someone else, until the entire community was aware of the visitors and the dark girl amongst them, and that they never forget. Consequently their glances held more than mere curiosity—a knowing—but they hid their smiles until a more appropriate time presented itself.

The two days of that earlier visit had been horrible. The sisters' grandfather had died unceremoniously, two weeks prior, in the nursing home where he had lived with advanced Alzheimer's. Angie—Holly's mother—had had to deal with the funeral arrangements on her own. Mim didn't have the phone on at her house and she wouldn't have come away from the island, anyway, detesting the old man as she did. Turned out he'd had money invested and had bequeathed it to his two remaining children— Mim and Angie—and Angie was determined that by rights it should be hers alone because who else had done all the running around both at first, when he'd been diagnosed, and later with the death and all?

Mim had said no way; that she deserved anything he left her due to the way he'd been towards her when she was young—a story unknown to Holly—before she had disowned him and moved away to live a real life.

Angie hadn't let up, so Holly hadn't had a chance to do more than hug her aunt when they'd first arrived. She'd spent her time away from the arguments, out along the cliffs, exploring the deep, moss swathed caves and the secrets that the island whispered to her. Until her brother came looking for her when they were due to leave. She'd never had a chance to ask about the talisman.

Holly dumped her damp backpack gratefully into the already open boot of the old Vauxhall that served as a cab before climbing in next to the driver.

"You goin' up Mim's?" He beamed at her, his round face ruddy and lined with years of too much drink, his whole head haloed in a flyaway mop of grizzled grey hair that extended down into a bushy beard and moustache.

"Ah...Yeah." She didn't feel in the least like entering into conversation, let alone be friendly, and ground her teeth into her bottom lip to avoid saying anything offensive.

"Ev'body calls me Woolly," he grunted, sensing her mood as he ground the old car into gear, "an' no I ain't got no idea why that'd be."

As they pulled out along the narrow strip of cobbles that led through the one street village he began talking about himself and anybody else he could think of, and by the time they broached the relative darkness of a track, lined thickly on either side with ash and thorn and elder, Holly doubted that any of the local folk remained unscathed.

They arrived at the cottage twenty minutes later. He pulled on the handbrake, got out of the car, opened the boot, surprising her with his height. Somehow, all scrunched up in the driver's seat in layers of warm clothing, she'd had an illusion of him as girthy but not tall. He was disconcertingly enormous.

His eyes sparkled and he raised an eyebrow as he passed her the case. He tipped his cap and held out his hand for the fare.

"Bound to see ya 'gain *mo chroì*," he smiled, turning away with an invitation to have a pint at the pub with him while she was around.

Holly ignored him, dropped her backpack to the ground and breathed the isolation and cleanness that the land emitted. "I, ah... I guess so," but he had already folded himself fluidly back into the cab.

THE ISLAND OF INISHRÚN WAS forty seven miles long and somewhere between sixteen and twenty miles wide. It was bordered by fortress-like, potentially unscaleable cliffs for the most part, all except for three miles on either side of the village that seemed as though it had just collapsed down on itself in some distant cataclysm, the huge granite rock slabs laying one upon the other like a fallen deck of cards. This was the most easterly aspect and the bay itself was relatively sheltered. Three high, steep hills (that the inhabitants called the Mothers) sheltered pasture land where long haired, black faced sheep reigned as monarchs of the glen, their thick silken fleece being their main sacrifice.

Amidst the dense, untouched copses of forest, and high up on the escarpments, deer still grazed—protected by tradition—and badgers, voles, small tan pigs and other creatures, rooted amongst the undergrowth, rustling unseen, or cawed, trilled and hooted in the thick overhead canopy.

The trade of the island was almost solely from fishing and wool but its heart was its music and the hidden mysteries of its faith to which outsiders were oblivious and which the heavily Christian mainland would have condemned had the people not kept it precious through their silence over the centuries.

THIS MYSTERY WAS WHY MIM had come here thirty years before. She'd met a man named Connor niUlchubhán, a Traveler.

He and his peculiar assortment of companions had camped outside the soulless steelworks town of Middleborough where she'd lived in ritual anxiety and futility with her sister, two brothers and her mother, all dwelling within the unpredictable shadow of George Tremenhere, her grandfather; an often brutal man, careless of his family and prone to bouts of severe alcoholic violence.

The Travelers had set up down by the river and she'd snuck out before anyone in the house awakened, biking her way in the freezing predawn to find them.

She'd been seventeen years old.

THERE WERE ABOUT TWO DOZEN people in their troupe and even at that early hour many were awake and gathered around open fires preparing the first food of the day.

Mostly ratty old cars and vans, and one dubious looking double-decker bus that had seen better days, were parked hotchpotch around the clearing.

Mim hadn't known what to do when she'd arrived. She'd felt very silly at her own impetuousness and had simply stood astride her
pushbike in a state of agitation.

Connor had been the first to acknowledge her. He'd detached himself from a huddle of others standing or sitting around what seemed to be a main hearth, and had sauntered towards her. He didn't appear any older than her (although that was an illusion) and was of middle height. He wore Levi's and scuffed steel capped boots, a nondescript blue pullover under a thick sheepskin jacket and a cream wool beanie pulled down over his ears. He wore his hair, as black as crows' wings, in two long braids that hung down to just past his chest—Mim would later discover that this marked him as a warrior—and he had odd, faded tattoos on his cheeks that looked like birds in flight. He'd kept his hands in the pockets of his jeans as he approached her, his shoulders hunched against the cold, and his eyes intent upon the ground as he walked.

He'd stopped right up close to her and raised his face with a quirk to his lips and laughter in eyes a disturbing shade of dark green that reminded Mim of a deep pool in a forest somewhere. "Are you lost, love?"

Mim had stammered something stupid—she could never afterwards recall what it was—but he'd turned back towards the camp calling *C'mon then*, over his shoulder and she'd left her bike where it was and waded after him through the thick dew covered grass.

At the fire Connor squatted down and poured her a steaming mug of tea, adding sugar unasked, handing it to her with a gesture indicating *sit*.

A few of the others had smiled and nodded in her direction but were too deep in conversation, in a language Mim couldn't understand, to pay her any attention.

After what seemed about an hour the birds began their dawn chorus and the whole campsite wound down its talk until the people were utterly silent, many with their eyes closed as though listening intently to the voices amongst the overhead canopy.

"What are they doing?" she'd whispered to Connor.

"Can't you hear it?"

"The birds?"

"What they're sayin'; the beauty."

She'd closed her eyes also, shocked that she'd never stopped and just listened.

SHE HADN'T BEEN ABLE TO KEEP FROM staring around herself at the strangeness of it all. The majority of the Travelers dressed in an odd assortment of clothing that looked as though it spanned the fashion of several centuries, and most of them had tattoos of some kind on much of their exposed skin. They reminded her, she'd thought, of something between rock stars and gypsies; while a scant few dressed almost like working folk. Almost.

Connor's close proximity unnerved her the most. He sat right beside her so that their thighs and shoulders touched, and it had brought a heat to her face and an unrecognized sensation to her belly. Once or twice as she'd sipped her tea, he'd turned to look at her and she'd been trapped in his eyes each time. She'd been certain he knew the effect he had on her.

The sun had just begun to penetrate the valley and shaft, in weak crisscrosses, through the branches of the trees that lined the river bank, dispensing the predawn chill, as more of the fey entered the clearing from caravans and other vehicles, bringing supplies to make up their morning meals.

"Sorry. What did you say?" She'd been lost in her own thoughts and it had taken her a moment to realize that one of the women sitting close by had spoken to her.

"You planning on staying?" The woman's hair was dressed in hundreds of black braids, each with a small bronze ring at its end, and her light grey eyes were ancient and haunting. She wore a large black sweater and baggy tweed trousers that looked like a man's pants and her feet were bare despite the cold.

"I..." Mim had stood as though to leave. "I didn't mean to interrupt or anything," and the woman looked as though she'd been about to laugh.

"Where's your gear?" Connor had whispered softly.

"I... I didn't bring anything. I just... I don't know why I came. Honestly."

The woman got to her feet and walked towards her, brushing leaves from her clothing before holding out her hand in greeting. "I'm Brighid..."

As Mim shook it a sense of acceptance flowed through her; a sense of kindness. They'd been eye to eye—same height, same lean body.

"And these are some of my company, and you *do* know why you came."

17

Mim *had* known. She could almost taste the magic that all at the campsite exuded. She'd wanted this.

"I don't think I can just up and leave Middleborough though." She whispered this, half afraid that she'd been wrong in sensing that she was being invited to stay.

"It's all easy, *mo chroì*," Brighid said, stretching, before walking off in the direction of the double-decker bus. "You've got until tonight to decide."

"What happens then?" But Brighid was too far away to hear her.

Connor looped his arm through hers and led her across the grass in the direction of where she'd left her bike. "'Bout sunset the cops'll turn up and send us on our way. Your town always does it same each time. Now let's go about getting your stuff."

"Oh, okay," was all she had to say. Her mind was in turmoil. It was true. The small voice in the deep places in her head had talked about the romance of just taking off with a bunch of Travelers without a care in the world but it had been easy to ignore until the words were actually spoken.

"Stay," Connor whispered into her hair, reading her thoughts as they pulled the bike off the ground.

She'd stood still, feeling the warmth of him, close to her, before turning in the direction of the camp.

MIM'S SUBSTANTIAL COTTAGE WAS of local stone, whitewashed, with a deeply sloping shingle roof strung about with ropes. Each rope held a fair sized rock attached to the ends for those few times in the winter months when the wind off the western ocean tore across the island threatening anything not tied down. It was situated at the end of the overgrown lane that led onto a small meadow on the edge of several miles of heath. To the west was the seemingly endless ridge that guarded the valley from the worst of the winds and, far off to the right, was a forest so thick that, to the untrained eye, it appeared impenetrable. It was a source of abundant game and wildlife that existed mostly undisturbed, although an occasional meal other than fish hunted by the local inhabitants, especially at the feasts of the sacred days. Close to the house was a small orchard of gnarly apple, pear and quince trees looking like they'd been planted forever ago. They formed a circle around an ancient walnut tree. Across the meadow, right out on its own where tame grasses met wild, was an unnaturally round hill, that Holly thought man made, graced by twenty trees, each different from the others and planted in a circle at its summit.

She suspected that the mound might be hollow like some of those she'd seen once or twice on the mainland but on both previous visits her aunt had warned her away from the place; she wasn't to climb it or go exploring anywhere near it and she was warned never to talk about it, or the standing stones, to anyone outside of the island. She remembered asking why, the last time they were there, and Mim had muttered something about the cliffs being safer (which she knew was not true as they were perilous indeed), and the fairies making her life a misery, before her mother had interfered to continue the money argument.

"Anyone home?" she called, but no one answered.

The wind picked up and a long feather of gun-metal nimbostratus moved in over the fortress-like ridge that bordered the coast to the nor 'west in the direction of an imposing, blocky circle of standing stones haunting the base of the escarpment and from which hewn steps scaled the rock face of the cliff.

From that direction Holly could just make out the figure of her aunt riding a pale grey horse at what must be full gallop, two huge dogs bounding alongside.

She shivered involuntarily and pulled her coat tighter around herself. She dragged the heavy backpack the rest of the way to the cottage.

MIM HADN'T CHANGED IN all the intervening years. Holly thought this a little weird, but then she could have used some of her father's inheritance to get cosmetic work done. She wasn't about to ask her aunt this early into the friendship.

Mim had known who Holly was straight away. When she rode up to the house she slid easily from the bare back of the horse and straight into an embrace with her niece as though she'd been expecting her. The bloody great dogs—one an Irish wolfhound named Oberon and Harry, some mix of bull-mastiff and a few other breeds but equally as enormous—near knocked Holly from her feet in enthusiasm at their new visitor and everyone was all a'tumble as they made their way into the warm and exciting kitchen beyond the back door.

There were racks of drying herbs and assorted unrecognizable other bits hanging from a wooden lattice suspended from the ceiling by ropes and pulleys, and others living in pots by the large southerly aspected window, enjoying the last of the day. The walls were lined with shelves on three sides stocked with bottles and jars labeled in a neat, flowing hand and a huge slow combustion stove that took up most of the fourth. This monster was banked up against the impending cold of the island night and was the source of the pleasurable atmosphere in the room.

Mim showed Holly through the house and up the stairs to where three doors opened onto bedrooms.

The room into which the two women pulled Holly's bag had its own small balcony looking out over the meadow to the forest in the distance, and a small but very modern ensuite bathroom. The room was decorated in a surprising mix of rustic Persian and art deco that Holly would never have thought to put together but that worked to provide a sensual earthiness, complimenting the harshness of the whitewashed stone walls. The bed was an old fashioned four poster covered in a blood-red velvet canopy while the bedding was a contemporary brown-on-brown that could have looked stark but didn't. Surprisingly the linen had been turned back, again, very weird, as though the visit had been anticipated.

"I'll leave you to get settled," Mim said. "When you're ready come on downstairs and we'll talk. You drink coffee or tea or something else?"

"I'd kill for a good coffee." Holly pulled a face of desperation which made her aunt chuckle.

"Then I'll be makin' you happy I figure," and she closed the door quietly, leaving Holly to unpack and explore her room.

THEY TALKED FOR HOURS—WELL Holly did most of it while her aunt listened, stroking the heads of her great big dogs that were nestled in her lap, asking only the occasional question. All the despair, the boredom, the sometimes desperation of what Holly described as a nonsense existence was laid bare. It was as though sitting there, with the storm crashing ominously around the outside of the sanctuary of thick stone walls, shuddering the windows but finding no entry and blanketing the last of the day in an opaque veil of water, they were outside of time and beyond the reach of mortal cares so that, even as she spewed out the reason for her visit, Holly also felt strangely detached.

Mim stood and stretched when it was almost too dark to see. She lit the old gaslights on the kitchen walls and two thick stubby candles that squatted in the center of the table.

"Over there behind that door," she pointed to a low dark oak door half buried in shadow along one wall, "is a pantry. There's a big bag of dry dog food on your left. Can you bring it out while I start on a meal for us? You eat pasta?"

"Anything," Holly agreed, getting stiffly from her chair, glad for the change of subject, embarrassed at having talked about herself for so long, wanting to be useful. When she dragged the bag from the well-stocked pantry, Oberon and Harry were sitting at attention beside their bowls, their tails drumming the floor in unison.

Mim set a large pot of water onto the stove to boil, and piled tomatoes and fresh herbs, garlic and olive oil, onto the table, along with a very large kitchen knife and a wooden chopping block.

"There's wine in there while you're at it," she called to Holly as she returned the dog food to the pantry. "Let's have a glass while I'm cooking, yeah?"

There was indeed wine. A whole rack. Holly grabbed a dusty bottle at random knowing nothing much at all about what went with what. As it was, she chose a fifteen year old cabernet that Mim approved with a nod and a look of surprise. Holly rummaged around in drawers and cupboards until she found a corkscrew, a couple of glasses, plates and other things that she thought necessary for their meal, before sitting back down, uncorking, and pouring them both a glass of the luscious red.

"By the way, I'll be going out later tonight." Mim was settling the pasta into the pot, her back turned to her guest.

"What? In this lot?" Holly indicated the gale.

"It'll have blown itself out within the hour. It isn't winter yet."

"Bad storms in winter?"

"Likely we don't much leave home until we can't stand it, and even then it's like challenging the gods. Anyway, I was going to ask whether you want to join me. There's music down in the village and you'll be glad you did."

"Yeah, maybe…"

"How about you save bein' unhappy till tomorrow?" And she laughed.

Holly took a sip of the wine, amazed at the richness of the taste. That was some kind of quirky logic, she admitted to herself. "Yeah, I'll come. By the way," she added as an afterthought, "I'm sorry to have just turned up the way I did without sending you a letter or anything. I won't stay more than a couple of days; won't get in your way or anything."

Mim turned at that, coming to the table and sitting down. "You'll stay until this shite all works itself into something that it isn't right now."

"I, ah—"

"I knew you were comin' anyway." She raised her glass to clink the younger woman's. "Been waitin' years for you to turn up, *mo chroì*. We got business, you and I."

Holly was confused. Waiting years? Business?

As if reading her mind Mim told her that it'd all come out in its own time and to let it alone for a while. "Let's just go dance for tonight. Can we do that?"

"Sure."

Mim stood and pulled down the big iron frypan from its hook above the stove, waiting until it heated up before pouring in a liberal flow of olive oil and the ingredients from the chopping block. The smell was mouthwatering.

CHAPTER TWO

THE SADDEST DAY OF ALL HAD been when the last person to speak believably of the gods of the land and the sky and the waters, and all the other places and things that mattered, was buried to the mopery of an uncaring clergyman of another faith who managed to get the old man's name wrong twice during the ceremony.

Nuala Tremenhere had sat dry eyed and negligible, in the back row of the claustrophobic little church building, remembering the stories her grandfather had spun of the glory days when their forebears had stood, hand-in-fist with the Welsh and other tribal resistance, against the forces of Rome that had sought to occupy the ancestral lands. They had been royalty in a land of ancient mysteries, affluent with allegiances.

How had it happened? For thousands of years her family had been host to Travelers from distant lands, had held the sea ports from invasion, and had worked with the traders from here and elsewhere creating a lucrative and affable territory. Their people had mined the tin for which they were legendary and had held court to merchants and mystics, dignitaries and seafarers from throughout the known world. They had joined houses with those of the Holy Isle and with clans from Eire and as far north as the tribal Picts whose appearance shaped who they were to become.

How had it happened? *It just does,* she mused. But it was insidious just the same. And the creeping apathy of the conquered had slowly eroded her ancestors' identity until even the memories and legends were treated with disdain in the most amongst them.

The first wave of attacks and subordination had driven many of the indigenous people across the sea to the west where they were accepted as refugees, settled inoffensively, and were absorbed into the common dye. But the second wave—taking place in Nuala's own time—was of a defeated and insignificant remnant. What was royalty when the Romans had won and the subsequent church government had acquired ownership, of what had once been simply home territory, by whatever means, including murder? What happened to the identity of a people when the barest of bones was all that remained to remember?

Her passage across the Irish Sea was booked for the spring tide; within the week. She would take the stories, the knowledge and magic of the gods, into the future by way of those who came after.

She tenderly stroked her swelling belly willing the child growing within to survive—it mattered not how cruelly it had been conceived—for this was all she had of family as far as she knew.

This does not end here, she thought as she stood and walked the length of the almost empty church.

The clergyman spluttered in disgust as the dead man's last remaining relative spoke a eulogy in reverence of her grandfather's love of all things 'heathen'.

MIM TOLD HOLLY THE STORY OF THEIR six hundred years dead grandmother while they waited for the music to begin. Five minutes into the monologue Connor turned up, as youthful-looking as Holly's aunt, and handsome in an unusual way. He sat beside Mim, putting an arm around her shoulders and hanging his head as though in mourning for the generations long gone, saying nothing throughout.

Holly wondered how her aunt could know such things; such detail about people and events of the past. She had no reason to make it up, but it did seem implausible. Who had told her? She'd ask at a more appropriate time; after all, she hadn't come to the island for fairy stories.

IN THE DARK NIGHT HEWIE Dowd, a short, stocky man of fifty who usually worked with Dairmid Tait down at the bakery, and who was known to be a bit *missing* (except for his skill at simple tasks and what he did tonight), stalked pheasant along the almost unseen trackways of the deep forest. He was allowed, the bird was not his dreaming.

The community of Inishrún had called the quarterly meeting the day before Holly had arrived, to choose the hunters that would gather the meats that the spirits of the land said they could, for the Feast of the Dead two weeks hence. Pheasant was always the first food hunted as it was necessary for it to be bagged and hung for quite a while for it to be sufficiently tender.

The *geasa* of each hunter was considered so that no ill luck befell him or her and no law broken unintentionally. Hewie's dreaming was the fox so he had no problem with pheasants.

He could see in the dark. He already had two birds—their necks wrung after he'd run them down—in the bag slung over his shoulder, and he was after a third. That'd do it; that was his quota.

He was on the very western edge of the forest when he saw the lights from over Mim's way. That stopped him. This should not be. He moved silently out onto the open heath keeping low because the cloud had passed and the moon was big and as fat as she could be, not yet turning to the wane and shadows stood out clear on such a night.

Pinprick lights—torches, he was sure—in a frenzied rock and roll all around the Barrow.

Horror.

Who would do this?

Run away, Hewie. Run as fast as you can to tell the others.

But he didn't dare yet, so he slithered on his belly, mindless of sharp stone and thistle and gorse, until he gained deep within the cover of the trees. He could not change because he had the bag and it would be a dire thing to dishonor the kill by abandoning it, no matter what. The death songs were incomplete; he'd never been able to remember all the words. So he ran as a man and was frustrated by the necessity of it when his true shape would have had him to the village hall in half the time.

The Community Centre was crowded. Anyone who could play an instrument sat shoulder to shoulder on the stage for the gig. There were fiddles and low whistles, tin whistles and two men at the pipes, one on the Uillean and one on the mainland's far north Border Pipe that had to be toned down so as not to drown out everyone else. There were two bodhrán players and Pete Neath moving from double bass to accordion when the tune required, an acoustic guitar, and Maisie Raith on mandolin. Dougal Beag played the plonky old in-house piano that he always claimed and that had probably been here since before the building went up.

There were around two hundred inhabitants of the island, many of whom had gone to other places, once upon a time, in search of adventure, but who had been unable to survive the ways of the mainlanders and had returned to leave, only occasionally, when necessity demanded.

Those not playing music or serving food and drink were dancing. It was impossible not to.

Except Holly. She sat alone, watching. Every so often someone would attempt to coax her from her seat to join the dancing, but she wasn't ready to relax her guard just yet and declined each offer with an inoffensive smile.

She had almost succeeded in putting aside her blues for the evening, because the music wouldn't allow for sadness despite it not being really to her taste, when Hewie burst through the doors in a sweat.

"Lights on the Barrow!"

He pushed his way into the crowd. "Lights on the Barrow!" he called, puffing with exertion. He shoved the bag containing the pheasants into Woolly's arms on his way through the press of bodies.

"Lights. On. The. Barrow!" he yelled as he attempted to pull himself onto the stage.

The music faltered and stopped, and the room became deathly silent as the words sunk in.

Faces turned to Mim.

"Get the hounds." She said it softly, but everyone heard, including Holly, who saw something in her aunt that scared her.

THE PEOPLE MOVED IN A FLUID, unhurried grace, out into the night where many of the dogs were already on their feet, sensing the sudden intensity in the air. Harry stood by the door awaiting Mim's exit but Oberon had already taken off at a run in the direction of home. He was the pack leader of the two and waited for no one, human or otherwise, to make his decisions for him. He knew the word "Barrow". He was fourteen years old, as strong and fit as a three year old and his kind had bred on Inishrún for generations, each successive litter inheriting the knowledge of its forbears.

He covered the twelve miles effortlessly, scenting the strangers long before sighting them, gauging the direction from which they had come to this, his territory. He lay down directly in the path by which they would most likely attempt escape; knowing strategically that humans tended to be predictable even when afraid.

They would not get by him.

CHAPTER THREE

CHARLES FREEMAN HUNG WAY BACK from the others because he felt both nauseous from the boat trip and with a sense that there was something not quite okay about this little adventure.

Professor Frank Harvey, the leader of the expedition, told him stuff it, if you don't keep up just don't do anything stupid like be seen. He and the other six members of his class followed the one member of the team who was into rock-climbing in a big way, and who led the expedition in the harrowing scale up the seaward face of the cliff where they had left him behind.

He was headed back the way they had come, towards the henge where they'd stashed their equipment, only to be confronted by the biggest, scrappiest looking dog he'd ever seen. It had its teeth bared, its hackles up, its front legs stiff and its ears laid dead flat against its head.

Charlie, me ol' son, he thought, sitting down to make himself as small as possible in the scrubby gorse, *jus' give up.*

This whole thing had been a bad idea from the outset and now he was going to be savaged by a bleedin' great wolf.

He chuckled softly at the irony, shaking his head, fumbling with his anorak until he felt the pack of cigarettes. He took one out, heedless of his movements, and lit it with the Zippo that his sister had given him last year for his twenty fifth birthday. The sudden light caused the dog to blink, but otherwise it didn't budge.

This was Charlie's first year in archeology. He'd already done a post-grad in linguistics and religious studies and the follow-up degree seemed like a good idea. Not bad for a red-haired, heavily freckled docker's son—late of the Highlands of Scotland—from the roughest of New Rathmore's downtown where most kids ended up on welfare. He'd signed up for this debacle because field work counted for mega-points towards his grade average. He had been the last of the group to be invited—whispered to as though this was some secret club—just two days before when Toby Saunders had come down sick and a last minute replacement became necessary.

He'd been fueled since he was a kid by dreams of Aladdin and treasure and Raiders of the Lost Ark and had had visions of deciphering the truth of the Western religious mind from a Canopic urn that held the secrets of the universe instead of dried out body parts, or from some ancient cuneiform tablet that no one else could fathom, and that he'd win a Nobel Prize and make his dad prouder than he already was.

He hadn't known, until the boat had been halfway across the channel and the storm had struck with a vengeance, that it was an unsanctioned affair and that he was definitely no sailor. In fact he had found himself willing death before they came anywhere near land. And here he was on some god-forsaken antediluvian rock in the western oceans' furthest archipelago, sneaking around like a criminal, all because his professor's wife had come here last summer to do bird-watching or some such shite and had gone home with the news of some seemingly unexcavated burial tumulus that she and her club had stumbled over and that could be worth a bloody peek!

Bugger.

"HOW'RE YA DOIN' ME OL' MATE?" Charlie spoke softly to the dog, not expecting him to become any less threatening, figuring for sure that he was smack-bang in deep trouble, so he was utterly surprised when the beast stopped slathering and cocked its head as though reading the man's frustration at being where he didn't want to be.

Charlie ground his cigarette out in his porta-butt, reached for his pack and went to stand thinking maybe it was okay after all, but the dog bristled again so he sat back down and pulled his sandwiches
and thermos from the bag.

Might as well have a bleedin' picnic, and he snorted with laughter at the situation. He poured steaming hot coffee into his cup and peeled the cling wrap from the food, biting deeply into the chicken, mayonnaise and lettuce sandwich.

The dog settled and dragged itself towards him by his front claws, his ears cocked.

"I *see,*" Charlie mumbled through a mouthful. He swallowed. *Don't talk with your mouth full,* he heard his mother say as sure as if she'd been there, and caught himself seeing the funny side of that.

"It's alright you bailin' me up and threatening to rip my throat out isn't it? But you wanna share my food too?" The dog merely looked at him in apparent bewilderment as Charlie broke his sandwich in two being rather certain that animals didn't eat stuff with dressing on it. He was mistaken. He was unaware that Oberon was a connoisseur of all foods, exotic or otherwise, and he wolfed down the proffered snack as though it was beneath him to bother.

Then Charlie heard it. The distant sound of baying.

"They know we're here, don't they?" he asked the dog, in more fear now than even the threat of the beast before him. Still, he realized, he wasn't going anywhere—he didn't need to be very smart to know that. He *was* worried though. These backwater provinces could be home to all kinds or folk with their own ways and their own laws and there was no knowing if they'd be simply annoyed at unauthorized intruders and would just send them on their way until they'd obtained the necessary permits or whether they could be much more dangerous.

Show no fear. He'd heard somewhere about animals picking up on a person's emotions, so he worked very hard to slow his thumping heart.

Oberon knew exactly what the man was feeling. He was partially annoyed with himself, however, because there was something just so utterly *nice* about him, and he kept his instincts in check because of it. It had nothing to do with the food sharing either—that was to be expected.

THE BAYING AND BARKING WAS closer now, coming from the direction of the house. He should be able to see them, and he was unnerved because all he could make out were silhouettes of black against the shadow and silver of the grass. There were people there with the hounds but none of them had torches, as though they only needed the moonlight to see their way.

Then he saw them. The green luminescent eyes of animals. Charlie started to shake uncontrollably, and sweat beaded on his forehead and lip and dripped from his armpits despite the cold, because they shone from the taller shapes that moved in the direction of his team. They shone from what could only have been people.

He was brought back to himself when the dog made a small noise in its throat that sounded suspiciously like a query.

This is too fucking weird! He forced his breathing to slow down, afraid that his anxiety and the tightness in his chest could herald an asthma attack. He hadn't had one of those for years so he had no medication and he thought that terror past history. *Just breathe, Charlie-boy,* he thought, counting in two three four, out two three four.

Oberon hunkered forward a little more and laid his great head on the man's leg as though in compassion and Charlie raised his hand unconsciously to lay it on the coarse fur of the dog's shoulder.

In the distance he could see torches bobbing: his companions were moving. They'd obviously heard the pack and as he watched, knowing with certainty that none of them were going to get away, the night went suddenly silent as though every dog heading towards the intruders had been issued an unspoken command.

"Oh fuck," Charlie whispered. He was going to throw up. He had such a bad feeling about this now.

CHAPTER FOUR

FRANK HARVEY USUALLY LISTENED TO HIS wife's conversations with a long-practiced set of automatic responses. Between the *yes dear's* and the *oh really's* she'd become a background drone of trivial inconsequence. He calculated his little inserts to time with the rising and falling of modulation because she was, ultimately, a very boring woman who substituted for a housekeeper, cook and hot water bottle sufficiently for him to remain married when, in truth, he'd probably be much happier alone.

But his ears had pricked up when the unexpected addition of the words "passage grave" and "mound" had slipped through the fangle of predictable rhetoric.

"What did you just say?" He looked up from his newspaper, pushing his glasses past the bridge of his nose and peered at Jesse over the breakfast things.

"A *mound*, Francis," she repeated, smiling to herself.

"What are you talking about? There are no tumuli—ah, mounds—on Inishrún. They've got a well-documented megalith of nondescript standing stones and a supposed holy well, Jesse. You're pulling my leg again, aren't you?"

She knew he hadn't been listening. He never did anymore. She'd been prepared to tease this along out of sheer bastardry.

"They most certainly *do* have a mound, Francis. Do you want more coffee before you go? I'm making a fresh pot." She stood and stacked a few of the things from the table onto a tray over on the sideboard.

"Please sit down, Jesse, and explain what you're talking about."

He didn't believe he was having this absurd conversation and he was going to be late for his first tutorial at this rate. *Bloody woman*, he'd thought, but she had him and he knew it.

"Yes dear, I'll do it in a minute," and she'd carried the tray into the kitchen, humming an old eighties tune.

She re-entered the dining room with a fresh pot of coffee five minutes later, just as Frank finished stashing the previous night's notes into his briefcase, preparing to leave the conversation unfinished.

"It's quite substantial and the summit's covered with trees."

Frank had sighed and sat back down. "I'm all ears, Jesse."

She told him that her bird watching group had camped out on the island overnight and had agreed, the following dawn, to do a last-minute bit of exploring before the ferry arrived later in the day. They had voted to avoid the numerous warning signs informing visitors against traveling the western ridge wall. They'd packed some supplies for morning tea and lunch (just in case they were gone for that long) and began the walk at just after 6 a.m. That would give them until the early afternoon, taking their time if the terrain was tricky.

"Yes, please don't give me the grand tour dear, I'm going to be late as it is." Her game was becoming obvious.

"Well it wasn't at all treacherous." Jesse had suppressed a smile. "We had no idea what all the warnings were about. It was very windy, certainly, but I doubt we would have been blown off the cliff in anything less than a gale. And there they were."

"There *what* were, Jesse?"

"A megalith of about forty uprights *with* a capstone on the inner ring, just below us, and the mound thingy a few hundred yards away all on its own in the edge of a heath."

"Well, did you go down?"

"There were steep, very scary-looking steps cut into the cliff on the landward side but none of us wanted to tackle them and get our necks broken in the process, and there was a house quite close by with smoke coming from the chimney and we all figured it was private property anyway, so no, we didn't go down Francis. Besides, it was time to turn back."

Frank had been disturbed by the news. There was only the one Neolithic monument as far as anyone knew and it was high up on the grassy hill inside the Catholic Church's graveyard just behind the village. Yes, he'd been most disturbed.

"How far did you walk before you got there, pet?" It was about time for endearments, he could see it in Jesse's eyes.

"Oh, hours, Francis. John Carey would know. He had his little GPS thingy."

"GPS tracking device?" Frank interrupted.

"Yes, that's it—a GP-thingamajig that fellows like him like to play with."

"I've got to run. We'll talk about this more this evening if you wouldn't mind."

"Dinner's at seven Francis. Derek and Amanda will be here. I *did* tell you twice. So don't forget or be late or anything."

Damn. He had no idea, let alone forgotten. He grabbed his briefcase and gave Jesse a perfunctory kiss on the cheek. He made for the door collecting his overcoat, feeling for car keys in its pockets. He was going to be ten minutes late for his first class.

Jesse sighed, finished clearing the remainder of the breakfast things away and phoned Paul Deering, her lover, to see if he still wanted to get together around ten.

FRANK CALLED JOHN CAREY AT his office mid-morning. He confirmed what Jesse had told him, and yes, he'd had a GPS and yes, of course, he'd kept a record of the exact location. No, he hadn't had a reason to discuss it with anyone—why should he? Birds and I.T. were his interests—he thought Frank's obsession with the dead, and old, rotting things, perverse and as far as he was concerned it did not serve the future one iota being merely a speculative science.

Frank had shut up until the silly man finished his rant. He then casually asked if he'd mind jotting down those coordinates and emailing him when he had a moment, and he'd disconnected as soon as it was politic to do so, spitting every profanity he could into the dead hand-set but with a rising sense of excitement behind it all.

John hung up chuckling.

FRANK CANCELLED THE TWO lectures that were scheduled for just after lunch and had spent the time searching the university records and the Internet for any and all information on the history and terrain of Inishrún, of which there was precious little, and no topographical maps whatsoever.

There was no mains power to the island and no phones. All communications between the residents and the mainland was by manned radio or delivered by mail. A small ferry brought staples and passengers to and fro three times a week in the months from March through October with nothing at all during the winter. There was no hospital, no school and the post office was annexed off the general store. There were the predictable two churches— one Proddy and one Catholic, the Protestant one having been boarded up years ago due to lack of interest—one pub, a small quarry that dressed local stone for monuments and such, no restaurants or hotels, certainly no accommodation for aircraft, and a small working lighthouse. Their only trade seemed to be fish, wool and honey.

As far as he could ascertain access onto or off the island was at Seal Bay, but he was certain that with the correct advice, another option could be discovered.

He had already made up his mind.

He hadn't been on an expedition of any notoriety his entire career. He was pushing fifty, had not written a paper in years, was not in line for any promotions and had no social life to speak of, all of which filled him with an abject sense of futility. To even begin proceedings for a sanctioned exploration would eat up months, with the perpetual risk of sabotage by other interested parties or a more affluent college, whereas if he got together a quiet little team and they made a significant find then the project would realistically have his name on it. Authorization and funding were a sure thing.

What he *had* found out from the available information was that the entire island was classified Crown land and all occupants were tenants-in-perpetuity, meaning he would not be open to private prosecution for trespass. Neither he personally, nor the university, would suffer one way or the other.

It was a win-win situation.

HE SAT AT HIS DESK AFTER saving his research in a *Utilities* folder, which was sure to dissuade anyone, sneaking around, from opening it, and considered the prospective ramifications of what he was about to do.

Stupid little island. Who'd ever have thought? Surely the inhabitants must have known they couldn't keep this to themselves forever, but how curious that it had not already happened? He would have thought that whoever originally recorded the existence of the first megalith would have explored a little more successfully. There had been a paper written on its significance (or insignificance) back in 1966 but there was no follow-up data just as there were no records of the anthropology of the islanders. No records of anything prior to 1779 when the quaint little nondescript Church of St Mary de la Mer was erected in close proximity to the henge, as though to enfold it in the bosom of Christ in denial of its pagan heritage.

He also sought out parish records of births, deaths and marriages to gain a more recent understanding of the population. But there were none. Either all of the residents went elsewhere to be born, get baptized, marry or die or the priests had not made that information accessible to the archdiocese on the mainland.

The potential for creaming this was enormous. Notoriety was a certainty. The press would be sure to find it newsworthy and with good coverage the chances of greater public interest was only a matter of time. With no property being in the hands of private ownership, the exclusive purchase was an entrepreneurial goldmine. Any subsequent development would broaden the tourist market immeasurably. He simply needed to be in on the perks from the outset.

The last thing he did for the day was to download everything he found onto an external hard drive and delete the file from his computer. Better to keep it as secret as possible; better to continue his research from home.

...

THE GREAT MYSTERY'S EARS PRICKED UP AT the unspoken word "development". Yeah, right... Like that was going to happen to her precious portal. She snorted her derision but figured she'd pass a warning on to the two people—well, only one of them was human, but hey, a technicality at best—whom she could trust to fix the situation should it actually look like turning into a reality.

CHAPTER FIVE

MIM, HOLLY AND CONNOR STAYED WITH THE others until just past the house where Harry veered away from the pack, heading for the henge, seeming to know exactly what he was doing.

The great moon-pale mastiff cross bounded ahead barking frantically, and the three raced to keep pace with him, with Holly lagging behind the others, her lungs burning from her not-so-healthy citified lifestyle.

Oberon stood up from the deep underbrush wagging his tail and whining a greeting as Harry covered the distance between them in bounds, and as the others caught up it was to find a red haired stranger, shaking uncontrollably, sitting cross-legged on the half seen track that led from the cliffs to the Barrow.

"Evening," said Connor, shoving his hands in the pockets of his jacket, ice in his voice. "Get up."

Mim stood back slightly, attempting to read the stranger as he hastily stowed a thermos and some discarded rubbish into his backpack and rose unsteadily to his feet.

"Me and my friends. We, ah—"

"Later," Mim hissed. "You come with us now, *mo chroì.*"

"But, I can't."

There was no point. They'd already turned their backs and were walking back the way they'd come as if knowing he would follow. He was very cold and very afraid and, shite, if it meant getting inside four walls and away from what he'd just witnessed moving in the direction of his companions then he was all for it. It kept going over in his mind, though, that as far as he understood it no one knew that they were here except the guy who'd driven them out here on the launch and he wasn't due back until just before dawn. He'd told the group that he had no intention of hanging around if they should get delayed or fail to be at the rendezvous point on time. The man had also insisted on being paid up front and as far as Charlie was concerned that meant he might not even show. It could be days before anyone realized they were missing and who'd think, in a million years, that they'd come here. No one, that's who.

So this is what helplessness feels like?

The three people and the other dog escorted Charlie back towards the cottage that he'd noticed when they'd first arrived. Oberon hung by his side the entire way like a friend and he found himself comforted by the big ugly mutt's presence, not realizing that he was as much a captive of the wolfhound as he was of the others. Oberon was *Mister I-Got-This*, that's all.

They entered into the buttery glow of a huge, warm, somewhat rustic kitchen and Connor pulled out a chair at the table and gestured the stranger to sit.

Charlie observed his captors in the newly-won light, noting the similarity between the two women and jumping to the conclusion that they were sisters except that the slightly younger looking one was dressed like a mainlander. The other, and the big guy with them, looked like his idea of hippies—in an eclectic kind of way—she with her hair in dreadlocks piled up on top of her head, with a thin silver cuff attached here and there, and one large, spirally black earring that could have been either bone or wood; he with coal black hair worn in two long plaits, with a thick gold hoop in each earlobe and uncanny tattoos, faded with age, on his cheeks, forehead and chin.

The slightly older woman busied herself pulling down jars from the shelves and putting pinches of this or that into a pot on the stove, with the man helping, while the other woman sat with him, keeping her gaze downcast.

"Get us some cups, will you Holly?" the man asked, "and the honey's over there by the fridge."

The tea was brought to the table and the scent of licorice and something indefinable wafted from the pot as it was poured into the odd assortment of crockery.

Mim scraped a chair over the flagstone floor, closer to the table, and peered at Charlie.

"I'm Mim. Who're you?"

"Ah..."

"Are you dumb then?" She steepled her fingers in interest. "Can... you... hear... me?"

"Sorry. Charlie. Charlie Freeman."

"Well Charlie Freeman," she nodded towards the others, "This here's Holly and Connor, and you're in quite a pickle. What are you lot doing on my island?"

"Look, I hate to think that we've upset anybody ..."

"What were they doing at the Barrow?"

"The..."

"Stop stuttering ferchissakes man!" Connor snapped.

"We're not gonna eat you, Charlie," Mim added, sipping her tea unsweetened, "and you look like the cold's got into you so drink."

Charlie took a big swallow, burning the roof of his mouth but finding the brew rich and fragrant. It hit his stomach like strong liquor, spreading warmth through his body but without the kick.

He began explaining, starting with his studies and ending with tonight's fiasco.

Holly looked up when he mentioned what he studied and stunned him with a beauty that would be sensational if she hadn't looked so tired. *Oh my*, and he faltered, a thing not lost on the others. Holly merely scowled.

"So I'm *really* sorry," he finished.

"Well. Fuck!" Connor sighed.

"They can't be allowed to leave," Mim added, turning to him, all seriousness.

"We'll be missed, you realize." Charlie hadn't told them everything. The situation was too unnerving.

Mim leaned so close to his face that he could see the pores in her skin. "That's the first lie you've spoken," she said softly, "and it had better be your last," but she was thinking about what a dilemma they had on their hands.

She sensed that the others had been plucked from the sacred site and were being escorted back to the village, but one thing at a time. She was very aware of actually liking her guest and that Oberon was quite the traitor, hanging by Charlie's side like a burr. Still, he *was* an intruder. At least he had not desecrated the Barrow like the rest.

"Unfortunately, Charlie Freeman," she rolled the sound of his name around in her mouth to familiarize herself with what it meant to her, "right now, you've got nowhere to go. And until such time as I figure out what by the *gods* I'm gonna do with you—and have undone whatever damage the others've wrought— you're to stay here. Holly, will you watch him until we get back from the village?"

"What on earth can I do?"

"The dogs'll keep you company," Mim finished her thought for her.

"Oh. Yeah. Okay."

When Connor and Mim left the house Holly and Charlie were sitting in an uncomfortable silence.

"Sparks," Connor commented smiling.

"Hmm," Mim had seen sparks, that's for sure, but not the way Connor meant.

...

FRANK AND HIS COMPANIONS HAD circled the tumulus several times seeking an entrance. To no avail. Up close the structure was enormous and it appeared well tended, each of the carved roundish stones that encircled the base, clear of undergrowth. There was a needle-thin upright stone facing due west that seemed of significance, however unconventional its placement, but its purpose was unknown.

They had needed to assist each other up onto the grass-covered structure as the unusual overhang of the stones allowed little ease of purchase. At the summit there was a circle of twenty different species of trees surrounding what had all the appearance of being an altar.

The ground cover within this living enclosure was ivy and pennyroyal, the latter releasing a sweet, sharp scent when stepped on.

Each person took notes by torchlight of every detail, and digital cameras took in the 360° panorama.

They were about to descend and do one more sweep of the circumference of the base in hopes of finding a way inside that was certainly there, if very well disguised, when they all heard the distant sound of dogs or hounds.

"Oh shit," Phil Laskay, Frank's most ardent student, swore. "You think the locals have found out?"

"Don't worry about it."

Frank had considered this possible scenario and had forged a letter of authorization just in case. How were these people going to know? "I've got it covered. Just don't any of you faze on me."

They packed up their equipment and started down the slope as the volume of barking and howling increased. Phil used his binoculars to see if he could get a make on who, and what, was headed in their direction.

He saw the feral eyes, both high and low and went cold, started to shake. "Hey Frank, check this out," handing over the glasses.

"Weird shit. I think it's just because they're not using torches.

Let's get away from here anyway." The fullness of the moon made strange the shadow and substance of the landscape and they kept their torches turned on. As they hurried down the hill the night went utterly silent.

They jumped onto the soft grass surrounding the base of the monument only to be confronted by an unsmiling greeting party of people ranging from middle aged to downright ancient. With them were several dozen canids ranging from small to huge. All were quiet.

"You have no right," Woolly stated flatly.

When the professor reached for his inside jacket pocket to produce the forged document several of the dogs snarled, their teeth bared, their hackles raised.

"Put yer bleedin' hands down," Woolly demanded, not caring what Frank had been reaching for.

"I do have a right, however."

"Did we say you could speak?"

Frank observed the grizzled old man, amused.

Woolly merely stepped to one side gesturing for the expedition to start moving.

"No—that's not what's going to happen." Frank had had just about enough of this threatening behavior. Even if they did not want to see his forged endorsement notice they weren't taking him or his associates anywhere they didn't want to go. This was public land. He ignored the gesture and turned to his class. "Let's get back to the equipment. This is Crown land and these people have no authority—"

But the dogs stopped them. The display of aggression was serious and each man in the team knew it.

"Ah, I think it might be preferable to not make enemies," mumbled Phil, deciding independently to accompany the islanders. Assuring his colleagues with an *It'll work out; we'll sort it* look as the procession made its way back in the direction of the village, the captives guarded on all sides from doing anything that would necessitate killing them.

ONCE INSIDE THE COMMUNITY CENTRE, FRANK and the students were politely asked to spread their equipment out for viewing; they were searched from head to foot, had all mobile phones confiscated, were provided with bedding and were told to make themselves comfortable as they weren't going anywhere until the banríon arrived.

Frank asked what that was but was handed a pint of beer instead, as were the others of the expedition. By the number of musical instruments on the stage, by the number of glasses and empty plates littering tables against the walls it was obvious that an event had been interrupted, but the intruders were unprepared for the band to begin again and for the party to continue.

"This is ridiculous," Frank whispered to the others, all of whom were huddled in the rear of the large stone structure. There were nods and grunts of agreement. "Let's just get the fuck out of here."

He went to stand, utterly offended at the old dodderers' arrogance, only to find his legs were like jelly and would not support him.

"Shit. We've been poisoned." He looked at his half empty glass with realization.

CHAPTER SIX

THE SOLE ACCESS INTO THE BARROW was by way of a tunnel that had been excavated millennia ago, shored up with solid rock walls and ceiling, each carved with trefoil spiral motifs or wave-like designs. The entrance was concealed only by the gorse and bracken that grew undisturbed around the base of a low rounded boulder, similarly carved, that sat virtually invisible in the scrubby undergrowth, nearly a hundred meters to the north of the mound.

Mim walked upright along the length of the tunnel accessing the deep chamber where the roots of the overhead trees had not yet reached.

The large space had niches carved into its walls, cradling the bones of ancestors and the remains of many of their possessions. Thick stubby beeswax candles rested in many of the recesses, along with talismans and gifts from the generations upon generations who had visited.

It was a rare thing for the fairies—the sídhe—to die. Most, like the island's inhabitants, lived for so long that they remembered events from before the counting of days—when the earth was ever-green—and further still, the *Imramma* into the Dreaming Lands, the Otherworld, where their particular mistress of Mystery still dwelt, the myriad of unseen realms thought of only as legend.

Those that *had* died had done so, always, under horrific circumstances: the ugliness of cruelty, the utmost despair, proximity to intentional depravity—all of these affected the sídhe by eradicating what is called the *shine*—the life force that burns most strongly in those who understand the wonder and mystery of life. These crimes were (and still are) perpetrated by humans, personally and collectively, on both their own species and the earth and her inhabitants.

The fairy folk of Inishrún had formed their own clan, *anFaoileán* (for the gulls, prolific on the surrounding cliffs), after fleeing to its long established sanctuary and escaping the world that had forged them into their aged forms.

THE BARROW FELT CLEAN. MIM breathed the scent of dry earth and stone and sat upon the enormous oblong dolmen that lay upon the floor. The only other furnishing to grace the place was a trident of narrow, upright, leaning stones that held, where they met at their tops, the crucible used to contain the broth brewed from the berries of the ancient rowan known as the Quicken Tree that bestowed near-immortality on certain fey mortals for specific purposes, like Mim.

She'd been included in the ritual for several reasons, the first among them being that Connor, of the Dé Dananns, loved her beyond anything else and had done since the first time he laid eyes on her. The second reason was the whatever-it-was that lay dormant in the blood of many humans—whom the fairies called the Lost—that was as awake in her as it was in Holly, and that those like her, those with official records, could be invaluable in dealing with the occasional clash with bureaucracy or the law. Of equal importance was the fact that it had been her ancestors who had originally inhabited the island and who had worked hand-in-glove with the sídhe establishing the monument within which she now sat.

Theirs had been a people deeply attuned to the land, waters and sky, their spirits and their gods. They had always had a *banríon*, queen of sorts, who had chosen her consort-kings—champions of protection and provision—in the sacred way. Many of their descendants had gone to the mainland, and even more distant shores, to intermarry with the chieftains of other clans, forging strong and lasting alliances.

The islanders had always supported themselves from either the bounty of forest and field or the graciousness of the sea. That had all ended abruptly, several centuries ago, when a small curragh carrying five Christian monks had landed on the shores of Inishrún bringing with them an alien and intrusive religion and, unintentionally, disease.

Within a week of their arrival the other human inhabitants had been decimated, plague ravaging the isolated population.

The monks, unaffected, had stayed to build their hermitage, calling the deaths the will of God.

The survivors had been the elder fairies—a thing not known to the priests—who were aged many years by the tragedy and who had wept bitterly as they sent each human body into the sea.

The priests were warned away from the proceedings and against any future contact with the survivors, under threat of slow death. Their curragh had been set adrift leaving them stranded for years during which time they had remained secluded and ostracized.

Many clans of the Tuatha Dé Danann had come, either from between-the-worlds—the access of which was the Barrow itself—or from over the sea in their guise as Travelers, including their mórbanríon Brighid, and Hunter, the forest god himself, and they had held a council that lasted for three weeks.

There had been much ceremony and feasting and cups of uiske beatha raised in toast to the spirits of the newly dead ancestors before the serious discussion had begun.

The bottom line was that the world outside was changing again and, whether they liked it or not, the new religion of the crucified god was looking like being around for a while. It would be pointless killing off the priests because others knew they were here and were bound to come looking for them eventually.

The worst-case scenario would be invasion by the non-fey mainlanders, so *anFaoileán* had better start acting like human old folk, and glamoring their appearances as time passed, so that no one became suspicious.

MIM PONDERED ALL THIS AND MORE AS the realization of what this current intrusion represented (that worst-case scenario) and how on earth she and the others were going to prevent it from snowballing.

CHAPTER SEVEN

HUNTER, THE FOREST GOD, POSED as a man.

He was well over six feet tall and as strong as an oak. His skin was dark—a little like leather or the bark of the trees of which he was guardian—and his black, black eyes were unfathomable. He wore his hair long and uncut in a mass of slender dreds hosting hundreds of small black feathers in honor of one of his favorite allies, the raven (the other being the wolf, the form he usually adopted to travel the Otherworld), with the sides of his head shaved and the dreds habitually tied up with strong cords at the crown.

Hunter, the Tuatha Dé Danann and their traveling companions were at their recently-won autumn tuath, high up top of the mountain that had the title of the Razorback, and earlier they'd driven into Brackenridge, the closest village, for an evening at the Hart and Horn.

They were enjoying a pint or two on a night without care or obligation. Feet were tapping and people were dancing as their band, the Fíanna, play rocked-up versions of reels and jigs, when a thread of need insinuated itself into Hunter's mind that he recognized as coming from the Isle of Secrets.

He sighed. Puck, his life partner, saw him stiffen and if, in human form, he could have pricked up his ears he would have done so.

"Trouble?" she asked.

"Not sure love, but I gotta go." He reached around her with gentle arms and enfolded her in a goodbye.

"You'll miss Robin's debut if you leave now." It was their only child's first night on stage singing the stories he'd written himself, that the others in the band had helped put to music. They were truly in the tradition of the ancient *seannachai*, the storytellers, and everyone was very excited.

"I'll hear the first one. Mim wouldn't have called if it wasn't dire but I'll wait. Rowan?" he turned to a younger man and asked him to get a note to Robin and the band letting them know that he'd been called away and so would only be around for another few minutes and was Robin ready and could they rearrange the gig so he could hear a song before he left?

A few minutes later and Willie, the fiddler, nodded in their direction as Robin put down his harp and took a stool at the lead mike. He sang a song called *The Gentry,* about the so-called mythic people that the Irish call the sídhe and the fair folk, warning that perhaps these figures of ancient legend were really still around, and he sang about a man he "was sure you've all heard of" named Oisín who'd spent a night in their company only to return to his home to find his clan long turned to dust, and so to never be fooled into thinking that there was no more to the stories than fiction. It was so well done, the meter so perfect, that tears sprang to Hunter's eyes as he remembered the old ways when this kind of telling was considered a holy thing and he applauded along with the rest, continuing to clap until the crowd died down and the band started an instrumental.

Puck kissed him lightly and settled back in her chair, smiling with her eyes, as he walked towards the rear exit of the tavern without another word. Robin had sensed his father's pride and picked up the harp, satisfied.

Out in the mist-shrouded alley Hunter slipped unnoticed into the Shadowland—the Dreaming Land, the Otherworld—and passed through it like a ripple, to enter into the Barrow soundlessly.

Mim had her eyes closed and she opened them with a start when Hunter cleared his throat to get her attention.

"What's up?" he asked, settling his bulk cross-legged on the floor, resting his back against the stone wall opposite her.

Mim let out a deep breath she hadn't realized she was holding. "Oh, Hunter, we've been found!" and the words tumbled out all over the top of each other as she explained the night's events.

"You know the rules, Mim."

She looked puzzled. What rules? As far as she was concerned the thing she loved about the sídhe was their unapologetic disregard for any rules. Then she remembered. *To influence the course of human affairs one of their own had to verbally agree to the interference of either the fairies or the gods of earth and water.*

"Well, me and Holly. We don't have to abide by that."

"True."

"So we can act, yes?"

"Two of you? You're kidding me."

Mim slumped. *Think, woman,* she upbraided herself.

Hunter sat patiently, a lopsided, canid grin on his face, as he observed her train of thought. She kept coming back, again and again, to a scared-looking, ginger haired man who sat at her kitchen table with Oberon's head in his lap.

"'Kay." He interrupted her concentration, "I better meet this lad. We'll see where his head's at on the situation."

He stood and took Mim's hands, helping her to her feet. "But you better fill Holly in on a whole lot more than you have done 'cause, like you said, the two of you *don't* have to abide by the rules so there's things that you might be needed to do that don't involve us."

"There hasn't been time so far, milord."

"Make time."

Hunter bent his knee and kissed the stone on which Mim had sat, in honor of the dead.

THEY WANDERED BACK TO THE house arm in arm, catching up on news (of which Mim had little and Hunter lots) and entered the kitchen where Connor was dumping the intruders' equipment unceremoniously onto the floor. He reported on events in the village, where he had gone after separating from Mim, before honoring Hunter with an irreverent "You're getting' taller me ol' son!"

Hunter ignored the greeting with dignity. "Tea would be nice, Connor."

He sat himself at the table where both Holly and Charlie stared at him curiously and a little warily.

"Hello Holly. A pleasure." He reached across the table holding out a hand in greeting, enfolding her smaller one completely. "Name's Hunter. I've heard all about you."

"Ah… Hi. Do I know you?"

"I'll get to that, *mo chroì*." He smiled his most charming smile with the intention of disarming her unease.

"It's just that…" Holly was experiencing an acute sense of déjà vu. He was very familiar. Maybe she'd met him here when she was small and had forgotten? He had already turned his attention to Charlie, however, leaving her to ponder.

"Hello Charles."

"Hi Hunter." Charlie's voice came out all crackly and Hunter realized that the man was very afraid.

"Now suppose you tell me what you're doing here."

"I came with a bunch from the university."

"I know that bit. That's not what I'm asking."

Charlie's brow furrowed in confusion. He attempted several similar beginnings and was cut off each time.

Eventually he shrugged. "I really can't tell you. It all just happened at the last minute. I just towed along I guess. Seemed like a good idea."

"You've got complacent, me ol' son." Hunter grinned, displaying disconcertingly elongated incisors.

"I don't follow."

"What about treasure?"

"What?"

"Aladdin and all that."

Charlie's jaw dropped and he went pale as his secret childhood fantasy—the reason his life had turned out as it had—was flaunted to his face and to the company who turned as one towards him.

"And you know that, how?"

"I read minds, Sunshine; I'm gifted."

Connor snorted a laugh as he placed a big yellow china pot in the middle of the table and went to rinse the cups from earlier.

Mim turned the teapot three times *sunwise* as she composed her thoughts. "Why didn't you go to the Barrow?"

Charlie stroked Oberon's head as the great hound snuffled at being ignored for too long.

"Dunno. It felt illegal-like; like we were trespassing but more than that. Just wrong, was all."

"Just wrong, huh?" Mim looked at their captive's clear tawny eyes, liking him. "You're not like the others."

"Sure I am."

"No, you're not. You're a dreamer."

"What? The buried treasure thing?" He was embarrassed but he brightened anyway. "They all want that."

Holly mumbled something under her breath as she stood to pour the tea, feeling defensive for the island even though completely at a loss as to what was going on; what she'd landed in. What she wasn't going to do though was to allow herself to feel excluded or dismissed from any of it. She examined Charlie again, antagonistic. All she wanted, just for a little while—just a few days—was some private time with Mim. He and his friends' little fiasco had stuffed that up.

She could, if she let herself, find him interesting and funny, and something else that was the very *least* thing she intended to feel right now. A disinterested and aloof attitude were not hard at all for her to adopt after years of forcing smiles at complete strangers, and she glared in his direction, fingering the talisman around her neck nervously.

"It was the trees!" Charlie suddenly registered what had unnerved him about the idea of accessing the monument. "It was the trees on the top of the tumulus. They're young and it made no sense."

Mim smiled. "Go on."

"Young trees mean the place is tended; that someone planted them on purpose not a whole lot of years ago. And the way they were in the distance; in the moonlight . . ." He left the thought unfinished. He'd felt like they were all headed towards a holy place and that those trees were telling him to keep away.

"*We* planted them. Me and the islanders and the others."

"What others. Why?"

Hunter watched Charlie's shine deepen as he relaxed, and his curiosity sparked. *Ah,* he thought, *Highland fey, is it?* And his eyes twinkled. His turn.

"We're going to tell you a few facts of life, Charlie, and you're going to listen, alright?"

The mortal nodded.

"And when I tell you, you're going to think you've landed in a nest of crazies, that's for sure."

Charlie squirmed on his chair, thinking inanely of his dad and wishing he was at home watching the match on the telly with him in one room and his mother singing to herself as she painted in the other, instead of being out here at the edge of the earth with these uncanny strangers.

Holly leaned a little more forward because Hunter spoke softly, and she didn't want to miss anything.

"But you'd be wrong in your thinkin'", Hunter said seriously, all pretense of amiability fled, "and if you listen deep, deep down you'll understand. And it's a reason that I have for tellin' you, and it's killing you I'll be doin' if you betray us after. Am I clear?"

Charlie went even whiter at this and Holly looked at Mim and Connor to gauge the truth of what Hunter said only to find their faces closed.

"Ah. Yes. Very clear sir."

"Well, Sunshine, you've gone and landed yourself smack in the middle of a mystery. And, sure, you've found your treasure, but you'll not be sharin' the realization and you'll not be spendin' it either. First thing to know is I'm a god."

And he proceeded to explain the island and its inhabitants—the Tuatha Dé Danann—and his eternal love for them, the Otherworld and what the Barrow represented, the Great Mystery that was their own special goddess, and the ramifications of this becoming known to the people he called 'the blind', and of the desecration of this outpost—this final, untainted, glorious outpost—by what would surely become just another bloody invasion and commodification.

"So do I have your attention, laddie?" he asked at last just as the first rose of what would be a bright, clear day lit the window sill and silked itself into the room.

"Shite," Charlie responded after an uncomfortable silence. He looked to Holly for some kind of reassurance, but she seemed lost in unspoken questioning, her gaze fixed on her aunt.

"Is it okay if I go outside for a bit," he asked Hunter. "I really need to be by myself to sort through some of this."

"You don't believe us do you?" The way Connor said it implied a direct challenge and the hackles went up on Charlie's neck and his jaw clenched. He'd met men like this. Hardcore men, quick to take offense. The sídhe had said very little all night. Come to think of it he'd hardly opened his mouth at all since Charlie had been captured.

"I didn't say I didn't believe it," Charlie said, as calmly as possible considering how he was really feeling—exhausted, scared, overwhelmed, probably in love, certainly in no condition to fight—and he stood up from the table and headed for the door, with Oberon as his shadow, letting in a blast of early morning cold on his way out, not really caring if they stopped him or not.

Connor moved to go after him, but Hunter put an arm across his body preventing any such thing. "He's being honest, *mo chroì*," and he sent a shot of calm. The sídhe backed off and went to stand with Mim, kissing her neck and holding her a bit too tightly for comfort. He'd thought they were safe here; he didn't trust any of it.

"Who wants to go down to the village with me and see what's happening?" Hunter suggested.

Connor moved to join him.

"What about Charlie?" Mim asked.

"Leave him, yeah? I got a good feeling about the lad."

Mim mumbled something about not going anywhere this early and set about gathering eggs and bread to make herself and Holly some breakfast.

Hunter and Connor took the track that wound through the countryside leading to the town. They passed Charlie lying on his back amongst the gnarly old fruit trees with Oberon and Harry sniffing at everything close by. He looked like he might have fallen asleep, though

Hunter had his doubts.

"YOU BETTER GET SOME REST." MIM DUMPED the barely touched food into the compost bucket, worried about Holly's silence.

"Like that's gonna happen. What else, Mim? What else don't I know? And why haven't you told me all this before? I feel so bloody shut out!" She was as close to tears as she could get, struggling for control and feeling that a whole world of inconsequence could have been avoided if she'd known about this when she was younger; if she could have been trusted, accepted; if it were all true.

Mim sighed. She felt that Holly was as fey as they came, that the two of them were like peas in a pod in a family so utterly dysfunctional as to seem alien. She also realized why both times when she'd had the opportunity to tell her niece, she'd kept silent. She was embarrassed. This was all so personal and to have risked seeing disbelief, or worse, scorn, in the eyes of the only blood relative she loved would have been too hard.

"Mim?"

"Holly, it's a bit much all at once, I agree."

"No it's not, it's you. What have you to do with all this?"

Where to start?

"Okay. You looked at me when you first came, and I sensed you thinking about how I must've spent your granddad's inheritance on a face job, but I didn't. I fixed the plumbing and put the rest away for you for later…"

Holly was startled that her assumption had been recognized and she blushed deep crimson. The corners of Mim's mouth turned up a little but she attempted to remain serious.

"It started out because of me and Connor."

"Yeah, I see you two together."

"Well the rest is about this thing called the Quicken Tree and the brew that the Dé Dananns make from its berries that confers longevity."

And she told the whole of it, only stopping occasionally when Holly asked a question. When she got to the part about being queen of the island because of their ancestry, and that ancestors' conspiracy to protect the portal to the Otherworld (always been in their guardianship; guardians of the secret) she realized that Holly had fallen asleep sitting up.

"Ah, love," she whispered, picking her niece up with unbelievable strength—one of the perks—and carrying her up the stairs to her bed, opting for a long hot shower before the rest of the day unfolded.

HALFWAY TO THE VILLAGE Hunter changed his mind.

"Look Conn, I'm not needed here—not yet—so you lot deal with this because it's going to be better if I'm not seen by the outsiders; you don't need any more conjecture than you've already got."

"But…"

"It's too soon. Stop and listen to me."

Connor had started walking off in a huff. He turned back to Hunter, his eyes sparking.

"*Mo chroì*, it's too soon," Hunter repeated. "This could die out or it could blow and if it blows I'm better off dealing with it from the mainland. Me and the Travelers there."

Connor sat down heavily on a rock by the side of the track, elbows on knees, face between his hands.

"What?" Hunter could not read him; the threads were too tangled. Too confused.

"Well that's just fine I suppose."

"Connor?"

"I'm so bloody torn, Hunter. I'm missin' bein' on the road so much I could cry but I love her beyond words, and I couldn't bear being apart from her."

Hunter sighed, thinking of Puck and of the few times of desperate separation. The Tuatha Dé Danann were like that—loved completely; hated completely; no in between—*he* was like that. The difference was that he was a god and could be utterly emotionless when necessary whereas his beautiful fairies were never still.

"Somethin'll come up Conn. Don't let it age you any more than it already has. It's two weeks till Samhain and the new year always brings about change, yes?"

"Yeah, 'kay." Moods like light on water, Connor shuffled to his feet and turned in a circle, his arms wide, smelling the day. "It *is* beautiful here," he whispered, "just sometimes it's too bloody quiet and there's nothin' to fight, no tricks to get into, you know what I mean?"

Hunter laughed, "I don't think that'll be your problem come a little while, me duck," he managed, having a fair idea that the Great Mystery would be sure to make waves when it was her special island that was threatened.

Hunter clapped Connor on the shoulder and leaned close to smell him and so reassure himself of the other's emotions; that he was in no danger of dying of despair. Then he moved between the worlds and was gone.

"Hmph," Connor grunted to the emptiness where the forest lord had stood. He hoped Hunter was right about the change.

He'd been a rogue fairy sídhe, a wild and often violent individual until a mere few years ago, not long before he'd met Mim, and he was sure his pattern would end up suffering from so much peace. Oh, well, he could always fight the invaders one at a time.

He strode off towards the coast, where the community center was situated, considering that option and smiling a little but feeling very un-magical at the same time. *Might as well be a bloody* mortal, as a fairy, he caught himself thinking.

CHAPTER EIGHT

A SÍDHE WITHOUT HIS OR HER OWN FOR company is always vulnerable—to loneliness, to confusion, to making mistakes—but the vast differences in the lifespan and experiences that existed between Connor and the elder Dé Dananns on the island meant that he actually felt isolated even from them.

Ah, Connor me boy, Connor me boy, his bright and shining mother used to say, shaking her head and getting older.

She'd known the rage within him; how much damage he could do when it took him. So did the others of their clan.

He'd never been able to laugh and stir the pot and bounce like they did. Not in those days anyway. Cursed, some said when his *gift* was recognized, because being an empath in a world being harmed more with each passing century was a cruel thing to have to bear.

Connor had been born sometime back in the eleventh century when all the magic and the mysteries in the home country had begun a seemingly irreversible slide into disbelief, or hiding, due to persecution.

But then things went from bad to worse.

By the time three hundred years had come and gone the invaders had diminished the forests, the wild places (to the point where hardly anyone remembered the great trees) and the spirit of the people to whom the land and sea were a birthright, more sacred in the deepest parts of themselves than any religion could ever be, and in the subsequent two hundred years the ruling monarch of strangers took their heart away and left ashes in their

Place.

That was Connor's youth.

He'd left the company of the Tuatha Dé Danann—an unprecedented step—because he couldn't shut out the mortal people's savaged desperation; he joined them in their fight for freedom and self-determination.

Hard-drinking, passionate men and frightened, courageous, rosary-beaded women had taken him in, knowing what he was and yet trusting it despite the possibility that they could go to hell for consorting with his kind. Heavily tattooed in the way of the elder race he'd kept out of the face of the queen's army, wreaking havoc on it from behind blockades.

He was the people's talisman—their memory—their grandfather's, grandfather's faith and they believed in the luck of him.

He'd killed so many of the off-landers that there came a day that he forgot *how* many. Just to stop feeling. Waiting not to feel for what was being done.

When the famine had struck, Connor knew every private death and humiliation as though it was his own and when the final battle, that followed as a consequence, killed off the last of the truly great poets of the times Connor lost hope.

So it was that a Dé Danann who looked thirty-something when he should have looked no more than a boy sailed away to another land in the company of ragged immigrants, mostly silent, when he should have returned to his own kind to replenish.

For a hundred more years he forgot who and what he was, and once within that time he took himself a human wife, Aggie, who had lived and died barren. He'd held her in his arms, loving her still for all that she was old and dried up by poverty and time, and he'd wept that he could not have aged and withered with her.

The new land was brutal in a different way. He'd skirted the raw wilderness of dense forest and mountains that could have soothed his jadedness, out of a perverse need to maintain the sense of who he'd become—hard-edged, capable, unfeeling. He had moved into the heart of the sprawling frontier city of New Rathmore, a place of cutthroats, women for whom he could pay without thought of love, moments of oblivion gained from a shot or ten of uiske beatha. Steam ships put to port continuously, spewing out refugees from other lands, itinerate workers and their families—desperate for a chance to begin their lives in a new land—into the hostile and unforgiving confederacies of already-established gangs: segregated ethnicities and cabals that had ruthlessly carved out their sectors of turf in others' blood, causing warfare of another kind and led by bullies, all guided by the same *gods*.

HE'D BEEN SHUNNED SINCE NOT long after he'd arrived. It was the swirls and spirals of his clan tattoos that caused it.

In a new world, where status and appearance went hand in fist with success, Connor's history, long acknowledged and accepted by the people of his own land, had all of a sudden become unwelcome. Loneliness was darkening his brightness to the point where he could hardly raise his head from the table of whatever pub he had slept at the night before. In fact some establishments had either thrown him out or barred him from entry because they mistook him for one of the land's indigenous people.

And it was the latter that turned it all around.

Dismal night it was, bone-numbingly cold, close enough to springtime for the gods of winter to wage their eternal battle for supremacy. The streets were slippery with ice and no one ventured out of doors if it could be avoided

Connor sat on a stool in a soot-blackened corner of O'Shanessy's, one of the only places down on the southside (known then as Irishtown) that knew what he was and who still accommodated him despite the proprietor thinking that the drink had finally taken him down, when several members of an uptown enclave entered looking for some excitement. They had two bronze skinned, black haired, black eyed people with them—a man in his forties by the look of him, and a younger woman—and they were shackled in iron at the wrist. They had been beaten, and a dark purpling above the woman's left eye still bled. They were utterly silent.

Both of them bore tattoos on forehead and cheeks and the man was looking straight at the fairy man, unblinking.

Nah, me ol' son, Connor told himself, *mind yer business*, but he knew by the waves of emotion and ancient magic that flowed towards him that it was already too late for that.

One of two big blonde men standing by the captives hit the chained man on the side of his head telling him to drop his fuckin' eyes or lose 'em and Connor sat up straighter on his stool, hackles raised, instantly sober.

The few women servicing the local custom moved subtly towards the stairway leading to the arrangement rooms knowing that the place was ready to explode, the interlopers shoving the Irishers forcefully as they sought access to the bar.

Connor felt unconsciously for the dagger at his belt as the first punch swung.

Within seconds fists, knives and bottles were making a mess of the inhabitants of the pub without exception. Connor rose swiftly. Ducking and shoving as he moved, striking out wildly, he reached the couple and pulled them roughly through the fracas and into the darkness that hid the back exit.

The woman stumbled, blinded by the blood in her eyes, but the man kept strong with both his feet and his courage, and the three managed their escape without attention, the fight at its apex.

At first all Connor could think to do was to get as far away as he could; bury as deep as possible into the winding slapped-up alleys of the dockland. He didn't have the energy for more than that. Once some distance had been gained the three sat, breathing heavily, behind a pile of discarded crates.

The shackles were a bolt and chain affair and with almost-numb fingers and a careful knife Connor forced them open. Both of the strangers' wrists were raw and suppurating leading him to realize that they'd been held for many hours, perhaps even days.

Ah shite. He knew that he could not just abandon them even after gaining them their freedom; what was freedom in a city like this to people such as these?

A healer. They needed a healer.

Think, ya fuckin' fairy, he growled to himself.

"Do you understand me if I talk to you?" He spoke in a whisper, not sure how safe any of them were.

"Yes." The man held out his hand in greeting and Connor shook it, careful of the wound. "I'm Bears."

"B…did you say bears?"

"My name. Bears."

"Well now Bears me ol' son you're in a right pile o' shit, are you not?" Looking from him to the woman.

"Mackawdebenessy is my name." The woman smiled when she saw the look on Connor's face.

"Ah."

"Just call her Mac," Bears sighed at his granddaughter, knowing she wouldn't budge an inch and knowing that these people could not get their tongues around their language.

"Nice to make both your acquaintance Bears, Macawdeb… deb… Mac," trying and failing. "I'm Connor and what's a lovely couple like yourselves doin' to get yourselves in trouble?"

"Mac is my granddaughter and she followed me without permission when I came down from the mountain after the trappin' season."

"You came to sell pelts?"

"Ngh." He nodded slowly feeling at a lump on the back of his head. "Yeah, that was the plan."

"Your granddaughter? Man you don't look that old."

"Thank you."

"Welcome."

"When I discovered she had followed me, we were too far into the crowded lands to turn back. The men attacked us just outside of Mornington."

Connor looked at Mac and sensed her abuse. She hid it behind a necessary dignity and it certainly had not diminished her spirit.

"Why the chains? Their idea of a punishment?"

"Humiliation."

"Aye, I know about that." Connor stood and staggered slightly as he assisted the others to their feet.

"I know a healer who'll clean those wounds up quick," he said, thinking of Walter McLeod who worked with horses and hounds but would sometimes take on people if he knew they had no place else to go.

"What are you?" Bears interrupted.

Connor felt the blood leave his legs. He didn't want to say anything.

"No time to explain. I'm nobody in particular, let's get movin' afore we freeze or get found."

It took nearly an hour of false turns and back-tracking before they came to the old stables.

Connor roused Walter from his bed, but it was no drama to the old man. He had never understood bigotry like he'd never understood the cruelty he'd sometimes have to fix for many of the animals that came his way.

Connor scrounged around for some wood, and summoned up a fire in the yard and brewed a pot of coffee from Walter's supplies, lacing it liberally with molasses. He poked his head around the door once to see if he was needed, which he wasn't, and let the others know to come out when they were done.

Walter graciously declined Connor's hospitality, choosing his bed instead when he'd patched the two up as best he could, and dawn saw the three outsiders huddled around the embers.

"So you gonna tell me?" Bears asked out of nowhere.

Connor chewed on his lower lip before answering. "No."

The big man stood, dusting himself down. "No problem. But if you're ever up in our mountains you'll be welcome amongst what's left of our people."

"How far away from here is that?" Connor had no idea what was pulling his reins, but the invitation seemed to promise a moment outside of his life as it had become.

"Well, if we gotta walk it'll take at least a week; if we steal us some horses. . ."

He left the suggestion unsaid but the two men grinned at one another and Mackawdebenessy, whose name meant *black hawk*, merely kicked dirt on to the fire, up for anything.

CHAPTER NINE

CONNOR DISCOVERED THAT BEARS' PEOPLE were very much like the earlier folk who had been the Dé Danann's joy before the envoys of the Christ had changed them from their true pattern into something very different.

The mysteries surrounded the village, and magic, was strong amongst the villagers—some more than others, like Bears—as were their family ties, their hunting honor and their connectedness to the spirits of the land. Their overwhelming totem was the horse and many of the clan who lived hidden in the rugged mountain depths counted these as family members and lived with them inside the longhouses during the worst winters. They had come together from several separate tribes around the region when disease and the gun had decimated their numbers, and their elders had outlawed alcohol because its initial introduction by the invaders had been devastating and so Connor's last drink had been on the night of the rescue.

The people reintroduced Connor to himself and it was a revitalized sídhe who greeted the Travelers three years down the track when they passed through that particular area of the mountains for the first time.

He had known them straight off.

He'd joined Hunter and Clan Fíach Dubh with mixed feelings of relief and regret that he was leaving the people who had healed him and for whom he felt great love.

He had stayed on the move with them for almost a hundred years until opting to join Mim on Inishrún, but he'd never lost his appetite for trouble.

A LIGHT MISTY RAIN DID NOTHING TO dampen Connor's spirits as he walked the last mile to the village; it softened the colors of the landscape creating a sense of being wrapped in silk, and it muffled the overhead screeching of the sea birds and the cac-cacking of the plovers into a melody, so that much of his fire was tempered by the time he reached the Community Centre.

The mainlanders were sitting huddled over a table eating a breakfast supplied by the sídhe. Woolly was their only guardian, but he had laid a spell of lassitude upon the group and they ate contentedly and only Frank looked up to see the new arrival.

"Top of the mornin' to ya," said Connor, grinning with mischief.

Frank grunted. He was unshaven and looked the worse for the night just gone and it took him two attempts to clear his throat. "Is it you we are to speak to regarding this matter?"

"Hah! Not likely." He turned his back and headed for the kitchen to see if there was any breakfast left. He filled a bowl with barley and vegetable broth, cut two thick chunks of fresh-baked bread and poured himself a mug of coffee from the percolator that sat steaming on the back of the range, lacing it liberally with honey.

He returned moments later and plonked his bowl and cup down opposite Frank, spilling a little of the soup, sucking it from his thumb with a fleeting memory of whatever legend the gesture reminded him. "Can you pass me the butter, *mo chroí*?"

It was well within his reach and Frank recognized the goad, choosing to ignore it. "Well?" he said as he slid the dish across.

"Well what?"

"Is it you I'm to talk to about this.. This matter?"

"Nah, me ol' son. You'll be waitin' for the queen."

"The—the *what*?"

Connor looked the other man in the eye issuing a clear warning. "Are you deaf as well as bein' an eejit?"

Frank's face turned beetroot with rage, his appetite forgotten, but he said nothing for several minutes recognizing the clear danger in the other man's body language.

Stuff it, he thought, just wanting this ordeal to end one way or another; hating feeling like he was dangling from these yokels' strings. "This is outrageous," he said, keeping his temper under control.

"Yer in the wrong bleedin' story to be puffin' up like that, I hope you know."

"This is kidnapping!"

Connor chuckled, fighting down the urge to slap the man.

…

"WHAT DO YOU MEAN 'WE HAVE RIGHTS'?" Frank spluttered, amazed. He was prepared, quietly to himself, to make this little uppity feral bitch, who had somewhere along the line acquired the title of queen, her long haired hippy boyfriend and these silly old fools, pay bigtime to the authorities when he got out of this—and he could see now that he would as there wasn't a tough guy amongst them, including the Irisher, as far as he was concerned. "You don't own *any* of this! I've checked. It's all the property of the bloody Crown! You're all *tenants*!"

That stopped the muttering.

Mim felt the ripple of rage. *Oh you fat idiot!* she yelled soundlessly. She didn't think he could have said anything dumber.

The room was icy with silence; deathly still, and Frank was oblivious.

"So unless you want some real problems, and believe me I can make that happen," he bluffed, "you'll let us go immediately."

"The ferry doesn't come by until three," said Woolly softly.

Mim had been about to say something but whirled instead, dumbfounded, to see Woolly lighting his pipe with deep sucks and puffs of rich blue smoke.

"Woolly . . ."

"Let 'em go love." His eyes met hers as he shook out the match.

Frank stood, a smug sneer on his face, and turned to his team with a look of triumph.

"And where's our man Charlie?" He asked Woolly, deciding that the old man was in charge despite their "queen".

"I'm here." Charlie strode through the door with Holly right behind him looking daggers.

"What the—" Frank looked from him to the others of the expedition as though they knew something he didn't.

"You go. I'm gonna hang here for a while," Charlie said, not affected in the slightest by the shocked looks on their faces.

Mim turned her attention to Woolly who, unbeknownst to the outsiders, was the most ancient and respected of the elder sídhe— almost a piece of the land itself that people called gods—who raised his bushy, grizzled eyebrows above twinkling grey eyes looking the soul of innocence. She passed him an *I trust you in this,* look and he made his way to the kitchen with nothing more to say.

IT WAS HE WHO PICKED UP THE mainlanders' equipment from Mim's cottage just past lunchtime, dumping it unceremoniously into the boot of the cab before driving to the jetty and leaving it.

Later, as the intruders took off heading back to the mainland, he stood alone atop a craggy ridge of escarpment at the very point where the domino of downed rock formed the eastern shore, watching the stern of the ferry boat diminish as it chugged out to sea. The day was so quiet that he could hear the distant susurration of the waves as they washed around the barnacled wall that formed the wharf. He picked up his pipes, filling the bladder with air as he'd done forever it seemed, and began to play a lively jig. Within seconds the wind picked up. Within the next ten minutes it was howling like a beast and Woolly stood unmoving, allowing the bag to deflate.

THE CAPTAIN OF THE FERRY HAD sufficient years at sea to have fought the storm hard. He'd mayday'd ahead when they started taking on water and they were within minutes off the coast when they foundered.

The boat had listed dangerously to starboard and he'd yelled for Frank and the others, white faced, bone cold and terrified, to make sure they all wore their lifejackets and to hold on, anticipating the inevitability of the danger they faced if she capsized.

The coastal patrol got to them and winched them to safety one at a time, moving in seeming calm, aware that things could go to hell in an instant. All the survivors were in a state of mild hypothermia, with Frank the worse for a painful constriction in his chest that he refused to mention, as they were taken in to shore where an ambulance awaited.

None saw the ferry break apart in the last fury of the storm.

FRANK HARVEY HAD A HEART ATTACK JUST four days after release from Intensive Care after the ferry incident.

He'd gone home and Jesse had feigned compassion and it was all so toffee and gooey and a lie.

He'd recovered sufficiently to decide to return to work, and to face whatever consequences were to be had. He'd been walking down the front steps of the house, heading towards his car, when his chest had felt like a bomb had exploded inside it sending shrapnel across his shoulder and down his left arm in the greatest agony he had ever known. *Cursed*, was his last thought before he'd blacked out; *cursed* was his first thought on awakening to the beep, beep of the quiet machine.

He lay hooked up to life support, its soft electronic rhythm letting him know he still breathed, with drips puncturing the back of both hands and an uncomfortable tube apparatus up his nose. He wondered with unexpected insight whether the island had cursed him for his arrogance.

He'd had an epiphany concerning the recent events. The details were missing, and he fought to bring the strands together.

A sacred place.

He'd never considered in all his years that the stuff he'd studied and taught was more than academic.

Somewhere he'd got lost if ever he'd thought about it, which maybe he had done once, a long time ago.

A sacred place.

What was he supposed to do with this? What had John Carey said about his work? Something about his interest in dead things? Well Inishrún hadn't seemed like that. It had felt operational somehow, as though the monuments were still in use. No. Leave it for a while. Get better. Think about it later.

He was in a predicament, that was for sure.

The sinking of the ferry had hit the news and the university had gone into strategic recovery mode, backing up his story that it was a sanctioned expedition only because it didn't want the affairs of the school handled outside of its own administration. But he was in big trouble and was due to appear before the board as soon as he was sufficiently healthy to sit through the tribunal.

He'd get the sack. No matter how important the find.

All the students had survived their ordeal and none of the families had so far sought litigation. There was still the matter of Charles Freeman and he didn't yet know whether he had returned or was still on that damned island.

He'd get the sack for sure.

He'd never known anything to turn so horribly wrong so quickly.

The word *ambition* insinuated itself into his head like an accusation, feeling like the fingernails of a demon raking across his identity and causing the beeping thing to quicken, bringing a nurse in its wake.

The stocky, efficient woman checked his vitals while asking him softly, "Are you in pain? What just happened, professor?"

He'd taken a ragged breath and said nothing.

CHAPTER TEN

ROBBIE FREEMAN HADN'T DONE ANYTHING for a couple of days after being informed of the incidents at Inishrún. Charlie was a grown man and could go where he wanted and do what he wanted to do, including staying on some island at the back of nowhere if he so chose. But it wasn't like him to say nothing or to get no word to his family; he and Kelly were always good like that. Good kids. Looked out for each other, looked out for him and Grainne; never had it tough like when he'd been a lad.

He'd come from a large family—mother and father, five brothers and two sisters all older than him—who'd been forced out of their croft when he was only six because the work had dried up. They'd lived at a place called Duntulm back then, on the far north east coast of the Isle of Skye where their family could trace itself back through his mother's line to the glorious reign of the MacDonald clan. On the day they had left their homeland Robbie had thought it the saddest day possible. Until they'd got to Glasgow and life went to hell.

His parents had died in a motor accident just after his fourteenth birthday and he was forced, because of it, to drop out of school and get a job or be put in a foster home, of which horror stories abounded, which was not going to happen.

He'd started on the docks that same year. He was, even then, well on the way to topping six foot and the men who'd trained him had worked him hard. Despite how tough he'd had to be just to survive, his sense of fun and justice kept him out of most scraps. He'd hung on, deep within and precious, to the way his family had always loved.

He was only seventeen when he'd met Grainne on a Friday night at the fun pier. She was two years older than him, a chestnut beauty working the ticket stall for the Spider at nights while studying art during the day. He'd never thought she'd say yes when he asked her to go for a drink after she knocked off, but she did, and he'd asked her to marry him within the week to which she'd also said yes.

Charlie was born nine months later, and they'd packed up their world, said goodbye to their families and emigrated in the hope of a better life for the lad.

Rob had got work straight away when they'd settled in New Rathmore and straight away he was earning more money than he'd ever thought possible. He'd been a Union man from the start and had earned intense respect for his quiet ways and his stolid values. Two years later Grainne had gifted him with Kelly, the bonniest daughter he could have believed possible, but then she'd said "no more" to any other children and had meant it. She was devoted to the two ginger haired, tawny-eyed babies, but her deepest passion was reserved for painting, and she said she only had just so much love and he'd believed her. He was a happy man.

Nothing had fazed him in all the years until the feeling that his son could be in danger.

GRAINNE OPTED TO STAY HOME IN case Charlie called or turned up and Robbie had driven off in his old Ford truck.

It took him several hours, with a few wrong turns, to make his way to Weary Bay. He drove down the Main Street to the wharf and left the motor idling as he strode over to two men who were loading empty plastic bins, which stank of fish, into the rear of their van.

"Who do I see about getting over to Inishrún?" he asked, hands shoved deep in the pockets of his anorak against the chill of the afternoon as the wind blew the feel of ice off the water.

"No one," mumbled the taller of the two, stopping what he was doing and reaching for a pack of cigarettes, cautious. "What're you wantin' to go there for this time o' year, not that it's my business?"

"My son was with that expedition that sank last Friday. Far as anyone knows he didn't leave the island."

"Not my business."

"Why "no one"?"

"The *Rosie Rua* is the only boat about and she's at sea. Ain't anyone else'll do the passage this time o' year."

Robbie's brow furrowed in worry lines, his thoughts working around possible options. "Where'll I find the Coastal Patrol? What about them?"

"Dunno. Maybe. Hang on a minute." The fisherman walked around the van to the passenger door and rummaged around in the glove box, pulling out an old invoice docket and a pen. He drew a hasty map on the back showing the way to the Tower where the patrol was based.

"Don't know the phone number; you'll have to look it up if you want to ring them. Always someone there though."

Robbie thanked him and got back in the truck, turning up the heat while he studied the directions.

...

THE COASTAL PATROL HEADQUARTERS was aptly named the Tower—a non-functional lighthouse a mile and a bit south along the coastline. Les Oldfield was rostered on radio in case of call outs which, as far as he knew, never happened at this time of year because nobody except the Travelers ever took off past the bay.

He was completely absorbed in watching the re-runs from last Saturday's match, hovering over a two bar heater, and was startled by the rapid series of knocks on the only door.

When Les opened up to him, the blare of the television disoriented Robbie. The silence of his trip and the depths of his thoughts had taken him a long way away and he stuttered as he introduced himself to the small, weedy man who kept turning away to look at the screen.

"Come in then," Les agreed finally, ushering the big Scot into the stale warmth.

He muted the racket of between-shows advertising with the remote, and dumped a pile of newspapers off the spare chair. "What do you want then?"

Robbie remained standing, explaining his request and offering to pay whatever was necessary.

"We don't do ferry," was the curt reply.

"But—"

Les worked at removing something that seemed wedged in his back teeth before opening the little bar fridge and pulling out a beer.

"You want one of these?" he asked distractedly.

"No. Mr., ah, Oldfield, what I want is a boat."

"We were told that one o' the party stayed on of his own accord Mr. Freeman, *and* we've had the *Rose Rua* back and forth for a couple o' days. If he'd wanted t'come out he'd ha' come out so there's an end to it."

"When's she due in port then?"

"Dunno. There's some event takes place ont' island this time o' year and she takes her own across t'that. Hardly anyone's here yet s'far as I'm aware though—too early. The skipper knows when they arrive—radio or summat. She'll turn up."

Robbie was flustered. "Isn't there anybody else?"

"Nope. Thanks for dropping by."

"He's my son. He could have been hurt or anything," Robbie

blurted, wanting to squeeze the little man's throat for not caring.

Les turned away from him, depositing himself back on the seat and picking up the remote, calling over his shoulder "And I'm not a ferry. Good luck and g'day to 'ee and mind you shut the door as you go."

Robbie thundered out of the room almost exploding the metal door off its hinges as he slammed it behind him, cursing the man's genitals all the way down the stairs and out into the bitter night.

HE DROVE BACK TO THE VILLAGE and found a pub near the wharf and parked the truck across the other side of the road in the car park. It was warm inside and the atmosphere seemed friendly. He inquired at the bar as to whether there were rooms available and was assured he could have his pick. He ordered himself a pint and dropped his pack onto a chair at a small square table close to the open fire and went to find the payphone—abrading himself for ignoring the push of the twenty-first century to purchase a cell phone—and put in enough coin to call Grainne. She answered on the second ring sounding worried, thankful that he was alright and telling him there'd been no word.

"I'm staying down here till the boat comes in. No, I don't know, nobody knows. Hang on, I'll ask." He went to the bar and asked the publican what the phone number was in case he got a call.

He gave the number to Grainne and said he'd let her know when he got passage and that he loved her and to trust him. He smiled at her reply and hung up.

He returned from the phone just as the publican reached the table with the beer. He introduced himself as Henry Poe, shaking hands with Robbie in a comfortingly beefy grip before directing him around to the office where his wife would take his details. Rob took a sip of the beer, decided against it for the moment, and shouldered his pack.

"How long you here for love?" Alice Poe asked.

"Seems I don't know." He filled her in about Charlie and she clucked and tsked in understanding.

"He'll be right," she smiled holding out his key. "Raurie'll get you there." At his look she explained that the *Rosie Rua* was his boat. He nodded as he took the key and turned towards the stairs leading up to the guestrooms.

"You want a meal when you're settled?" she called after him.

Robbie grinned; letting down his guard. "I'd love a meal."

"Fish and chips alright?"

"That'll be bonny."

HE DUMPED HIS BAG ON THE CHAIR near the old-fashioned floral curtained window, without unpacking it, and sat down on the edge of the bed, taking in his surroundings, his hands between his knees.

The lump in his throat threatened to choke him and he fought it fiercely. Charlie was his pride; his peace. If anything happened to him…

Patience, y'old Celt, he thought, rubbing his face with his heavily calloused hands, sighing. He stood after five minutes, pocketed his key, and went downstairs for his dinner and that pint.

…

ROBBIE WAITED FOR TEN DAYS, HIS WORRY and his impatience put away on the shelf of his single-mindedness.

He used the time to explore the village and surrounding hills, coastline and woodlands remembering his boyhood in a region strangely similar. The smells of kelp and wood smoke and the decomposing of the summer's garments filled his senses. Something within him awakened that kept struggling for life as he, equally, fought to deny its right to be.

But he couldn't.

There was poetry in him.

Songs and stories recalled in snippets and strings—a thread here, a thread there—came to mind as he waited and wandered. He formed whole verses or passages that he spoke (or sang) aloud believing no one could hear and so embarrass him.

Except he *was* heard. By local folk just out of sight; by Travelers passing silently towards the village along ancient wooded tracks; in the Dreaming Lands where Brighid often wandered, causing her to stop her vigils on more than one occasion; by the ravens—the little magics—who actually remembered the whole of the stories that Robbie unleashed, unconscious, onto the wind.

Hmm. The Mystery smiled a quirky smile and kept her lips shut tight so that she might not join him. Yet.

Within those ten days his presence at the local pub for his dinner invited conversation with the villagers to whom a pint in the evenings was an institution.

They weren't shy about asking him to talk about his life and Robbie was friendly, easy-going and open, so they knew pretty-much all there was to know by day three.

And he knew most of their names and many of their stories, the history of Weary Bay, its legends and its quirks.

By the seventh day the whole town had begun to exhibit a festive feel with craft and food stalls beginning to appear, and cut-out gourds lighting many of the town's windows on dark.

Then the Travelers began arriving. And to Robbie they looked unnervingly like the same ones he distantly recalled as having passed through Duntulm when he was a boy, despite logic telling him that was impossible.

The villagers accepted them as a custom and greetings were exchanged while names were not and one or two of the exotic women, and several of the men, seemed to know that he was an outsider and eyed him quizzically as he tried hard not to stare back.

The publican distracted him when he deposited a large bowl of seafood chowder, and a couple of hunks of thick, dark, liberally buttered bread, on the bar where Robbie sat with his pint.

"Thanks Henry."

"The hooker'll be coming in now this lot's come." Henry tilted his head towards the big corner table, where the crowd of Travelers chatted and laughed. Robbie spooned the rich creamy broth into his mouth, smiling, feeling better than he'd felt for years.

Later on in the evening several of the strangers struck up an impromptu gig with traditional instruments and voices that sang a lament in an unknown tongue.

The patrons of the pub went quiet. All listened. Robbie felt that his heart would break as the foreign words awoke long forgotten, long denied emotions of the years of hardship his family had endured at the hands of poverty and landlessness: even beyond his lifetime it seemed he could sense the slow erosion of his ancestors' rights; the extinguishing of their pride.

He shook himself, roughly wiping his sleeve across his eyes as the song finished and the fiddle and whistles began a trivial jig, but not before he noted how many noses were blown.

What was that about? He was confused and slightly unnerved; a shiver of fear coiling around his sense of identity.

ROBBIE WAS PACKED AND READY. HE'D settled up his bill the night before and Henry had cut ten percent off the total, suggesting he was welcome back as a friend anytime which caused Rob to think briefly that moving away from New Rathmore could be a really good thing and determining to talk it out with Grainne when this lot was settled.

The *Rosie Rua* came with the high tide just after dawn. She was what is known as *anbád mór*, big boat. She was forty four feet long with main sail, foresail and jib all black and made of calico in the traditional manner, and he watched, impressed, as she maneuvered her sharp splendor—like something out of myth—around the curragh, small craft, fishing boats and trawlers moored in the harbor.

He hummed to himself as he stood amongst the crowd of fairies waiting their turn to board but when he finally reached the top of the gangplank he was stopped by the skipper, a heavily muscled, freckle-faced man with a shaven head and the look of a pirate, who appeared to be somewhat about his own age.

"What do you think you're doing?"

"This your boat?" Robbie adopted his most affable face, suddenly aware that he could hit obstacles yet again.

"She's mine. And she's not a public vessel."

Robbie reached into his jacket pocket to pull out his wallet, eager to pay whatever was asked. "My son is on the island."

Raurie's eyes widened and he grinned, taking a step back. "Sure it is, I can see who y'are! You'll be Charlie's kin is it?"

Robbie nodded, encouraged.

"You're expected, boyo, and I don't want yer coin. Give us that." He gestured for the pack. "I'll show you where to plonk yerself for the passage."

There were about thirty others aboard making up the limit of passengers, and Raurie shoved his way happily through their business, settling Robbie in the shelter of the cuddy, suggesting he hold onto whatever he could.

CHAPTER ELEVEN

WOOLLY WATCHED AS THE BIG MAN MADE his way through the
turnstile on to the cobbled main street of the village. He pulled his
chin in and snorted at the shine of the stranger.

Well, bugger me, he swore under his breath.

Not much surprised the masterful Dé Danann but this did. Not
wanting to miss the opportunity to find out more he pushed off
from the bonnet of the cab and strode in Robbie's direction, his
hand reaching out to grasp the other's as he closed the distance.

Robbie watched the grizzled old man move towards him, and
felt a sense of déjà vu. What had he got himself into? Fate seemed
to be doing a merry dance around what had begun as a simple
quest to ascertain Charlie's wellbeing.

The old man's hand shot out as though in a greeting to
somebody already known and Robbie clutched its dry cool
strength, returning the vigor of the grip.

"Name's Woolly me ol' son."

Robbie introduced himself and asked if Woolly knew of his
son.

"I know where he's stayin'. You want a lift?"

"Is he—?"

"S'far as I know he's orright, gettin' might chummy w'all an'
all."

Woolly turned back towards the taxi with his arm around the
other's shoulders, the equality of height satisfying him as though
a challenge had been met and won. Robbie shoved his pack onto

the back seat and climbed in front beside his companion who grumbled something about *bloody ol' bitch* as he pumped the clutch and ground the car into first gear. They crawled along the village street, back-firing all the way, and up the slope that led onto a tree-lined, heavily-rutted road that wound inland from the coast.

CONNOR HAD RIDDEN CLOUD, MIM'S MARE, OUT into the Mothers the night before. He'd slept in the wild stony protection of Loch Dearmadach, in the company of his little mysteries: hounds and owls and bits o' this and bits o' that, that made up the company of his totems.

He was to call in the horses; bring them down from the high places to the relative shelter of the heath and the forests of the lowlands for the winter months. He knew they'd find their own way, that was not the point. Being away from everyone and everything, especially now that the crowds were coming was the point. Running with the herd. *That* was the point.

He woke well before the first hint of dawn and placed more wood on the embers, summoning up the fire to join him in the morning. The Mothers ran rich with underground springs and he filled his billy from the one that bubbled from the mossy stones a mere few yards from his camp and placed it on the coals to boil, adding a handful of ground coffee before pulling out the thick dark loaf that Mim had slipped him, and the neatly parceled soft white sheep cheese, liberally studded with peppercorns, that he spread decadently on a broken off chunk of the bread.

The Mothers were all but bare of trees, so as the first of the dawn insinuated itself onto the air around him he could see the whole of the island.

He breathed in the smells of cool water, wood smoke, Cloud, the heather, bracken and rocks and the myriad other ecstasies as the first of the birds called the day.

He closed his eyes and felt the Mystery bless him.

COME MID AFTERNOON HE'D SUNG in seventy three horses and they ran at what to an average rider would have been a perilous speed, but to the Fáidh and his company was exhilaration. They galloped down off the mountain and onto the flat ground, following the edge of the forest until they separated just before sighting the first of the Travelers' pennants—russet and cream, over a blue background, for the Fox clan—flying above the outermost campsite.

Whooping a farewell he and Cloud continued their breakneck ride right through the Dé Dananns' makeshift hearthrights and only slowed, much to the horse's disappointment, as they approached Mim's place.

He noticed Woolly's Vauxhall parked outside and wondered at how full the house was by now. He sighed.

Love ya and hate ya all, he thought, looking around at the gregarious display the fair folk presented—no extravagance was spared where their tents were concerned, no fabric forgotten, no color ignored—and he took note of the banners, depicting the totems and symbols of each clan, that rode in the westering wind defiantly proclaiming *We're still here*! And he wondered where his friends from Fíach Dubh were, as no pennant of ravens on a background of forest green could yet be seen.

He dismounted and walked the mare to the stable at the far side of the cottage where he filled her bucket and rubbed her down while she munched. He crooned and hummed to her softly, taking as much pleasure as she in the ritual. By the time he'd finished teasing out the last of the burrs and snarls from her tail the day was almost full dark, and he realized he was both cold and hungry, the wafting scents of roasting meat and something delightfully spicy making his mouth water and his stomach growl.

He nuzzled Cloud's neck as she whickered *get outa here* n horse. He left the Dutch doors wide open, as usual, knowing she liked to wander in the night, and with the new boys down from the Mothers he realized he might not see her again until the herd wandered back to the camp for the race. He grinned as he thought of the probability of a foal in the coming year.

As he rounded the corner he sensed the new person. *What have we here, me ol' son?* Whoever it was they were mortal, but they sent out a clean emotion; a sharp, vital, tangy emotion.

In the kitchen were Holly and Mim, Hunter and Woolly, Raven—another rogue sídhe and an old, old friend for whom he held the deepest respect—and Brighid. Locked in a dance of embrace were Charlie and one of the tallest, strongest looking mortals that Connor had ever seen, with a fey shine that caught his throat and made his eyes water.

He stumbled over his own confusion. Were they related? The resemblance was obvious, but he didn't understand. What was more, Charlie still looked as ordinary as ever despite the omnipresent grin.

"Charlie's dad," said Mim, reaching up to kiss Connor's cheek. Hunter pulled a chair noisily from the table and spread himself out asking if anyone would be gracious enough to honor the formality of *an aíocht*, guesting law, and make a pot of something.

"You wanna get yourself a maid," Holly responded only half in jest, jumping down from where she perched on the chopping block and swinging the kettle from the stove to refill.

"Used to be I'd have 'em," barked Hunter, reaching out to tickle her as she passed. She slapped his hands away, brandishing the kettle as a weapon and warning him with a look. Brighid snorted back a laugh.

Robbie pulled away from Charlie, smiling warmth across the room.

"So what's the story?" he asked.

THE EVENING WORE ON INTO THE night as the events were told. Rob was silent throughout as one person after another added bits and snippets.

Connor and Brighid set to, around 9 o'clock, making pizzas enough to feed everyone and then some, and Woolly opted to go into town to the pub and buy beer and whiskey for which he was applauded.

"WHAT'S THE WORD ON THE MAINLAND?" Hunter was concerned that this was a one-sided conversation and attempted to steer it to where the danger to the island would come from.

"Right," Robbie began as everyone settled into the food. He took a bite from his slice of pizza and a long swig of golden ale before continuing. "What do I know? Well not that much really. Papers got hold o' the story and I'm right surprised no one's been here so far. Inquiry by someone about the ferry sinkin' and all. That professor o' yours," he tipped his glass in Charlie's direction, "is in the hospital last I heard and is in a bloody right bad state."

"What? From the ferry going down?"

"No. Bloke's gone and had a heart attack, so rumor goes. I got told by the coppers who come around to let me know about you bein' with the expedition and not comin' back wi' the others so here I am. I got to get back soon as I can, too, so your mum don't worry."

"She okay?"

Robbie laughed. Last he'd spoken to Grainne she'd been out back in the shed banging and kicking away at her old punching bag that she'd had from her days doing karate or aikido or whatever other thing she'd studied to "keep fit and keep the mind alert".

"She's ready to fight somebody, Charlie, if you're not alright."

"Tiger-mum," Charlie smiled with pride.

"Hmph."

Charlie grinned all the more so at the thought of his mother— all of five foot tall—sparring out in the yard with her mates when he was younger, when she wasn't painting or protesting something.

"You heard from Kel?"

"Not since I came down here." Kelly lived a wandering life by choice, going where the seasonal fruit or vegetable picking was and living out of her mobile home with Phoebe, her two year old daughter, and a feisty little Jack Russell that guarded his mistresses ferociously.

Rob turned his attention to Hunter. "So you made some deal with Charlie, he mentioned."

"If anybody thinks to harm our island he's given us permission to interfere." Hunter had held nothing back, informing the Highlander as he felt was right, trusting him from the first.

"And so is that why the ferry sank?"

The occupants of the room looked from one to the other not quite knowing how to respond to the canny conclusion.

"Eh-hem." Woolly cleared his throat, attempting to appear contrite, scratching his beard before patting his jacket for his pipe.

"*You* did it!" The corners of Robbie's mouth tilted with humor. "You old bugger!"

Stunned silence. Robbie burst out laughing.

"Dad?" Charlie was confused. It came from never having lived in the old lands; never having grown up with the tales of the Gentry's penchant for vindictive behavior if offended.

"Bloody fairies," Rob chortled, which ruffled a few feathers amongst the gathering but sent both Hunter and Brighid into peals of laughter.

CHAPTER TWELVE

CHARLIE GLANCED ACROSS TO WHERE Holly had repositioned herself on the chopping block. He fleetingly wished that he was the wood before being caught in the reality of her glare. Why did she always have to look at him that way; thin-lipped and mean?

Tonight had been really happy. *He* was really happy. He knew he had choices; decisions to make. He'd been thinking about it for days. He could go back to his study—that'd sort of be okay—but the thought of it seemed dead somehow, as though it could never replace being around a living magic; a living history. Mim and a couple of the Dé Danann had told him stories—they called them *scéala*—of things long past, that bit like fleas at the traditional way that history was written. He was yet to puzzle out the big picture but was fast coming to the conclusion that all the things he'd been taught in school, and much of what he'd learned in college, leaned heavily towards two things: the bias of a militaristic and heroic might-of-right, and that somehow humanity had come from a less civilized linear past that put our progress ahead of all other considerations. Not enough was documented of the suppressed or conquered people: the way they thought, the ways in which they related to reality, or it was presented in such a way as to patronize. Charlie was beginning to glean an alternative viewpoint altogether. He concluded that the majority of the academic accounts of history were a justification, a presumption of superiority that seduced people into an acceptance that was really very unhealthy; very one sided.

He wanted to discuss it all with Holly. He wouldn't be able to with many other people; he'd been sworn to secrecy and he understood why. But she was here, a part of it. Another mortal. He had no idea why she disliked him.

"Can I talk to you?" The rest of the gathering were enjoying themselves around the kitchen table, and Hunter, Brighid and his dad were locked in a conversation about Skye that he probably should be listening to but wasn't.

"Go away." She watched the others, refusing to meet his eyes, noting as Mim picked up on her voice, no matter that she'd spoken in a hiss, sending the younger woman a piercing challenge.

To Holly's mind, Charlie had been incorrigible over the past two weeks, refusing to be put out by what was very often rudeness on her part, enjoying his time on the island and gathering stories from Mim who seemed to take to him easily (in difference to Connor who remained antagonistic) with the two usually spending a couple of hours talking in the afternoons.

He'd realized from the first day, walking from the house to town, how unfit he'd become because of his academic lifestyle and had driven himself at whatever task he'd been set, loving how he felt and refusing to be disheartened by those who seemed to dislike him. He'd been put to work from the beginning, chopping the firewood that was now stacked in rows right up to the eaves of the woodhouse roof and he was glowing with good health and humor. Only Holly brought him down and he really wanted to know why that was.

"Please Holly." Charlie shoved his hands in the pockets of his jeans and scrunched up his shoulders thinking he should just leave it; that he was wasting his time.

She hopped down from the bench, sighing, and wordlessly wandered down the hallway to the tiny sitting room where a turf fire smoldered.

She squatted down to add more fuel as Charlie entered the room behind her, with a stubby of ale in each hand that he placed on the low table before sitting cross-legged on the carpet.

"So what?" Holly took up a beer and swigged from the bottle.

"There's a million things I wanna talk about with you. Why can't we be friends?"

"Do I look like I give a shit about what you want?"

"Can you drop it?"

"Damn! Why should I? You came here when you had no right; you take over any space you occupy… And what's with the *Oh, I'm such a nice guy* attitude? I don't trust you and I'm willing to bet *they* don't really trust you either!"

Once she'd started she didn't seem able to stop. Yes, she'd met guys like him before, always wanting something and pretending otherwise. Liars. Sneaks. Sucking up to whoever to get on their good side; to get on the inside. Charlie sat through it without saying a word—questioning his motives for any truth to what she spat—while she veered off on tangents, tirading this or that, most of which he figured had nothing to do with him, until she wore herself out and snapped her lips shut, glaring at him, defying him to defend himself.

"You done?"

"Whatever," she said, turning from him and studying the fire.

Charlie considered the consequences of what he wanted to say to her and concluded it didn't matter. He stood up and picked up his untouched ale, deciding the last thing he needed was to be anyone's whipping boy, or anyone's savior.

"Go fuck yourself, Holly." And he walked from the room.

Holly stood, still staring at the flames that licked delicately around the slowly disintegrating turf. She was shocked. She had anticipated any reaction except that. She replayed what she'd said to him. Replayed and replayed, and she felt quite sick. The knot in her gut tightened and her eyes burned as she realized, abruptly, that most of her venom had nothing to do with him.

She slumped down onto the thick, gaily-colored rag rug that served as a hearth mat, considering the patterns that wove about each other in evident randomness, glad, for the moment, to be on her own, and crying until her nose clogged up and her chest hurt.

CHARLIE STALKED BACK THROUGH THE cottage and out the kitchen door like a dark thing. Everybody noticed. Robbie went to go after him but Brighid laid a hand on his arm as Connor slid from the room, following.

Hmm, thought Mim, wondering what had happened; wondering about what might be being woven on what loom, knowing Connor had been almost as antagonistic towards the Scot as Holly whilst being aware that he was an empath and that his true feelings could be overshadowed. Was *that* why he'd been so hostile? That it may have had nothing to do with Charlie hadn't occurred to her until now.

"What's going on?" Robbie asked aloud.

"Women," whispered Hunter up close so no one else heard.

"Oh." And he returned to a conversation with Brighid.

The night was icy. Charlie's breath left him in great clouds and he instantly regretted not having grabbed his coat that had hung to hand on the back of the door. He was over-reacting, he told himself, attempting to rein in his disillusionment at her attack.

Connor caught up with him just as he reached the heart of the orchard where he'd taken on the habit of going when he needed to think.

"You'll be wantin' this, me ol' son," holding out the jacket. The fairy man was smiling, which unnerved Charlie a little after the hostility since he'd arrived.

"You like her don't you?"

Charlie snorted. What was the point? He knew Holly was hurting but he didn't want to be the one who healed. His last two attempts at love had been that way. Rebound ladies. He'd filled them with their own beauty until they felt good about themselves again. Both had left him for somebody not so helpful. What was wrong with him? Women, he'd decided, didn't fancy nice guys except maybe to dump on.

"Cheer up! She'll come 'round."

"What's with you then? You hated my guts just half an hour ago."

"Ah. Well then. It's me curse, Sunshine." He grabbed two overhanging branches of the ancient walnut tree under which they stood and pulled himself up, climbing until he could wedge himself comfortably between two branches, and took out a pouch of tobacco.

"Nice up here," he commented, rolling himself a thin cigarette and lighting it carefully to keep the wind from the flame of the match.

Charlie clambered up after him, not quite so agilely, using his feet to help him, until he sat opposite the sídhe ignoring the niggle of altophobia that trilled along his spine. "So what's this curse?"

When Connor completed the fairly lengthy narrative Charlie's expression had gone from a glower to something else. "So you were aggro at me because of *her* mood?"

"Guess so."

"You're not sure?"

"Nah. That's why it's a curse." He pulled a bottle from the pocket of his pea jacket, fighting away the lining. He unscrewed the lid and handed it across to Charlie who took a liberal swallow unaware of the potency of the liquor. He spluttered, almost choking, as the impact of the whiskey took his breath away.

"Warming up are we?" A look of sheer impishness crossed

Connors face, and he chortled with delight as the bottle was handed back. The two slowly became very drunk, oblivious to the cold. As the night wore on they stayed talking. About women, about war, about very old things.

Charlie was aware, at one point, of lying flat on his back on the rock hard ground with Connor laughing as he pulled him to his feet, but he couldn't recall if he'd fallen out of the tree or merely slipped getting down to empty a painfully full bladder. He wasn't to know the truth until the following day when the aches and grazes were realized.

Connor, staggering slightly himself, hefted the Highlander to his feet and sang some garbled tune under his breath as the two swayed, arms around each other's shoulders for support, back to the cottage where only Mim remained awake.

She crossed the kitchen and helped Connor get Charlie under control and up the stairs. They tucked him into bed leaving him, fully clothed except for his boots, smiling in his sleep and snoring softly.

She pulled the door closed soundlessly and they made their way down the stairs to their room.

"You're drunk," she said tightly as they pulled the covers back.

"Yeah, but I made a friend *mo chroì*." He grinned at her as he stripped and dove for the blankets.

"Well then…" But it might just have been a very good thing, so she cuddled close to him as his hands began their journey of exploration.

...

CHARLIE DIDN'T WAKE UNTIL AFTER eleven the following morning. His brain did a lurch in his skull when he sat up—sending a shaft of pain across his temples—and his mouth tasted like something had died in it not too recently. He walked very carefully into his little bathroom, looked in the mirror and groaned at the image. Everything hurt. He remembered some of the night: all of what had happened between him and Holly and some of what was discussed up in the tree which caused him to grin and invoking even more pain.

He stood under the hot shower wincing as bruises and grazes announced themselves, recalling a rare glimpse of himself looking up at Connor who'd been laughing like a fiend at whatever it was he had done.

Ah well, boyo, another day. We'll see, feeling relatively certain he'd made a deeper enemy of Holly but a grand friend in Connor.

He rugged up in thick socks, jeans, sweatshirt, pullover, scarf and beanie and went downstairs for coffee and, perhaps, some commiserations. His dad was alone with Hunter; his backpack beside the door.

"You leaving already Dad? Is there any coffee anywhere?"

"Mornin' Charlie. You look like shite."

"Thanks Dad." Charlie saw the coffee pot on the back of the range and shuffled to the cupboard. He filled the biggest mug he could find and sat at the table spooning in sugar, saying nothing.

"I've got to get back to your Mum."

Robbie sat carefully beside him as Hunter left them to themselves calling, *You won't forget now?* after him.

"What was that about?"

"Not that matters a' the moment. You made up your mind what you wanna do?"

"Aye. I'm hanging here a bit longer. I've a few things I need to think through."

Robbie smiled a smile to light the day. "You're not the only one. I'm about to challenge your mother to a move."

"Not here to the island?"

"Don't be daft. No. Weary Bay."

"You're *joking*! There's nothing there to do. She'll never come, Dad. There's no work from what I know. What on earth—"

"Well, och. Shall I bet my career on her comin'? You want somethin' other than coffee for that headache?"

"Sure, Dad, bet a career you'd not have if you come down this way."

Robbie's eyes merely twinkled. He wasn't about to tell anyone at all the rest of his plan either. Not yet anyway. "You think you'll come home before the island closes down?"

"Probably. That's three weeks away. I can do a heap in three weeks."

"What *are* you doing?"

"Compiling." Rob looked confused but Charlie just shrugged and hugged his father goodbye. "Tell Mum I love her."

Tires sounded on the gravel path outside and Woolly tooted the horn urgently. Rob shouldered his pack and headed out.

"Wait!" Charlie gulped the last of his coffee. "I'm coming with you to the dock."

Holly was outside sitting at one of the Travelers' clan hearths getting to know several of the 'younger' fairy women as Charlie climbed into the cab behind his father. As they drove off towards the village the sudden, unbidden thought that he could be leaving the island struck her with the oddest sensation. Fear that he might not return? Don't be ridiculous. But it was. She was disgusted with herself for the feeling. She turned away from the receding vehicle and worked at concentrating on what the women were saying.

CHAPTER THIRTEEN

THE ELEGANT, BLACK SAILED HOOKER, THE *Rosie Rua*, would occasionally, in high summer, deem to transport enthusiastic tourists around the coastline of the island so that they could go back home and tell their friends and show their photographs of the mystical boat. Her skipper, Raurie Mór, would embellish already graphic tales of what ship had sunk where and when, how it had foundered upon the dangerous rocks that lay submerged in the high tide like broken teeth, what they had carried and who—if at all—had survived.

The long nights had begun, and the waters around Inishrún were far too treacherous for any boats other than the Hooker to navigate. Three more weeks and the last of the provisions would be hauled in and the island would become a virtual fortress of inaccessibility for the following four months, disappearing into the mists.

THE TUATHA DÉ DANANN HAD BEEN arriving for several days. They came from everywhere, to the village of Weary Bay on the far west coast of the mainland, and the *Rosie Rua* was kept busy transporting the arrivals to the isle of secrets. Raurie gloried in reunions with past companions who only ever came at this time of year unless extreme circumstances summoned the need for a grand council. This was the Great Fire Festival where the many worlds, both seen and unseen to the mortal eye, overlapped and became obvious and accessible to anyone fey and open enough to sense and recognize the shift.

The Travelers drove into the fishing town in every sort of vehicle imaginable and they parked on the field just up the hill from the village as they had always done knowing that the villagers would never go near. They'd shoulder their belongings and instruments, dress in all their unpredictable finery, and wander the docks exchanging hellos and news both with others from around the country and with the locals. They bought the traditional sweet pumpkin pies from one stall and hot dogs from another, admired the local crafts that were up for sale just like on any other market day, and played a pipe or two, inviting dance, while they waited for Raurie.

Many of Weary Bay's residents had their own traditions around the time of year they called *oíche shamhna* and were used to this annual pilgrimage, and as a result there was a carnival feel to the docks. No one knew exactly what the deal was, and if they did they kept it close amongst themselves, but their grandparents, and those before them, had thrilled the children with spooky tales of supernatural beings and ancient spirits that wandered abroad, and remnants of legend intermingled with talk of saints and ancestors, of witches, of the Gentry, the fairies, the Good Folk, riding on eldritch, bedecked magnificent horses. The occasional bowl of milk and plate of barley cakes was still left on door-stoops as old custom decreed even though it was thought by most to be mere superstition and by a few as downright heathen.

THE SÍDHE HAD A REVERENCE FOR the sea but would prefer to honor it from the land.

Those up for their turn on the decks mostly exhibited various shades of grey and green around the mouth, controlling an ancient and instinctive fear by paying each other out over how ill they looked; knowing they'd be sure to laugh about it later when their feet were on solid ground, and as soon as the boat docked and they were on shore, they got to chatting like magpies and a whistle or a bodhrán would start up on exiting the turnstile.

They made their way, mostly on foot, from the wharf to the site of the festival, setting up tents and other makeshift dwellings as far off as the henge to the west, and the forest to the east and into the heath to the north, with the majority in the vicinity of the meadow between Mim's house and the Barrow.

WITH THE EXCEPTION OF HUNTER AND Brighid, who'd taken the journey through the Dreaming Lands several days earlier, Clan Fíach Dubh left their autumn place the day before Samhain. Black Annis was behind the wheel and she drove the bus as quietly as possible through the village of Brackenridge just as the day began stirring.

Smoke from many chimneys mingled with the scents of frying bacon, brewing coffee and the bakery on Girrell Street, intoxicating the Travelers into momentary regret. The bus crept, barely noticed, through town and out along the winding, badly pitted back roads that led to the highway that merged with the western arterial.

They'd picked up several others of their troupe who'd converged on the outskirts of New Rathmore: Raven, who'd been goodness knows where, Vincent and Kathryn—two of the newer members of the group who'd been staying at her farm at Falconstowe with several other permanently-based clans—and Willie, a sídhe, and his girlfriend Merrin, a witch and recent participant in the quicken brew, who'd both been staying at her old friend Dimity's flat, where the two had spent several months looking after the bookshop while the latter went off on some pilgrimage or other into her past. They'd brought Dimity's van which was just as well because the bus was overcrowded and several of its occupants had needed to be unloaded.

They arrived at Weary Bay just after half past one in the afternoon, parked the bus and the van and bundled themselves with all their equipment and provisions, knowing that Raurie would be agitated at their lateness as he didn't ever like to be at sea near to dusk "just in case".

The Fíanna were booked for the first gig at the pub that night and they knew they'd be cutting time very thin what with having to set up their hearth beforehand, but Woolly had foreseen their need for haste and was waiting for them at the wharf with the boot open and a makeshift trailer tied up to his rear bumper in anticipation of their equipment. The band had gone with him while the others accompanied Seamus Beag who'd come along with his horse and cart to take any of the stragglers up to the field.

There were hundreds—perhaps more like a thousand—of the eccentric visitors moving from tent to tent, busy and joyful, and the last arrivals were greeted as though they were royalty.

HOLLY WATCHED FROM HER BEDROOM WINDOW, pondering how like a riotous colorful, strange garden everything seemed from this distance. Fires bloomed like chrysanthemums as late afternoon stole the light and pale mists crept like ghosts' fingers from the sea onto the land from all directions.

Two weeks.

If a person's life, and everything that persons understands of reality, can change by denying one lie about the way they've been living—can change in one night—how much more can two weeks achieve?

Holly was granted her desire for time with Mim. She was taught about the spirits of the land, the waters, the winds. She was told about the mysterious link that always exists between fey people and certain plants and beasts and how they can unlearn the blind spot in themselves that most in society have had imposed on them by insistence.

The secret protection from that mass illusion was in the talisman that she wore: the thread that bound the feathers was the thread that bound her to her birthright, to Mim, to their ancestors through Mim; the raven feathers linked her to the birds themselves, sacred to the Great Mystery, her messengers, whisperers of prophecy and warning; the two pennies had been gifted to Mim by Brighid, queen of the Tuatha Dé Danann, who'd taught her how to move back and forth between the gates of time by a ritual called the *Penny Spell of Power* which she'd shown to Holly just last night for the first time and that she was certain would be the first of many such journeys. The small white stone held the soul of Inishrún within it so that the sweet song of the island could guide her back when she was ready.

So logical really. So simple.

"Are spells always so easily done?" Holly had asked.

They'd climbed the zig-zaggy hewn steps up to the ridge above the henge and had spent the morning talking and watching the sea birds dive bomb a shoal of mackerel amidst the seals that inhabited a small rocky islet, called Cloch naRon, frolicking and hunting undisturbed.

"If the intention's clean of coercion. Sure." Mim replied.

"You ought to write a book someday," she'd said in all innocence.

Mim barked out a laugh, looking at Holly in disbelief.

"What?" Holly was confused. She'd meant it. There were bound to be others who would benefit from the kind of knowledge she was being told and who didn't have any other way of learning about it.

"And have it sit on some fiction shelf?"

"No. Yeah. I guess so."

"I *know* so! Anyway, that's not how this works."

"Not how *what* works?"

"Knowing and remembering are the links between the so-called past and future. When knowing and memory are spoken they're truer."

"How so?"

"When you speak a thing or sing a thing in a certain way it

joins the wind; it's breath upon the breath of earth. I guess that's the best way to put it. That's why the old traditions were always oral. There's only so much a person can learn from books. The part of us that's capable of being a storehouse for vast amounts of information, understanding and lore can get lazy like a muscle that doesn't get used—over time it withers and becomes useless.

"You're learning really easily with me. Why do you think that is? You could have read about it in one way or another. The books are out there."

Holly had laughed and shaken her head. "Not like this. There are no books about this."

"You're wrong. They get labeled myth or legend. They get thought of as fiction. They're not thought about as real stuff."

"There're books in the New Age shop near where I lived. I looked through a few. Even bought a couple but they didn't ring true somehow."

"And why was that?"

Holly had thought about it. She'd *wanted* to believe what she'd read: the books on witchcraft, the books on druids and shamans and other magic people. She'd loved the content and the concepts; sensed herself in the words but she didn't.

"I guess it's because I didn't know the authors; didn't know if *they* were real." She tilted her head, looking away from Mim to where the rocky coastline misted with foam. When she turned back to Mim she rolled her eyes as the understanding became clear.

Holly stood and reached for Mim's hands. "I'm *starving*. Can we go?"

"Can I ask you a question first?"

"Sure."

"It's a bit personal."

Holly squatted down to avoid the bite of the wind. "What?"

"Can you drop the snarkiness towards Charlie?"

Holly didn't say a word, just radiated all snarly and snarky.

110

"He's not an enemy you know. And he likes you. It's getting so it's really uncomfortable to be in the same room with you two what with him trying to be nice and you being the Ice Queen."

"I don't want to be nice back, okay?"

"But why?"

"I don't *know* why!" She clamped her jaws, refusing to be drawn.

Mim wasn't in the least put out by the attitude. "Well I think you're lying."

Holly whirled on her. "*Please* don't wreck the morning by talking about this! I'll try. Okay? For everybody else's sake. Will that do?"

Hiss, thought Mim, shrugging.

After an uncomfortable moment Holly took a small breath. "I'm sorry, Mim." She snuggled closer. "That was really rude. I'm *so* sorry."

"S'okay. Good to know there's fire in there," and she snorted and made cat-snarl noises in good humor. "Food?"

"Food!"

SHE WAS DEEP IN THOUGHT, AND was startled by the light tapping on her door. Charlie's muffled voice asked if she was awake. She stood from where she'd been nestled amongst a pile of cushions on the wide windowsill, stretching lazily and calling for him to come in.

"It's amazing out there." Charlie was joyous, barging into the room all smiles. Much to Holly's disgust with herself she was finding it difficult to hold onto the detached attitude that she had determined to maintain. He was like a big kid—a highly intelligent big kid—and his fiery, straightforward outburst the other night had left her feeling dangerously interested. The last thing she thought she desired, however, was to be approached on any personal level so she had avoided being alone with him since.

"What do you want Charlie?" She yawned, heading to the

bathroom.

"Mim sent me up to get you; she wants you in the kitchen."

"Tell her I won't be long. I gotta have a shower first."

Charlie strode to the window, watching the scene below. "Can I wait here?"

"Suit yourself. Just don't touch anything."

She scooped up a change of clothes from the chair beside the unlit hearth and pulled the bathroom door closed behind herself.

Ten minutes later they headed downstairs and along the hallway to the kitchen where a frenzy of baking, food preparation and liberal drinking was underway.

The uproar and hilarity between the visitors went quiet as the couple entered, mainly because Charlie was obviously not one of the Lost and, at first take, seemed very un-fey. Until they probed. It was there then, after all, buried deep in the blood, dormant or simply slumbering. They understood that he wouldn't be here if it was not okay with the banríon and the Elders. As for Holly, well she was Mim's blood, so she was okay, wasn't she?

"Who's on the beer?" shouted a punkish Black Annis as the din rose again and a fiddle started up from Willie niFíach Dubh, also known as Red-Haired-Willie, who sat warm and smiling on a corner of the kitchen table, back to back with a lean dark haired Goth-looking girl who was introduced later as Merrin, late of New Rathmore.

HIGH UP ON THE WIDEST PART OF the ridge on the western escarpment, accessed by the ancient foot-worn stair that wound precariously up from the henge, overlooking the raging ocean on one side and the whole of Inishrún on the other, a great bonfire was being built as processions of Tuatha Dé Danann defied the encroaching gloom and the bitter cold to ascend the cliffside with their bundles of wood, and bones, thick with discarded hopes and savage memories of the things seen and done throughout the previous year at the hands of the greedy or the violent or the ignorant.

The same thing was occurring at the far north, east and south with debris being constructed into towering beacons.

AS THE LAST OF THE DAY SLID BEYOND the western horizon all of the hearth fires across the island were extinguished in preparation for the creation of the 'First Fire' deep within the heart of the Barrow where Hunter, the Gentry of all the fairy folk, Mim and other invited guests, were gathered in ritual. Brighid, the greatest and most ancient of the Dé Danann knelt at the keystone, her hands held gently, as though in a caress, by the sídhe that most called Woolly—because of the glamour he chose to adopt in common time—who was actually Aengus Óg, the lord of love, who had shed his grizzled stubbly illusion, as was only proper, and appeared in all his beauty and power.

The gathering raised their voices in song, calling to the spirits of wind and earth, sea and spirit to bless the future seasons and to remember to continue to be beautiful, letting them know that the fires would be lit in their honor to remind them that the pact that existed between the fey folk and the world—to protect it, to keep the magic alive and to care for the mysteries large and small—was as strong as it ever was.

Hunter sat all rugged up in a worn, ex-army greatcoat, with his long legs, in old denim jeans, drawn up to his chest, his scuffed, steel-capped boots just visible beneath the frayed hems. His knees were bent, and his arms were wrapped around them. He looked like he was asleep but wasn't; he roamed the Otherworld in search of the Great Mystery in the annual attempt to entice her to the Barrow.

STRANGE THINGS—APPARITIONS, enchantments, things half seen, veils between a myriad of realities—permeated the Otherworld as they did at no other season and Hunter wandered aimlessly not knowing where to begin his search for her.

"Are you here milady?" he called every now and then. No answer. He could feel in his gut that she was close; would want to be enticed as always. He was down by Forgotten Lake perched, for a spell, on the thick trunk of a long-fallen tree, simply basking in the loveliness of the perpetual twilight that thickened over the surface of the never-still water, when she came, in the body of a huge white hound, ears red, tongue lolling, in the company of a pack of dogs of every size and breed, all sniffing and grinning after some unseen quarry.

She broke from the hunt and sat beside Hunter as the others went their way, oblivious to her absence. He chose not to look as she morphed—she always did it in such a fashion that his insides lurched—into the appearance of a woman whose skin and ragged hair were white but whose eyes were those of a seal with eyebrows and lashes as black as night. The semblance of clothing she concocted was as fickle and unique as her sense of humor: knee-high lace-up boots, black and white striped stockings, short black skirt with a plaid shirt tied around the hips and a fox skin jacket that still moved, indicating that the foxes were alive in there somewhere, over a man's old-fashioned, crisp white opera shirt fastened at the collar with an ancient bronze pin.

"Hi Hunter, waz up?" she grinned.

"It's Samhain again, love."

"Again?" Feigning shock, she shook her head sending icicles flying in all directions.

Hunter smiled. He knew she had a deathly serious side to her nature that she shared with no one except him, but it did not please her to show it often.

"Will you come?"

"Do I *have* to?"

"It's what you do," and he scuffed the pebbly ground with both dangling feet.

"You want my fire?"

114

Hunter nodded, looking in her direction, being careful not to get lost in her eyes.

"They're going to try to steal my Barrow, Hunter. What're you going to do to stop them? And Aengus? What's his trip making things more complicated than they were?"

He shrugged. No plan. He told her that they had an ally in the young Highland exile and that he'd agreed they could interfere—a kind of loop-holed way of working the situation, to be sure, but why not? —but until the fire was back in the world there was no way they could be inspired to come up with a solution.

"'Kay," she mused. Hunter sensed more.

"What else?"

"Oh, nothing."

He waited for her to continue; she seemed lost in thought. "Milady?"

"The world is in such a mess, y'know? Sometimes it gets hard to not just drown it all and start fresh." She sighed and looked at Hunter with damp eyes before perking up. "But it's okay y'know; we're on it. Me and the weather. You and the others; we're on it aren't we?"

"Sure are. What else?" knowing she would take as long as she wanted to talk things through.

"I'll maybe tell you some other time." She grinned, exposing small shining white canines. "We off to do the fire thingy then?"

Hunter hopped lightly from his perch, shrugging off her distraction, and the two passed into the Barrow.

PEOPLE STOPPED WHAT THEY WERE saying mid-sentence. In the cottage, in the village, around every hearth. It was as though some mighty bell tolled causing the island to go quiet.

And all the fires died.

And the mists crawled across the land from the sea.

And everyone moved towards the Barrow, unlit rush torches in their hands.

From deep within the tumulus the gathering heard the bódhrans begin. Five hundred drummers. Drawing magic up from the earth's core, opening up the gates of time, breaking down all thought and separation.

A flame formed within the upturned hands of Aengus Óg and Brighid (also known as White Eyes; also known as the Banríon Mór), that burned green and violet. This was the form the Great Mystery took.

Ramparts had been laid, like bridges, between the ground and the Barrow. Hand in hand, the flame between them, Brighid and Aengus emerged from the tunnel beneath the earth, followed by the others in procession, and they walked to the ramparts and climbed to the summit. They wove sunwise around each of the twenty trees before moving to the center of the ring where the great stone altar lay, a cauldron of oil upon it to which they touched the flame.

As the light flared, so the drummers were joined by pipers, and the throng proceeded up the sídhe mound to light their torches from the Source.

Most scattered back to home and hearth, including Mim and the others who were not Dé Danann, to kindle the need-fires that would not be allowed to die out until the same time next year.

Samhain was always a blessing but also a warning to take nothing for granted, as too many things go wrong when that happens.

The procession made its way over the land to the henge where a béansídhe waited, her brand ready to take the flame to the top of the cliff, to the first sentinel fire, from there to be relayed by runners who would link every pyre, from the ridge around the island, to the wharf where wood had been piled high upon a barge to be sent out to sea to Manannán Mac Lir and from there back to the henge where it would complete the great circle and light the final blaze on the king stone within.

THE FIRST OF THE RUNNERS, LIATH Leannán, had been born in the days when the Dumnonach clan were in their prime, a thousand years before the Romans had invaded her home country.

Her mother had been a mortal—the chieftain of her tuath—steeped in the ways of the mysteries and a great warrior.

In those times the people were governed by mother-right and the elders, and both sexes, acknowledged the oldest woman amongst them as their Wise One.

Liath Leannán's birth had been prophesied by this old woman who hadn't known the whole of it but had seen the "man" who was to be her father in the Dreaming Lands only and never upon the ground that graced the people's bodies' needs. That he was of the Gentry she hadn't known but that his daughter would one day be caught up in a great destiny was certain.

So when Sila had met the stranger with milk-white skin and deep brown eyes and hair the color of night who had spoken little of the language but seemed to understand it, and who, when asked from where he'd come, had pointed out over the Western Sea, she had taken him as a foreigner. And she took him as a lover.

He hadn't stayed long but while he'd been with her Sila's happiness was complete. He had learned to speak the language unnervingly quickly and so was able to say I love you and every other tender thing beneath the sky.

The night he left he sent her a dream of their daughter, and said he would love her forever but could no longer live away from the sea, which had made no sense upon waking except that he was gone, and she had cried.

But her courses did not come and nine months after she gave birth to Liath and called her also *Leannán* (which meant 'lover') because her father had never given Sila a name by which to call him except that.

It had been recognized from the start that she was fey. The old woman had said, *Ah…* The same coloring as her father, a beauty yet to unfold. She walked early, she talked early, she ran like a deer, absorbed stories and lineages, poetry and songs and could recall them word perfect when asked, and had an eye for the bow and a swift arm for the staff all before her twelfth birthday when her menstrual time began and the rites of womanhood were bestowed.

But it didn't stop—the strangeness—because instead of rounding out, with budding breast and softened hip, Liath stayed lean. She braided her hair in warrior braids and took for her totems not one beast but four: the seal and the hound and the horse and the raven, so that her tattooing was abundant. By the time she reached late adolescence she was corded with lean muscle and was skilled with most weapons including the sword and slingshot, bow and long pole; she could swim as well above the water as she could beneath and had been given the task of teaching this skill to the younger children.

Many of the tribes' young males tried in vain to bed her but she remained with her mother and retained a strange distance from her peers.

Her favorite place was the tiny cove at the most westerly tip of the mainland where she would often sit for hours watching the sea and yearning for something she could not name.

Four more years passed, then four more, and the people of the tribe began to look at her sideways and avoid her often because it had become obvious to all that she had ceased to age.

It was the night of her twenty-fifth birthday that the Wise One came to Silas door in the late hours accompanied by her apprentice who carried a small box carved all over with sacred spirals and trisceles.

Liath was still awake, as was Sila. They were disturbed from a game of *brándubh* when the old woman's leathery voice called from beyond the heavy bull's hide door flap.

The old woman's name was Una and she was ushered into the chieftain's home and seated close to the fire. Liath was asked by her mother to awaken the servants but Una said no, this visit required no guesting laws, merely a small offering of *uisce beatha* which she drank in one mouthful.

"Sit." The three women joined her before the hearth and she reached for the box that her apprentice still guarded, pulling it to her knees and placing her gnarled hands lovingly upon its lid.

"What I have to say—what I have to show you both—is not to leave this room."

The others nodded in acknowledgement. "Except for you, Liath Leannán, except for you."

"Why, Greatmother?"

"Because I think you must go away very soon." Liath looked to Sila and back again to Una, confusion and disbelief written on her face.

"But I don't want to leave, Greatmother. What could you say that could change that? I'm happy enough."

"Are you?"

"Yes, I am happy. Tell her Sila." But her mother was silent.

"As happy as the others?"

"I don't know how others feel."

"You know you're not like the others."

"Like the other women you mean. As a chieftain's daughter I choose my differences just as I choose not to wed or bear children.

"That's not what I mean, and you know it!" the Elder snapped.

Liath Leannán closed her mouth but could not shed the defiance in her eyes.

"You are too like your father to stay."

Now both Sila and her daughter looked confused.

"I learned very little of Leannán while he was with me. No one knew more," the chieftain spoke quietly.

"No one could. I have dreamed the truth at last."

"What truth?"

"That he could walk back into your life today and that you would look like his mother." As she spoke she undid the locks on

119

the box. "Do you know what's in here?"

"I've never seen that box before."

"Because it's a mystery; a secret of the keepers of the lore. It's very ancient." She lifted the lid and both mother and daughter leaned forward to see better in the shadowy room.

"Here, Sila. You first. Run your hand across it and tell me what it is." Sila sank her hand into the box and touched a pelt. She ran her hand over its softness wonderingly.

"Now you."

The old woman gestured to Liath Leannán who placed her hand in the box and pulled it back quickly with a look of horror on her face. "Who have you killed? Who have you killed that he should be flayed!" She was becoming more upset by the second and her mother took her in her arms and shushed her and stroked her.

"You see?" Una smiled toothlessly.

"See *what*?" Sila was out of her league. She had simply felt the soft hide of some long-dead beast, beautifully tanned and supple. Liath's reaction was bewildering.

"It's the skin of a selkie."

Sila's heart beat faster.

"Many generations before my birth he came onto the land because he'd seen a woman whose beauty enchanted him beyond belief. But another also loved her and when the stranger had looked upon her, and she'd looked back at him in such a way as to light a fire without flint, the rejected man slew the selkie.

"As he lay dying in her arms he'd begged her to get him his skin so that he could pass to the Otherworld in his true form. She'd run as fast as she could to the cove where *you* go Liath. She found the skin and returned to her lover, but it was too late, and the body of the man shriveled before her eyes, dried out and blew away like dead leaves in the wind. So she kept his skin.

"No one remembered her name. It was long ago and yet that fact is unforgivable…" She left the rest unsaid.

Sila paled but Liath Leannán was still; composed.

Una's eyes were as bright as blue glass as she watched the young woman. "You know don't you? Have you always known?"

"I've always known. I have memories that are not mine," she laughed, "and I smell things that others can't smell. And often at the cove they would be close. That they were family."

"You *knew* them?" Sila trembled at the knowledge; fought to believe it was not so, that *he* had not been so.

"I didn't know for sure, Sila, only that they came close to shore and would watch me. I felt their spirits so strongly which is why I took the seal as my first totem."

It all made sense. That Liath Leannán was not a selkie was certain, but that she was fairy—or half of her was—was also certain.

Una entered the Dreaming Lands and set a talisman for any of the fairies to read and they came for Liath not a fortnight later—a band of Travelers heading north while the passes were still open.

LIATH LEANNÁN HELD HER BRAND TO that of Aengus Óg and began the climb. He grinned as he watched her take the ancient and treacherous stairs two at a time like one of those mountain sheep from the northern isles.

She reached the ridge, hardly raising a sweat, and passed the brand into the bonfire before a sídhe, known only as O'Toole, lit his own torch from it and ran off along the rocky escarpment towards the next pyre.

Liath looked over the night and the throng that moved deliciously in and out of wraiths of fog. Her sight was sharp and clear, and it wasn't long before she recognized Hunter—by the sheer size of him—sequestered amongst a cluster of Dé Danann whose pattern she knew. She whooped as she took off back the way she had come excited at the prospect of reunion with Black Annis, her old ally in many an indiscretion.

Annis saw her approaching at a lope and grinned as she closed the distance, throwing her arms around her friend. It had been many years since the two had met up and snuck away from the rest of the clan to pub crawl through New Rathmore stirring up the menfolk wherever they went, even so far as to instigate a brawl in a toffee-nosed north side club at two. in the morning.

They strolled back to the others, Liath Leannán receiving a fond if wary greeting.

"So who are the new people?" She didn't know Rowan who snuggled into Annis in obvious passion, and she'd heard about Robin and Puck but had no idea which they were of the many.

"Shall we go back to my place?" Mim suggested, having rejoined the group once her hearth was re-lit. "There's a ton of food to go 'round."

"I'm easy. Sure."

Entering the kitchen was like walking into a contradiction—cozy and warm after the chill of the night but with Charlie and Holly, both busy with last minute feasty things, lending an ice to the room that felt like it could be cut with a knife.

"Oh my," Liath whispered to Annis, looking from the one mortal to the other, her gaze settling on Charlie and a heat spreading up her cheeks.

"Liath! I wouldn't…" but Annis' warning went unheeded as the selkie half-caste glided across the room to introduce herself.

Her sense of her own identity rested very strongly on never allowing herself to fall in love. She had done, twice over the years, and she'd lost herself as the emotion of it had consumed her—something in the power of the fire of the fairies. She'd had the self-fortitude to leave, both times, when she'd recognized how many of her other passions she'd rejected. It was some deep, unconscious thing; *the selkie in me*, she thought. Too much water!

So she'd stuck with mortal men as lovers ever since. She could take her pleasure and walk away unaffected, in difference to her ancestors who'd been the opposite.

You are a very pretty man, she thought, turning on her full glamour to entice his interest.

"What's your story?" she asked, pouring herself a shot-glass of whisky.

"You are?" Charlie asked, out of his league.

They struck up a light conversation. His humor was infectious, and he kept her laughing as he told about his encounter with Oberon who'd helped him eat his sandwiches while he'd waited for the death that he was sure was to come. The others gathered big pots of food and loaves of yeasty bread and *barm brach*, crates of wine and beer and whisky and musical instruments, heading out into the night for the great feast.

"Come on you two, give us a hand with this lot!" called Brighid balancing an armload of cushions with still more piled against the far wall to be gathered.

The troupe chattered like birds as they made their way to a central hearth. All except Holly who felt like an outsider. *What's wrong with you,* whispered her inner demon, over and over and over, as she lagged behind.

…

CAMERON BLANE WAS ON WATCH AT THE tower when the first of the fires was lit across the waters to the west and he phoned through to the pub where most of the town was gathered awaiting word.

Grainne had driven down, in her battered old Jeep, at Robbie's request and they were sitting at one of the tables as the hurrah was raised. The pub was a little on the chilly side as, thought Robbie, someone had either forgotten or neglected to light the fire in the great hearth. Grainne observed, in slight confusion, as Henry Poe, behind the bar, lit a taper from a disposable lighter and walked over to the hearth with great ceremony and bent to light the kindling beneath a great stack of wood. A cheer went up from the crowd of locals and someone began to sing *Auld Lang Syne* whilst still others kissed and slapped each other on the back calling greetings of *Happy New Year*.

"What's going on Rob?" She was smiling, though, as the publican called out that the first round was on the house and Alice came from the kitchen out back, along with several of the local lasses, carrying trays covered in fruit and nut cakes and great platters of butter, telling people to help themselves.

"Well, see, that's what I wanted to talk to you about." She tilted her head to one side, waiting for him to continue.

CHAPTER FOURTEEN

THE CELTIC DAY BEGINS WITH THE SUN'S SETTING and not with its rising, and the night of the first day of the new year on the island was spent in feasting and catching up with long distant fairies, but the tunes played by the many musicians present were mostly laments as things that had passed 'into the West' were sung to, toasted and placed into the legends of remembered things.

Most did not sleep until dawn, or even not at all, so the first day was as quiet and preparatory as it always was. That night, however, was the night before the beginning of three days of games, challenges, championships, races and pageantry and from late morning the practice areas had been marked out, and many of the folk were stripped to the waist and sweating with the exertion of their training whilst still others roamed, mumbling the paeans, songs and stories they had created for the challenges that took place in the evenings, judged by the champions of past generations—the eldest among them.

Hunter, Willie, Connor, Liath Leannán, Raven, Black Annis, Puck and Robin were all practicing with the quarterstaff and Charlie watched for a good hour, amazed at their skill, before asking desperately to be allowed to join them.

Connor and Willie laughed a little at the idea of the scholarly mortal wielding a big stick but agreed just the same to show him a few warm-up moves, passing him a lightweight staff. He copied them as they went through a series of strikes and thrusts, leaps and turns, stopping them every so often to have them repeat a pattern. They left him alone then to practice the unfamiliar maneuvers.

Holly sat away from everyone watching; brooding. She felt like she was slipping further and faster into some pit of despair that she could do nothing to prevent. She watched Charlie having fun and her jaw clenched painfully. She'd seen him and Liath flirt into the night and at one stage they'd gone off together and she'd felt a stone in her gut. She felt like some crazy woman obsessed with the need to dislike the annoyingly intelligent and amicable Scot yet unable to dismiss him from her thoughts.

Mim had tried unsuccessfully to pull her into a playtime mood telling her not to be such a Pisces but she could not escape what was happening. The new magics that she had been introduced to were exciting and she really wanted to learn more, but her self-focus—her life-long sense of inadequacy—engulfed her in self-pity. She had no creative skills whatsoever. That was the most troubling thing. Other than being social and disliking it (in the past) and reading prolifically, she hadn't initiated any learning or acquired any skill. And there was the demon laughing at her. Why? She understood. She'd always blamed everyone and everything else for being colorless and boring when it was her. Her.

She didn't belong no matter what Mim thought; she figured her aunt had planted this fantasy of her involvement when she'd given her the talisman. Maybe she'd needed Holly—family—to be a part of her world because she couldn't stand being the only one?

It's all very wonderful, she thought, *but it's all just too far out there for me*. She realized that she required something a little less extravagant than all of this. It was just too alien. She just couldn't do it. The whole thing was playing havoc with her sense of herself; with her emotions. She felt like she was drowning. She was caught between wanting to lash out or disappear into her own malaise.

Down on the training field Liath saw Charlie hit his staff up and down on the ground, drop it to the earth, put his hands on his hips and walk around it abusing it for being unhelpful. She was delighted with his antics. She stopped partway through a complicated pattern of her own and walked over to him.

"What's it done now?" she asked in a conciliatory tone.

"It keeps telling me that *I'm* the one who's forgetful. I'm just trying to establish a pecking order here." He stared stonily at the staff, *tsking*.

"Come on. Pick it up." Charlie did so, shaking it in warning; Liath laughing so hard her cheeks began to ache.

She went over the simple set of strikes and blocks, explaining where his footwork was wrong and catching him out when he made the moves difficult by shifting his grip at the wrong time.

They went over it and over it for a good ten minutes until Charlie relaxed and the form came more naturally. He was sweating hard by the end of it. Liath stopped him.

"Take a break *mo chroí*. When you get back to it it'll be easier. You wanna come get a bite to eat?"

Charlie stripped off his tee shirt and wiped the sweat from his face. Here it was, almost winter, and he was hot!

They walked over the field together, arm in arm, towards one of the cooking hearths where fish were strung along a spit wafting out a succulent aroma, and several pots of coffee, boiling water and pots of tea, were arranged around the coals. There was also, at this hearth, a mountain of fresh dark bread and several cheeses, soft or sharp. Liath was dressed simply in loose black pants and a white men's singlet. She had a grey and green plaid shirt tied around her hips, and soft leather moccasin-type boots on her feet. Pressed up against him he could feel the warmth of her—the strength of her—and he was unnerved. Surely this was just a buddy thing? She was certainly a woman to draw attention, being

127

built the way she was, but that in itself was enough to make any man wary. I mean who could deal with a woman stronger than most guys? Yet still the blood rose within him and he found it necessary to think about stacking bricks so as not to have his body betray him.

Liath Leannán could sense what he was feeling. But she also was unnerved. This was a mere boy, albeit a big one, and she'd planned a little pleasure for herself at his expense but was experiencing an altogether unexpected sensation. He was just so bloody likeable.

As they sat by the fire she attempted to keep the conversation casual, but he continued to boggle her with completely unexpected off-the-wall comments and suggestions that had her falling down laughing several times.

When she asked him about himself he'd given her a brief rundown of his history and his family's history, and his shine brightened as he talked, to the point where she was bathed in its beauty as were several others who'd been drawn closer by its proximity.

Liath found herself shooting out a warning thought to several other women at the hearth, when she sensed their rising interest, and was as surprised as they were. This was not like Liath Leannán at all, not at all.

By the time they bounded back to the practice field her reputation with mortal men was in tatters.

Charlie was a mess. She was beautiful. She was funny; she was very, very sexy. She was a fairy for goodness sake. Oh, but she was bonny. His reserved, mild-mannered joy at life was blossoming into something quite amazing and what he didn't realize was that it released the *shine* that the Dé Danann saw, to their delight. It usually slumbered contentedly within him because he'd never really been truly surprised by anything before coming here.

Recollections of Holly's complicated meanness were rendered

ineffectual in light of the moment and he was relieved. He'd been very attracted to her at first but that had eroded as she'd continued the hostility. He'd felt obligated to apologize to her on more than one occasion for some offence that he hadn't committed, and he *had* wanted them to be friends. Well he would just stop trying. He wanted to savor the uncomplicated. Charlie liked to laugh. Being happy was his natural state. Growing up with a family that honestly loved each other was probably the reason for it, he supposed.

Hunter had been right about treasure and he felt good about swimming in it for a while. And Liath was also right—when he took up his staff again it did behave itself.

"YOU WANNA TAKE A RUN TO THE lake?" It was only mid-afternoon, but the twilight was already beginning.

Charlie had exhausted himself an hour ago and disappeared. Liath found him covered with Oberon and Harry in the heart of the orchard where Connor had told her she would probably find him.

She grinned as she noticed the little line of dribble that had formed at the corner of his mouth.

Charlie opened his eyes fully, noticed where she was looking and wiped his chin. He groaned and buried his head into Oberon's ruff mumbling *How bloody embarrassing!*

"Walkies!" Liath called to the dogs, slapping her thighs. Charlie stumbled to his feet as they deserted him leaving cold patches along his body.

"What do ya want to do woman?"

"The lake, Charlie; I'm gonna run to the lake."

"An' how far is that?"

"Not far. A mile. Maybe two. It's beautiful I promise."

"Run?" The look of horror on his face did not deter her at all.

"C'mon Charlie, it'll be fun!" Oberon and Harry were alternately panting and closing their mouths and he could almost hear them prompting.

"What if I die?"

"Oh, Charlie."

"Orright but don't wait for me if I get lazy," and he pulled himself to his feet and staggered into a half-hearted lope that Liath matched and only the dogs bounded with any sense of haste.

Mim and Connor, Black Annis and several others were all seated around Selkie Duffy as she told snippets of the poem that she was preparing for the competition, when Charlie and Liath and the hounds ambled past heading for the forest and the lake within its heart. The two emanated a closeness that took Annis aback.

"Well what's that then?" she said to no one in particular.

"Liath's got herself another toy." Willie had seen this happen on several occasions but hadn't recognized the difference this time.

Selkie stopped the verse she'd been telling and looked in the direction of the others.

"Oh dear," Mim responded softly.

"I thought it was Holly he fancied?" Connor asked of no one in particular.

Mim had seen the way he'd looked at her niece on the first one or two days but that had faded as she'd continued her antagonism towards him. She'd thought it would have blown over though, but she'd been wrong.

Brighid looked at Willie and shook her head. "You're way off about him being a bit of sport, Will."

"You think?"

"Well *I've* never seen her behave that way with a mortal man before," piped Annis. "She's never that easygoing; it's always a hunt."

"You don't think maybe it's a tactic?"

"She's happy, Willy." Brighid looked amused. This was interesting.

Mim seemed sad. "I don't know what to do about Holly. It's not working out the way I'd hoped."

Hunter understood that Mim's desire had been to see Charlie and Holly as allies—representatives—on the mainland when the threat to the island's sustainability became a reality. "Let it play itself out *mo chroì*. Nobody's sure of the pattern of this whole thing and the goddess isn't saying everything she knows, as usual. Something's in need of changing, else she wouldn't have gotten involved at all," he'd assured her.

"But Holly's getting angrier. Darker. I'm worried for her."

"Some people have to go there, Mim." Connor was able to say this in all honesty knowing that there were times when all the help in the world just seemed to take the sadness to a deeper place. "Are you going to keep teaching her?"

"It's up to her. Not until the festival is over though, I intend to enjoy it to the max."

She turned to Hunter who had distanced himself from the conversation already, and was fiddling with Puck's hair. "You're probably right, Hunter."

"Huh?"

"I said you're probably right about letting it play out."

He snorted, his black eyes twinkling. "Probably right? Oh ye of little faith. You wanna get ready for work," he gestured to Willie and Annis. "Aren't you due up for a gig?"

"That means me too," Puck said, kissing him tauntingly before joining the others to go in search of the rest of the Fíanna who were doing a session with several other musicians before the nightly feast.

BY THE TIME LIATH LEANNÁN AND Charlie reached Loch Dearmadach he thought his lungs would burst and his legs would be permanently damaged, whilst Liath's breathing was normal. The wonder of her, he thought.

She moved ahead of him to the lake's edge and knelt in the

damp mossy shallows. With her palms down she ran her hands over the surface of the water without causing a ripple. He thought she blessed it or was blessed by it. She stood then and removed her boots, then her other clothing, and the sight of her took his breath away.

She walked into the water until it reached her buttocks before diving.

Charlie waited. And he waited. *No way,* he thought as the minutes passed alarmingly.

He wasn't thinking as he stripped frantically after what must be too long no matter who or what she was.

As he hit the water, naked and running, he screamed at the coldness of it and yet kept going. As he dove in after her his mind was a chaos of underwater weeds or monsters or rocks to break one's neck upon. It was blackness. It was impossible. He lasted thirty seconds before breaking the surface, his teeth chattering and his body feeling as though it was on fire from the cold.

"Shit! Shitshitshitshitshitshit!" he mumbled as he dragged himself up onto the shore, falling to his knees, and cutting one open on a jagged stone.

He crawled up to his clothes, certain he was going into hyperthermia, just as she breached the water, black hair streaming, an angelic, beatific smile lighting her face beyond his endurance. He went into battle with his jeans, struggling with them because his skin was still wet, embarrassed at what the water had done to his genitals and angry at himself for falling for the trick. He shook until his teeth hurt, registering the look on her face as she realized what he had done and how she had scared him, and she ran until she could grab him and stop him from leaving.

She clutched him to her, feeling his bones rattle and his teeth chatter.

"Oh Charlie I'm so sorry..." but he stopped her with his mouth.

HE WAS SO TENDER. HE EXPLORED every part of her as though she was the most precious and dangerous thing he had ever experienced; as though she was a wild animal that he had the honor of being trusted by. The heat of the two of them drove the cold from him quickly until the fire of it all defied description.

Normally men were not like this with Liath. Normally she kept it a romp. Normally she was predatory. Whenever she sought to lighten up the exploration of Charlie's hands or mouth he would stop and wait for her to settle before continuing. *Ah well*, she though briefly, *all new experiences are a good thing at my age*, but the longer they lay together the more intense it all became. He smelled like summer; he smelled of the salt from the sea, as the night mists wove in off the Western ocean permeating even here in the depths of the forest. He smelled of the dirt beneath them and the grass their bodies crushed.

Then they fit together and still he wouldn't hurry, and he loved her; she knew he loved her and damn if she didn't feel it back and what was she to do now? She'd always been so careful.

Between the worlds the goddess purred like a big cat, and Holly watched from the shadow of the deep trees, horrified that she had followed them; horrified that she spied upon them; devastated that it wasn't her wrapped around his body so.

OBERON WALKED AT CHARLIE'S SIDE, and Liath and Harry played tag between the trees, as they headed back towards the gathering. It was fully dark and his two-legged friend's eyesight wasn't like the others yet, and he understood and so chose to be the bigger man leaving the moon-pale mastiff-cross to have his fun for the moment.

Charlie was glowing—anybody could see it—and Liath basked in his shine as he and the great hound caught up to where she waited at the tree-line.

"Can we do that again later?" she grinned, draping an arm around his shoulders.

"Only if you teach me the next bit with the staff, ya wanton fairy."

Liath stopped and turned towards him and saw the wicked glint in his eyes and the lips that attempted to be serious.

"Oh *you'll* wait," she challenged. "Shall I race you to the food then?" and she bolted away knowing he could never catch her, thrilled at the sheer gall of him.

The curious glances of the Dé Danann who were not dancing would have caused her to blush if she'd been capable of embarrassment, but she smiled instead, stretching lazily as Charlie caught up to her.

The smell of roasting meat drew them over to the cooking fires where several people who had agreed to do the hosting for the night carved direct from the boar that had turned on the spit for the past several hours, basted with wine and oil and honey and herbs. The two filled their platters with roasted vegetables and green beans and several slabs of the meat and grabbed a mug each of Guinness before looking for a place to sit close to the music. Charlie's eyes caught Holly's as she watched the two of them pass towards the stage and the look she gave him would have killed him if it'd been a blade. He shrugged at her and smiled and kept on walking.

CHAPTER FIFTEEN

WHEN DO YOU GO back?"

Raurie Mór was pretty drunk. The Samhain gatherings reminded him of the old days when whole clans of people would sit around the great fires of the halls at Teamhair, in all their glory, sharing food and respect with the Tuatha Dé Danann. He knew that Holly was related to the banríon of Inishrún but that didn't make her any easier to like. She stood—overshadowing his conversation with Gemma O'Maile, a full-bodied, stunningly sexy and quick-witted fae—with her hands on her hips and a look of bitter willfulness not lost on any of the company.

"Excuse me, but yer blockin' my view." He reached out to touch her arm and move her aside, but she avoided his touch.

"When do you sail next for the mainland?" She repeated her request differently, refusing to be dismissed.

Raurie looked up at her face. Behind the rudeness she looked like she was fighting tears. It wasn't much in his nature to be compassionate towards the short-lived, their minds were too complicated, full, mostly with too much contradiction, too many agendas. But she *was* Mim's family.

"First lot's leavin' in four days. High tide's at first light. You want passage you'll need to be at the dock afore that 'bout an hour."

"Thank you," and she turned and walked away like a storm.

"What was all that about?" Gemma moved across to sit beside Raurie, snuggling her ample bosom into his side.

Raurie sighed, content. "Seems pissed off, *mo chroì*," and he turned his full attention to the task of the moment.

Holly was a black cloud. She entered Mim's house, passing her aunt and Connor who were laughing together over some private joke, without saying a word, retreating up to her room where she pulled shut the door on their world. There was no lock and she pushed a chair under the knob knowing, as she did so, that no one would enter her private space without her invitation. No. It was merely a gesture, as though she had already been invaded and sought to protect herself "just in case." She knew it was irrational and didn't care.

I'm going mad, she thought angrily as she curled up on the bed. She registered the beauty of the room; thought about Mim and how much she truly loved her and what the hell was she doing being such a bitch and why was she hurting so much without anything real to back it up and what was this horrid obsession with Charlie all about? It made no sense. She'd never been so unhappy in her entire life.

At least you're feeling something, sneered her inner demon.

What's that supposed to mean? she though back.

All this craziness; all the huff and puff... at least you're more fun than you were before.

Oh shut up! And she slammed her mind shut as sleep took her.

A field. Bodies everywhere. The blood of the dying sun doing little to soften the images of silent people, grey and bent, wandering amongst the dead and almost-dead, searching for their loved ones.

Ravens in clouds. Some in the air, many on the ground, a midnight movement amongst the lengthening shadows; horror at the sight of them, knowing what they did.

Where she moved they hopped and cawed to avoid her passing. She could hardly breathe.

He hadn't returned with the survivors to take the long march north so she knew he was here somewhere, and she had to find him; would not leave him so far from home.

Ye' silly wee boy. She whispered it over and over like a litany of love, holding on to that rather than allowing herself to drop into the agony that was sure to come; still hoping he had got away somehow; that they'd crossed wires somehow.

Bonny red head after bonny red head, from either side, until it seemed full night was to become her enemy after all.

Then beneath her feet the ruined body of a man she recognized, beside him another, beside him Laughlin McAlpine's son. Curled nearby, as though in sleep, lay Alex Donald, bravest of them all and there… oh sweet Jesus… bent above another as though in protection, the blood upon his face and neck staining his plaid black in the dying light.

Charlie, what've you done t'yerself? She acknowledged his death as the sound of drummers, started up on the field of the slain.

HOLLY'S EYES FLEW OPEN, tears unchecked as she brought the dream with her, registering the knock that came again upon her bedroom door.

"Go away!" Far from sounding authoritative her voice came out in a crackle and she worked at clearing it.

"It's Mim, Holly. Can we talk?"

"Please go away."

"Not this time. I'll wait here then shall I?"

Holly wiped her eyes roughly, causing mascara to smear beneath them. As she stood from the bed her legs gave way beneath her and she had to grab for the bedpost to stop from falling as the last words of her dream screamed through her mind.

She took the chair from under the knob and opened the door without looking at Mim.

"Make yourself at home." She could have bitten her tongue to stop herself from sounding so snide, but her mouth seemed to belong to someone else lately.

Mim came into a room that was in complete disarray. Holly's clothes were strewn everywhere, and several unfinished meals and dirty coffee cups sat upon every surface. She was aware that it had not been this way in the beginning, and it seemed to her that it coincided with her niece's abrupt behavior change.

In her gut she wondered if she hadn't taught her too much too soon; if it all wasn't way out of Holly's league.

"What's *happening* to me?" Holly slumped on the edge of the bed, looking ragged and disturbed. "I feel like I'm being haunted."

"It's Charlie, isn't it?"

"Oh Mim, I've been awful. I just now dreamed..." and her breath caught in her throat.

"If it's not too much like prying?"

"I have been behaving like a bitch, haven't I?" she snorted, none of it funny.

And like on the first night of her arrival she blurted out everything she was feeling, concluding with the dream.

"I think," Mim began after Holly ran dry, "that the *Penny Spell*, especially at Samhain, was probably a lousy idea." She sat down beside her niece and took one of her hands in her own, stroking the fingers.

"Why?"

"Samhain. You remember what I told you?"

"Yes. The *Gates of Time* and all the ancestor stuff."

"I think you've known Charlie, or someone very like him, some other time; some other way. Nothing else makes sense. Especially since at the start we all thought you liked him."

"That's the worst bit, Mim. I *do* like him! I thought, at first, that I was afraid of liking him because of Patrick; because of not wanting to get caught up in something so quickly after leaving him. But it turned into something else.

"Mim? I followed him and Liath," and the look of self-loathing on her face was almost unendurable.

"And?"

"And I saw them together." There. She'd said it.

"Oh dear," was all Mim could reply.

"So I'm leaving on the boat when she sails in four days."

"It's too soon."

"Mim. I've got to go back to the city."

Mim sighed. She couldn't disagree. Her intuition told her that Holly wouldn't just snap out of it. Winter on the island? It was too hard alone.

"Will you come down and let me make you a cup of coffee?"

"No. I really can't. I just want to stay here for a while. I'll come later; I promise."

Mim withdrew, leaving Holly walking to the window, seeming to forget her aunt's presence; lost within herself.

THE FIRST DAY OF THE CHALLENGES DAWNED clear and biting and still. And the horses had come. The Travelers awakened to snuffles and whinnies as the animals explored the campsites for whatever treats they could find.

Those who were to ride in the great race were already spending time amongst them, checking wither and fetlock, muscle and stance, knowing through long association which were ready to be ridden for the first time and which, of those raced in previous years, would enjoy the challenge again.

That Mim would ride Cloud was certain. She had done so at every carnival since the horse had been old enough to put through the paces.

The great grey mare had won twice in the past five years but this season Mim had her doubts—she seemed more interested in a big roan stallion than being around people and Mim suspected he had covered her already.

All across the hearth-holdings the fires were stacked, and cooking pots bubbled with stew or oats and the smells of bacon and eggs and fresh-baked bannock wafted on the bright air.

Connor and Liath Leannán were both at the hearth of Clan Fíach Dubh, under the pennant of ravens on green, along with the many others who would compete with quarterstaff, bow, sword and spear, and those who were to participate in the great run—a race that would circumnavigate half the island, including the forest and one of the Mothers.

These events would culminate in the evening with the *comórtas labhair*, a grand challenge of word-magic where poets, storytellers, singers and satirists would cast their enchantments. Selkie Duffy was competing for the title of *ard-fhilíocht* with an epic that she had memorized—sure to break the hearts of the judges—determined to take the crown from Shiela ní Dubh, who had won year after year.

The games were set to continue for days, with music, dancing and feasting on each of the nights, much of which was to take place away from the fields down in the village where residents of the island had organized the Community Center, the pub and the Village Green as the venues for the occasion.

PART TWO

The Gathering of the Clans

CHAPTER SIXTEEN

FRANK HARVEY SAT WITH HIS HANDS PRESSED tightly together in his lap, staring into his cold mug of tea. The hustle and bustle of the lunchtime crowd jangled his already throbbing head as students and faculty found their way to favorite tables throughout the cafeteria.

He looked at his watch. He had been sitting there for half an hour while both the Board of University Trustees and the Office of the Dean deliberated his fate.

His cell phone burred for his attention.

"Harvey," he announced abruptly.

"Professor Harvey could you return to the seminar room please? The board will see you now." Susan Ringer was Dean Hazlehurst's secretary and knew everything that went on anywhere at NRU.

"Susan?"

She paused on the other end of the line. "I'll let them know you're on your way." If she was aware of their decision she was not about to be drawn on the matter.

"Thank you Susan, I'll be right up." He disconnected and pocketed his phone, surprised at how calm he felt. There was, after all, no point stressing.

The office of the Board of Studies was paneled in walnut on three sides, while the fourth, constructed entirely of windows, looked out over the park-like quadrangle and the library opposite. The trees were mostly barren of their foliage; forbidding silhouettes against the backdrop of a sky the color of a sheet of lead.

A brown and tan-flecked Berber carpet was almost entirely obscured by a polished wood table that ran the length of the floor to where a whiteboard stood naked and pristine. Subtle lighting lifted the spirit of what would otherwise have been a rather bleak room, highlighting several postmodern artworks that made Frank's stomach lurch. Potted plants, lush and luxurious despite the season, were strategically placed on low benches providing the only relief from the blatant masculinity. *Susan's touch, I'll wager,* Frank thought fleetingly.

He took his seat back at the table, noting how amicable and pleasant the others were. Making light. How typical.

"Thank you for your patience Harvey." Dean Hazlehurst began, and Frank sighed, resuming the contemplation of his hands.

"We sincerely regret that there is nothing we can do to keep you on here. The fact that you have not given us any reasonable justification for having gone to Inishrún, let alone provide this institution with notice of intention, has caused us to appear negligible in the eyes of the public. If it had not been for the accident at sea—putting the lives of your students at risk—we could have gotten around the whole incident and set you up with a fully funded and sanctioned expedition.

"Unfortunately that is no longer an option. I shall hand this meeting over to Mrs. Blake, Head of the Board, to deliver their decision." He looked distracted and slightly annoyed as he gestured towards the well-groomed fifty-something woman who barely glanced in Frank's direction.

"Professor Harvey, you are no longer a member of New Rathmore University's faculty. Your dismissal revokes all rights to a pension and under the circumstances we cannot supply you with letters of reference. The Board is deeply disturbed at your unprofessional actions, and at the harm to the reputation of our institution that has occurred as a result.

"You will be paid one month's severance and your dismissal is to proceed immediately. Kindly remove your possessions from the university upon leaving this meeting. You may go."

She snapped her mouth closed, looking across the table at him for the first time. There was no hint of mercy in the icy, thin-lipped slit she pretended was a smile.

"Fair enough," he responded. *Bloody old bitch!* "Can I go now?"

Dean Hazlehurst stood and adjourned the meeting before walking to where Frank packed the portfolio of today's meeting into his briefcase looking lost; empty.

"I'm so sorry Frank. If it had been up to me ..."

"Thanks Richard. That means a lot." But it didn't, not really. He picked up his briefcase and left the room. There was nothing else to say.

HE SAT IN FRONT OF THE TV, STILL in his suit and tie, as the 6 o'clock news talked of famine and terrorism and what political leader said what about what. He wasn't listening but the ritual helped.

Jesse was not home which was unusual, and he was hungry despite himself, so when the weather came on he raised himself slowly and made his way to the kitchen, half-heartedly, knowing he really should eat something; should really take his doctor seriously about being conscientious concerning his health. He pondered other aspects of his new circumstances as he gazed absently around himself. He was not really in trouble financially, his superannuation would see him through even if he couldn't get another teaching job and, besides, something was sure to come up. He could look after himself and perhaps even enjoy a time of

145

doing nothing for a while.

Cursed.

Who was he kidding?

That damned island.

He forgot about being hungry and went to the sideboard to pour a glass of scotch, sighing deeply.

Think, Frank. He sat at the kitchen table and went over everything that had happened.

All of the members of the expedition had agreed, while being held in the Community Centre, to keep quiet about the exact purpose of the excursion, both to the local inhabitants and upon returning to the mainland, the carrot of future involvement assuring their allegiance. Frank had managed to keep his baby—a high end digital camera—undetected and had enough images to form an impressive presentation along with his recommendation for funding. He still had grunt as long as the others stuck by their agreement.

I'm not dead yet. And he snuffled a laugh as he considered his options.

Private enterprise. That was the go. He got up and went to the fridge. He pulled out a half-consumed cold chicken and several salad items, depositing them on the table. He cut two thick slices of bread and laid them open on a plate. He carefully peeled back the skin of the chicken and cut out the lean breast meat, adding it, along with the greens, to his sandwich. He decided against butter or any dressing, smiling to himself as he took the first bite. No. Not dead yet.

JESSE CAME HOME FROM HER DATE WITH Paul Deering. The house was dark except for a thin line of light that escaped from beneath the study door.

"I'm home Francis," she chimed. No answer.

She tried his study door, but it was locked from within.

"Are you alright?" she called, rattling the knob.

"Go away, Jesse."

"Have you eaten?"

"Go *away!*"

Drop dead you old bastard, she hissed under her breath, turning and heading upstairs, vaulting them two at a time. She'd used the excuse of his illness to take over the guest room and had slowly moved all of her things into it, pleased for the first time in years.

She refused to leave him. Divorce was messy and she would have it all soon enough anyway. She'd watched Frank deteriorate over the years, becoming overweight and slow, and she was determined to wait him out. She was young enough and attractive enough to keep Paul's attention and, besides, marriage was never going to be the way for her in the future. Too much ended up being compromised.

She had a whole other life that Frank knew nothing about and sooner or later she would shuck the shell of "good wife" and be real.

Jesse Harvey was a witch, even if a slightly negligent one.

She had talked about her domestic situation with Wolf Kain, the high priestess of her coven. Wolf had been angry; said it was a copout—the deceit, the pretense—and that nothing wholesome could come of it and that their gods did not put up with fools. Jesse had been offended but kept it to herself. She had the greatest respect for the slightly older woman who'd never had to hide the fact and could be so bloody honest and straight-forward that it hurt. Still.

She'd taken the slight with a grain of salt and said nothing more about it.

Now she wondered what Wolf was capable of. Whether she'd had a hand in the ferry accident; in Frank's ill-health. She wasn't about to ask though. Perhaps there were spells done on her behalf?

Wolf had dreamed it: a place where magic dwelt unspoiled, vital and rich from lack of human exploitation; dreamed of a race of people—almost gods—that academics had relegated to myth and fable; had dreamed of shape-shifters, laughter, music of the haunting, uplifting, goose-flesh-raising kind.

She'd dreamed the name *Inishrún*.

Wolf's dreams were not always within the land of sleep. They happened when she sought inspiration. When she sat in her tiny, overgrown garden—a haven amongst terraces and back lanes— and stopped thinking, zoned out, it was as though some gate to *other* opened. People she knew used such things as crystal balls, scrying mirrors, other tools, to look beyond the recognizable world; to seek their visions. Not Wolf. She simply sat. Things came to her unbidden and she would instill their meaning into her art. As such she considered that her gift was a way of communicating the unspoken voice of magic through *its* will, rather than her own. She considered herself its emissary.

The afternoon after she'd dreamed the island she'd gone onto the Internet to find out if there was such a place or thing as Inishrún and discovered that the obscure little island *did* exist and that it was off the west coast of her own country.

She'd decided it was worth the journey to see if the magic really was there and had organized several members of the coven to accompany her. Jesse Harvey had been one of them.

JESSE HAD FED THE BIRD-WATCHING-THING TO Frank two years ago when she'd initially been accepted into the coven, and it allowed her to be gone for days without questions.

Would he have asked anyway? No. He couldn't care less.

Paul had taken initiation the following year and she'd been set the task of teaching him the basics, setting Wolf free to work with other, more advanced witches. It had been a very natural progression from being friends to becoming lovers and he was not at all bothered about her relationship with Frank. It wasn't as if she had sex with the old bastard, after all.

She phoned Paul now, and he answered just before it rang out, sounding groggy from sleep. "Nyeah?"

"It's me."

"What's up?"

"Did I wake you?"

"Nah."

"Liar." She could hear him shifting the phone on the other end and imagined the bedside light snapping on.

"Frank's locked himself in the study."

"Is that supposed to be interesting?"

Jesse chuckled. It wasn't the same, when he said things like that, as with Frank. Paul always wanted to hear what she had to say. "So what's he doing?"

She'd contacted the university earlier in the day and spoken to Frank's department who told her the whole story because he had refused to answer his cell phone. Her gut instinct right now was that he wasn't about to let the matter of the island drop.

She'd been a fool to tell him about it in the first place but it had felt so good to goad him with something she knew that he didn't.

She'd got in trouble over it, too, especially when the whole shebang had hit the papers. Wolf had intended to return to seek out the mystery of the place, sooner rather than later, and that would now have to wait until the spring.

"If he's looking to stir up more on Inishrún it'll mean big trouble from Wolf." Paul said it softly knowing that she was touchy about her tenuous standing with the coven because of her stupidity.

She huffed down the phone at him.

"I'll get into the computer as soon as I can; see what he's up to."

"What can he do now, with the sack and all?"

"I don't know him at all, Paul. No idea what he's capable of." Frank's trick with the secret expedition had shocked her. She didn't think him capable of initiative. "Never a good thing to underestimate. Isn't that what Wolf always says?"

"Yup."

"G'nite Paul."

"G'nite love."

HOWEVER QUIETLY FRANK CLOSED HIS BEDROOM door it was still sufficient to rouse Jesse from her light sleep.

She sat upright and felt for the cigarettes on the bedside table. She swung her legs out of the bed and sat smoking in the dark. The luminous digits on her clock told her it was almost 5 a.m. and Frank would probably take a while getting to sleep unless he took one of his pills. Better to wait.

Half an hour later she silently called on the goddess for her blessing and stole her way barefoot down the stairs, carefully avoiding known creaky spots.

She waited until she'd closed the study door behind her before switching on the desk lamp and booting up the computer. She was desperate for a cup of coffee and another cigarette, but they would have to wait.

She sat staring at the request for a password for a good five minutes, her mind racing. It was pointless entering her own as she could not access Frank's files with it. What? Think! She knew it. She'd been with him the day he had had the upgrade.

She smiled as she typed TOMBRAIDER and clicked enter.

She accessed his Word Documents but needed to go into every file, entering *Inishrún* into FIND, as none of his filenames gave any indication of their content.

She almost bypassed the folder named *Utilities* but decided to look just in case.

"Oh shit," she whispered several minutes later. She pulled a couple of new disks from the drawer where they were stored. This was bad; this was *really* bad.

She snatched a few more hours sleep after downloading all of Frank's research and ideas and went to the local library around 11 a.m., bought an hour on one of their public PC's and printed out all fifty two pages of the document.

WOLF SAT AT A TABLE OUT IN THE COURTYARD area of Dimity's, a secondhand bookshop and café that'd been her favorite meeting place for many years, with Louise Carmichael, Jesse Harvey, Paul Deering and Fingal Connolly, all initiates of Three White Trees Coven.

The big yellow umbrellas had been stowed away to allow the late autumn sun ultimate reign over the chill in the air. The red brick walls surrounding the courtyard glowed scarlet with Virginia Creeper, dotted here and there with the last pale blooms of a climbing Floribunda rose, its scent still a hint in the afternoon.

Wolf was in her middle forties. She had short spiked red hair and slightly olive skin with an unnerving pair of green eyes that missed nothing and that could, under a hooded gaze, never be read easily. She was not beautiful in any traditional sense but the chiseled bones of cheek and jaw, and full lips that broke as easily into smiles as snarls, set her apart and drew men's eyes.

She was dressed casually in a black high-neck jumper and old jeans with sheepskin-lined boots that came up past her calves. She wore no jewelry, which was rare amongst the coven members, and sported only a small spiral tattoo on the lobe of her left ear and another, in the shape of crow in flight, on the inside of her right wrist.

She had begun this coven eighteen years ago and had spoken publicly, by invitation, on several occasions, at universities and colleges, on the true nature of witchcraft in difference to both the popular idea and the more recent lookalike fashionable excuse that eroded the spirit with its self-interest.

SHE HAD WRITTEN ARTICLES FOR JOURNALS THAT she considered serious and was well respected within the wider pagan community although, on the whole, she preferred to remain out of the public eye.

Wolf made her living from making masks. She used several mediums including plaster and resins, but her best works were through the use of fine leather, molded and sculpted whilst wet, into exotic faces and partial bodies—breast, hip, throat. Her use of materials from enamels and gemstones, to feathers and gold leaf, depicted a merging of human and beast that was both disturbing and fulfilling, seeming to remind the viewer of mystery lost; a magic denied. Her work attracted interest from galleries around the country, and twice in the past three years she had exhibited at Tackerbys in New York, calling her collection *The Masks of Kain*.

Wolf passed the pages around the table for the others to read after she had finished each one.

"So I figure he's going to find himself a backer to finance the excavation privately," concluded Jesse who hadn't stopped talking, nervously, since arriving.

"How's he going to do it?" Wolf stretched and thrust her reading glasses up on to her head before draining the last of the by-now cold coffee and asking if someone else would order another round—she'd pay—to which Louise agreed, asking who wanted what before going to the counter.

"Well?"

"Dunno. Other than the university the only place he goes is to his club once a month."

"What club?"

"I think they're Freemasons or the like. Boys' club stuff."

"Shit." Wolf tapped her fingers softly on the table, looking around at her companions.

"What?"

Paul stacked the papers in order, chuckling.

152

Jesse dug him in the ribs with her elbow. "What's so funny?"

"The Freemasons aren't a club, Jesse," he offered.

"Well, you know what I mean!" She was put out. She'd well and truly stuffed up with this whole thing and was feeling pretty tender around the edges.

"If he's in a Masonic Order he'll get his backer." Wolf looked at Jesse directly, pinning her. "You're going to have to keep some very late nights for a while, you understand."

"You want me to keep snooping?"

"Definitely!"

"You know where this club is, Jesse?" asked Fingal, taking his mug of coffee from the waitress, a dark haired Goth-looking girl that he knew as Merrin and whom he'd attempted to chat up once and been rebuffed, all very friendly-like.

"I've found matchbooks from Straub's. Maybe it's connected to them?"

"Bloody Freemasons," grinned Paul. "That exclusive club in the CBD?"

"I know somebody," Wolf hinted, "and we need to contact Inishrún somehow."

Merrin finished serving the coffees to the table, keeping her interest hooded as she registered the name of the island from which she had returned the previous day with Willie and the other Travelers. *This is too bizarre*, she thought. She hadn't even heard of the place before this year. What did this lot have to do with it? She returned to the counter, casually studying the members of the group. The young blonde woman who'd placed the order was adorned with several pieces of jewelry, one of which was a small, but heavy, crescent moon, hanging at her throat by a leather thong. Maybe.

She had seen Wolf here on several occasions and been drawn by her aura of confidence and power and Dimity had told her that she was the mask sculptor. Merrin was impressed. The artist's work was exquisite and intensely magical. She also knew she was a witch, having read a couple of her articles over the years admiring her clean slant on things: *Witchcraft,* she'd said, *is an animist, totemic way of knowing the world of myth.* Merrin remembered that. It was deeply akin to her own viewpoint. She also respected the *Songline* idea of ancestral relationship. It explained how people could be as strongly connected to plants and stones and animals and natural formations—shite, even the weather—and that illusions of separation were what prompted many of the human species to wantonly destroy whole ecosystems and habitats. It was all so freakin' shortsighted!

That they should be here, today, was way too much like kismet and she wasn't about to leave it alone.

Two of the party left soon after but the others remained for a further hour.

Wolf paid the bill and headed for the French doors as Merrin approached her. "Have you got a moment?"

Wolf appraised the younger woman, and at a glance, sensing her feyness and something altogether unrecognizable, liked her immediately. "Sure."

"Alone?" She turned to the others and apologized. Wolf took her by the arm and steered her back out to the courtyard, calling a goodbye to Fingal and Louise over her shoulder, striding to a bench over by the far wall where the sun hit in heatless color, away from the remaining customers.

"I overheard a little of your conversation," Merrin began after introducing herself.

"Which bit and why?"

Merrin grinned. Straight to the point; no *Oh?*

"You mentioned Inishrún."

"And?"

"Well, I've just come from there."

This time it looked as though she had surprised the artist who stared and was silent for several heartbeats.

"What exactly did you overhear, ah... Merrin, is it?"

She nodded, pulling out her pouch of rolling tobacco and offering some to Wolf who declined.

"I heard mention of Freemasons and having to make contact with the island, is all." She proceeded to roll a thin cigarette and light it before crossing her booted ankles, leaning back against the wall.

"The thing is," she continued, blowing out blue smoke, "the place is closed till the spring tides."

"What were you doing there, if you don't mind my asking?"

Merrin grinned. "Visiting."

"Relatives?"

"No."

"Okay Merrin, I'll tell you. I have other ways to make contact besides physical ones.'

"I've read some of the articles you wrote for *The Spell*."

"Then you know."

"That you're a witch? Takes one to know one, wouldn't you say?"

"Ah. Well blessings then, Merrin," Wolf smiled.

"Slanté," whispered Merrin.

"About Inishrún. There's a problem, and I'm responsible in part."

Merrin waited while Wolf delved into her bag, extracting a slim folder of A4 pages which she handed across.

"Do you want to read this here or would you like to come and have some food at my place? I'd welcome hearing your side of things if you're willing to discuss it."

"Sure. I'd love to see your work too if that's okay. I'm a major fan. One problem ..."

Wolf raised her eyebrows in query.

"My boyfriend's due any minute."

"Does he know?"

Merrin laughed. "Oh boy. You'd be amazed at what he knows."

"This gets more interesting by the second. But yes, he's

welcome to come if he wants to join us."

"Let's go inside. It's *freezing!*"

The last of the sun had dropped behind the steepled roof of Dimity's shop, plunging the temperature by several degrees. The women had been sufficiently engrossed to have ignored the chill until then.

Merrin stood, wrapping her arms around herself and thinking of her big old woolen duffel coat hanging behind the counter in the bookshop, while Wolf struggled into her own jacket and turned up the collar. She slung her satchel over her shoulder and hooked arms with Merrin as they headed indoors, leaving only a few diehard stragglers who were seated up close to the portable coal burner under the shelter of the awning near the kitchen.

"JUST GET HER TO DELETE THE file. Bloody simple if you ask me." Willie sat with Merrin and Wolf at a wrought iron table on the little balcony of Wolf's renovated inner city terrace house overlooking Bacon Street, a leafy pre-Victorian, sandstone-housed road—recently bespoke and reclaimed by established artists or the rich—just one block away from the chaos and debauchery of William Street Square where the trade consisted of drugs, prostitution, strip and gambling clubs, fast food outlets and tourists on the hunt for danger.

Wolf had turned the whole house into just three rooms: downstairs, which was her workshop—benches housing works in progress, paints, thinners, feathers, a dying tub, a computer shoved to one side, files, notepads and stacks of art books; shelves lined with materials of which only she would have been able to make sense; a big old blue coin-fed payphone, several fans, a corkboard on a wall littered with scraps of paper that Wolf assured them was her diary, several chairs and a mattress on the floor for when she couldn't even be bothered to go upstairs which happened when a frenzy of inspiration struck. And mannequins and wig stands everywhere sporting her masks: from uncannily lifelike forms to provocative morphings of human and beast, bird or reptile. Upstairs was a large living area that had had the inner walls removed so that the kitchenette and bathroom were as much a part of the décor as any other furnishings with the toilet providing the only private nook, surrounded as it was with red and gold enameled Chinese screens. The third room Wolf kept locked. She explained that it was the room in which she worked her rituals and that she allowed no one access unless they were initiates of Three White Trees.

Wolf had stopped around the corner at the Middle Eastern Bazaar where they'd bought falafels to take home and, having eaten their fill, sat drinking spiced chai tea and tiny triangles of baklava that Merrin had purchased at the last minute.

"WELL THAT'D BE MY SOLUTION AS well," Wolf replied, sitting back on her seat, wiping the last flakes of pastry from her chin, "and that was the first thing I suggested to Jesse Harvey but she's a bit of a problem child, witch or no witch."

"Why?"

"You know them: certain women who, despite all their abilities, all their talents, find it impossible to live without a relationship. She told me that; feels as though she's not a real woman blah, blah. She stays with her husband—who's twenty two years her senior by the way—because he's stable." She shook her head in disbelief. "Her description of him is that he's downright bland. But she's in his will and he's not poor, and she's got Paul on the side. She was horrified at my suggestion. Said he'd know it was her that had done it."

Merrin pulled out her tobacco, rolled a cigarette and passed the pouch to Willie.

Wolf observed Merrin's boyfriend in the momentary silence. He had long red-auburn hair that he wore in two plaits—*Like a fox*, she thought—strong jaw and dancing hazel eyes under birds-winged eyebrows. He wore a black tee shirt, jeans and leather steel-capped boots and his face and arms displayed a virtual eco-system of tattoos. She'd asked him *wasn't he cold* and he'd grinned saying *Nah, I've got the old blood, mo chroì*, which had made the little hairs stand up on end all down her arms. If Wolf had been envious by nature, which she wasn't, then now would be when that particular demon reared its ugly head. He was utterly charming, impossibly magical and had a sense of humor like a runaway train. He looked to be about thirty-something except…

"Anyway," she continued, "he's more than likely backed up the information. He'd be stupid not to."

Willie took a deep breath of the night. He could smell the river even from here and its solitude beckoned him. He loved Merrin, and Wolf Kain was special, but it'd been weeks since he'd had any alone time and now winter was coming and the Travelers would be in New Rathmore for most of it, playing gigs and scenting out the Lost. This human business was all too much for him.

"Look I gotta get goin' ladies." He stood and stretched. "What you wanna do Merrin?"

Merrin had come to know him pretty well over the last year or so and could sense his distraction and his distance. "Is it okay if I hang here for a bit longer?" she asked, looking to Wolf who nodded. "Then you go Willie. I can make my own way home."

"You sure?"

"I'm a sponge, *mo chroì*. I'll remember all the stuff about Inishrún to tell the others."

He grinned, relieved, and kissed her deeply before saying his goodbyes to Wolf.

"I'll show you out."

"Nah, me darlin'. I'm already gone," shoving his hands deep into his pockets, heading for the stairs.

When he'd left Wolf asked about him and how the two had met but Merrin seemed uncomfortable with the question, no matter how innocent, and she settled for the answer that she'd heard the band, in which Willie played fiddle, and fallen for him right off. The high priestess knew there was a bigger story; probably a whole lot bigger.

The two moved inside out from the cold, closing out the night, and Wolf fired up the convection heater.

"So why *were* you on Inishrún?" she asked finally, gesturing with a bottle of wine to which Merrin nodded.

Merrin didn't want to lie to the witch; wanted very much to talk to her about the *draíocht*. She would tell her as much as she could without giving away the sídhe's secret. So she began to talk about Samhain, the witches' New Year and what it meant to the island.

CHAPTER SEVENTEEN

WILLIE WANDERED THE STREETS FOR hours, heading south to his favorite thinking place in New Rathmore, down where the river met the bay.

He jumped over the metal railing on the side of the road and onto the causeway that ran down the littered embankment to the narrow track bordering the slow-moving Penance River. He turned east, past the pylons that supported the MacLean Street Bridge, and loped along another three hundred yards to where a tumbled mass of discarded concrete acted as an unnatural promontory.

His spine tingled as he sensed another presence and his shoulders slumped. He saw the silhouette of a small figure sitting scrunched up against the cold with its back turned to him. Something in the minute hint of scent that wafted towards him on the slight breeze informed him that the person was no stranger.

What're you up to sweet Mystery, he sighed. There were so many setups; so many seeming coincidences occurring. His goddess had to be behind it somewhere. *Typical*, he thought.

The figure on the rubble tensed, radiating fear, as Willie crunched along the towpath in her direction.

"'S'only me Holly," he called, "Willie. From the island?"

The small woman stood and turned in the direction of the voice, scrabbling in her bag for the small torch that had guided her there before realizing it was unnecessary as she noted the slight luminosity of his eyes as he closed the distance. Sídhe for sure.

He hopped easily onto the mess and scrambled across to her, squatting on his haunches only inches away.

"Y'er in my spot."

"What?" Holly sat back down, wrapping her arms around herself for warmth.

"My spot; yer in my spot."

"I…" but Willie grinned so she relaxed.

"I heard you'd left the island."

She said nothing.

"Right mess you got yerself into."

"What? So everybody knows?" she bristled. He ignored her and pulled out the leather pouch in which he kept his rolling tobacco and papers and proceeded to roll himself a cigarette before offering the makings across to Holly. Willie lit his cigarette, blowing blue smoke into the wind as a gift from the spirit of the plant.

"I thought you hailed from Middleborough, me duck?"

Holly *hmphed* as she struggled with the unaccustomed rolling tradition. She hardly ever smoked but occasionally it seemed a pleasant thing to do.

"Did," she said, holding out her hand for his lighter. "Bloody dirty old town."

Willie laughed. "Can't disagree with you there, love, so what made you come to New Rathmore?"

"Big enough to get lost in I suppose. Big enough to change in."

"Change how?" Did he really want to know? *By the gods people talk a lot,* he thought. He tsked in his mind telling himself to have a heart.

"I'm not even sure myself, y'know? Maybe I went nuts on the island; maybe I was nuts before that and the island just brought it out. One thing I know though—I'm not going back to the way I was before."

"Pretty bleedin' dull it was too by the sounds of it."

"You wouldn't know about *pointless* would you?"

Willie snorted and turned to her.

"You serious? Half the human race is pointless, mo chroí," he spat.

She was stunned. The bitterness in his voice was unmistakable.

They sat in silence for several heartbeats while Holly considered his outburst. The air was so cold it stung her eyes and made the skin on her face feel tight, yet he wore only a tee shirt.

"Aren't you cold?"

"Bloody freezin' but it won't kill me," he smiled.

"I thought if I came here where no one knew me, where nothing was familiar, it'd give me the space to digest everything that's happened so far; to start to work with the things I learned from Mim." She stubbed out the cigarette and almost absently put the butt in the pocket of her coat rather than allow it to join the other rubbish along the river.

She stood up and looked out to the lights of the city across the bay. "I've started, you know."

"What?"

"I signed up to study writing at Richmond College. Night school, three nights a week for three years."

"That's good, mo chroì."

She couldn't see his face and she wondered whether he was sincere.

"And there are a lot of things to learn, Willie, other than that."

He didn't answer. She moved to leave, and he caught her hand. "Mim felt bad when you left like you did."

Holly's throat constricted with the tears she would not shed yet.

"Will you ever go back?"

"When I can laugh," and she pulled her hand from his and rummaged for her torch. She found it and flicked it on, shining the beam across the concrete hill so that she wouldn't fall. Unlike them, she couldn't see in the dark.

"Slanté, *mo chroì*," he said softly as she struggled down the small mountain of rubble on to the towpath. But she didn't hear him.

Holly had the *shine*, that was sure. Even if she didn't know it herself. He sent out a silent request to the little mysteries and magics that still lingered in the secret places of the city to watch out for her if it wasn't asking too much.

He sat alone after that, listening to the sweet gurgling music of the river, smelling where she'd come from. Loving her.

HOLLY FELT STRANGE; UNNERVED. SHE'D originally seen the spot out on the promontory—sensed it like a beacon of peace—from the railing of yet another ferry as it plied its way across the harbor from Port Albert, where she'd been staying in a rundown youth hostel since her arrival in New Rathmore, to the Bank Street docks. She'd been on her way to the southside after having answered a *To Let* ad for an inexpensive but spacious bedsit down by the storm-water canal that fed into the river.

She hadn't known, when she'd spoken to the landlord on the phone, that this part of town was considered almost squalid and, initially, had wanted to turn around and not even bother to look at the place for rent. She'd wandered through the maze of streets, disheartened, until she'd turned into Copperhead Lane and been overwhelmed by the smells and sights of vendors hawking everything from fresh fruit and vegetables to fire-sticks. There seemed to be an entire community of inter-racial ease, sitting on stoops that led into low-rise tenement buildings or on benches outside the Lebanese take-out, the old-style pub, the cafes. There were many tiny shops, of old red brick, with grime and graffiti everywhere, that sold everything from kosher foods to bongs. The air was thick with too many smells, from the delicious to the corrupt, with an overriding miasma of maritime fuel, bull kelp and marijuana.

She'd asked directions from an old woman, dressed in the black of mourning, who'd directed her down Left Bank Road, straight ahead a few blocks to Napier Lane, then left onto Canal Street.

Mim had been distressed that her niece had become so antagonistic and upset as a result of her time on Inishrún and had almost begged her to take the thick wad of cash with her when she left. Holly had refused, disgusted, but Mim had blackmailed her, telling her she'd contact Patrick; her family; someone. You won't be able to find me, Holly had said. Her aunt had smiled at her then and said of course I can find you but if you take the money, which is yours anyway like I already told you, I'll not be sending Connor and a whole bunch of other Dé Danann to hunt you down.

So she'd taken the money. There was sufficient to pay a month up front on the bedsit with enough left over so that she wouldn't need to find work for several months. She'd used it, instead, to pay for the Creative Writing course and had found some part-time work, three days a week, at Solly Schlieberman's little bakery up on Copperhead.

She'd rediscovered the promontory almost as though she'd been led there by magic and she liked to go there around dusk to be close to the water where no one was likely to disturb her, the soft hiss and susurration of water on shore calming her spirit and allowing her to think clearly.

And the only person she'd encountered this far along the towpath, over the several weeks since she'd been coming here, ended up being a Sídhe! It was almost funny, or it was Mim checking up on her. When he'd questioned her she'd felt her barriers rise up like a razor-wire bastion. There was no reason to distrust him—she'd seen him often enough over Samhain—but she also didn't really know him, and Dé Danann or not, she was not about to confide in anyone about her current situation.

So she'd only told part of the truth, and of that she'd been sparing.

Her job and her studies had left her with plenty of opportunity to spin the pennies. She'd arrive home just after 9:30, take a shower and a small meal, light the ring of candles and work the mystery that took her between the worlds.

Like a visitor to some giant spider's web she'd travelled threads that passed through time that was no time, to places not known on any map.

And she'd made allies.

She'd been found, wandering some errant thread that had led her to an arroyo with no recognizable landmarks that might inform her where she was, by a small horse no taller than fourteen-two hands high and the mottled color of wheat and rust. He'd sensed her lostness and had guided her back to a recognizable thread that had led her home. He'd been waiting for her the next time she'd spun the pennies and they'd explored together, becoming bonded through a mutual pleasure in each other's company. He was the first.

Then just last Tuesday night he'd seemed agitated; determined to take the lead on their journey. They'd followed a thread that had led them into a dark forest that had appeared trackless and forbidding to her eye but sure beneath his hooves. He'd led her to a grove of birch and aspen where a cottage, built into the overhang of a three hundred foot cliff, sent out a thin stream of smoke from a thick, squat stone chimney. Initially Holly thought it looked slightly ridiculous; stylized; like it had come straight out of some children's book, and she had laughed thinking that Rocky, which is what she'd decided to call the Galloway, was being playful.

She had changed her opinion when a woman had pulled open the door, flanked by Irish wolfhounds. She appeared angry at having been disturbed and the hounds had bristled and snarled a warning. Holly had wanted Rocky to turn around; had willed herself back in the sanctuary of her own apartment, but neither had happened. The gelding had pranced on silent hooves towards the little house, oblivious to her distress. Or ignoring it.

The woman had her head shaved and bore a scattering of tattooed dots and swirls peppered across her forehead in seeming random. She wore small heavy-hooped earrings of bronze and amber and she was dressed in finely tanned moss-green leather *trews*, and a long sleeved marmot fur jacket, buttoned to the chin with small bone buttons, and heavy leather, thick soled boots. Over it all she wore a *breacan feile* of blue and gorse-yellow plaid and a dark brown *brat* trimmed with blue, yellow and pale green embroidery, clasped at the shoulder with a tarnished silver brooch depicting a many-tined stag. She held a quarterstaff casually in her left hand with a look that said she knew its use.

"Go away," she said softly.

Holly attempted to telepath to Rocky her desire to leave but again he moved closer.

Her throat was dry and would not obey her and she worked to clear it, to apologize for the intrusion. "I'm sorry. This isn't my idea," she finally managed, embarrassed.

"I'm not talking to *you* little girl," the woman had snarled.

The hackles rose on Holly's neck as she realized the woman was looking beyond her towards the forest, sensing alien eyes boring into her back. She slowly turned. Behind her, barely concealed by the darkness of the wood, was an apparition with almost all the semblance of an enormous boar—tiny eyes glittering, tusks filthy with what could only be dried blood. Almost all, because there was an unnerving intelligence in the eyes and an arrogance to its stance that hinted at humanness; something uncomfortably and uncannily familiar.

Silently and swiftly, seven hounds bounded from around the woman, into the clearing and straight past her in pursuit of the beast that squealed in agitation before turning and fleeing, tearing up the forest floor with its sharp, sharp hooves in a bid to gain speed.

"Now you."

Holly swung back to the woman who stood haughtily in the doorway, one hand on her hip, the other still brandishing the staff. "Get off that bloody horse and come inside before all the bloody heat escapes."

She did as she was told, sliding from Rocky's back and whispering that he better not go off and leave her, to which he answered by lowering his head and cropping at the lush, short grass.

The inside of the house appeared larger than she had guessed from its exterior, made more so by Spartan furnishings: a workbench on which sat the remnants of an interrupted meal, a clay or stone cup, an iron pot and several tallow candles on round flat stones. There were three stools, one stark, high-backed wooden chair and a rumpled bed. The floor was strewn with rushes, and a large walk-in fireplace, its fuel down to the embers, gave the room its warmth. The only things to break the seeming poverty was an enormous and vividly lavish tapestry upon the stone of the far wall, telling a story that Holly could not even begin to interpret, and a coat of arms above the fireplace depicting, again, the motif of the many-tined stag on a gorse and heather background, beneath which hung a Claymore in a dull brown scabbard—fortified many times over with bands of bronze—and a yew longbow hung beside a quiver of black-fletched arrows. There was only one door other than the entrance, and it was closed.

The woman busied herself stoking the coals beneath a blackened iron kettle.

"You want some coffee?" she asked.

Holly's jaw dropped at the incongruous question and the warrior woman chortled. "It's either that or uiske," she teased.

"No. Coffee's good."

"Then make yourself useful and grab us a couple of cleanish mugs from that box." She pointed to a plain wooden cupboard under the window beside the front door in which Holly found an assortment of crockery, pots and utensils, none of it matching and all of it having seen better days.

"You'd better be Holly Tremenhere then," the warrior said, opening the unknown door as the younger woman *Uh-huh*'d an assent. She entered into what looked to be a well-stocked pantry and storeroom, returning loaded with a jar of instant coffee, a bag of sugar, a small jug of milk and a box of biscuits.

"This is all very confusing," said Holly, pulling one of the stools up to the workbench.

"No it's not. Your world's the one that's confusing; mine's bloody simple!" She placed her armload on the table and wiped her hands on her plaid before holding out her right to Holly. "Name's Scathach," she grinned, shaking hands briefly.

"And that's supposed to mean what?"

"Shite, girl, haven't you heard of me yet? I thought you were supposed to be learning about the legends and the past and all. I'm not *that* bloody obscure! Tsk. A bit bloody slow!"

"You sure do swear a lot, Scathach," Holly grinned.

The room had warmed again, and the warrior removed her brat, throwing it carelessly over the back of the tall chair, exposing muscled arms with wide bands of tattooing along their length, chuckling low in her throat. "Shit. You should hear me when I'm pissed off. It's bloody disgusting! You want milk and sugar?"

"Yes please. A bit of both."

Scathach busied herself spooning coffee and sugar into the mugs, pouring in the now-boiling water, adding a dash of milk to one cup and a good nip of golden liquid, from a stoppered flask that she pulled from a soft leather pouch that hung from her belt, into the other.

The two sat in companionable silence for several heartbeats, the biscuits untouched, before Holly placed her mug back onto the table directing a curious look at her host.

"What?"

"Can I ask you a couple of things, Scathach?"

"Shoot." She balanced her stool on two of its three legs and lifted her booted feet up onto the table.

"I mean, apart from the obvious things like why did Rocky

bring me here, and where exactly *here* is, and who are you besides your name, how it is you know me and what's instant coffee doing in the Otherworld … what time frame are we in?"

"Oh stop it. Bloody clusterfuck all that is."

"Sorry, it's just that…" Holly was shocked.

"Don't you know there's about to be a war?"

"What?"

Scathach pulled her feet from the table and dropped the stool back onto its three legs. Standing, she headed for the door, opening it for the hounds that Holly hadn't heard approaching. They bounded into the cottage, pushing past each other as they vied for a spot closest to the hearth.

"Little spirit-sister, you don't get it, do you?" She sighed deeply and returned to the table taking both Holly's hands in her own heavily calloused ones. "I'm not your ancestor if that's maybe what you're thinking, but I *am* Charlie Freeman's."

Holly stiffened at the mention of the man who was the reason she'd left Inishrún, embarrassment and a sense of betrayal causing a flush of red to stain her throat and cheeks as she sought to understand what this portended.

"No need for you to be bothered by all that nonsense back on the island if that's your angst, my friend. It's no wonder to me that you got all pissed at him after he went and died on you so many times. That'd be enough to send any woman batty."

"You know about the dream?"

"Not a dream Holly; a memory. One of a whole bloody heap that you probably don't want to ever recall if you're sane. Oh, and by the way, he's not going to get away with it again which is where I come in. And not just for him either. And who am I other than my name?

She pulled her hands from the other's unconscious grasp and touched them to her heart. "I'm your guardian-bloody-angel."

Holly saw the sincerity in Scathach's gesture and felt a longing to go to her and hold her tightly even though she was still confused by the whole experience.

"The war?"

"The Shining Isle looks set to be fought over like she's a piece of bloody meat, *mo cridhe*; just like has happened everywhere else." She waited for Holly to respond but she was silent.

"The magic could go out of your world for good at that, *and* if the pieces don't come together just right. You're one of those pieces, Holls, and what you need to know right now, before we get on with things—and be very clear about what I say—is that what you are *not* is a pawn."

"What happens next then?" Holly asked, ignoring what she didn't understand.

"We get me into your world is what." Scathach stood and grabbed her *brat*, draping it over her left shoulder, and reached above the fireplace for the sword, bow and quiver. She thrust the former through her wide belt and slung the latter over her right shoulder as she walked towards the door. She grabbed the quarterstaff from where she'd placed it and called *Whishta* to the dogs that padded out into the clearing ahead of her.

"You coming?" she said over her shoulder.

"You can't take that lot into my world," Holly said, stunned and disbelieving.

"I can."

"But I live above a restaurant!" She wondered, momentarily, if she'd fallen asleep during the *Penny Spell* and would wake up and have a good chuckle at the dream. *Well I'm about to find out,* she supposed, walking out the door into the washed out afternoon sunlight where Rocky waited, eager to leave.

They were deeply within the forest, headed in the direction that Rocky had led them, when Holly remembered the boar.

"Scathach?"

"Yep?" she replied, not turning from her brisk pace.

"That boar…"

"Not a boar, *mo cridhe*, a human with a strong totem. A possible threat, maybe not, it's bloody hard to figure with some creatures."

"Can you tell who?"

"No. No bloody idea who it is."

IT WASN'T AS CRAZY AS HOLLY IMAGINED it would be. She'd considered the consequences of having seven very large hounds cramped in her bedsit but that's not what happened. As she and Scathach followed the thread back to Holly's circle the wolfhounds become more and more insubstantial. When she opened her eyes the pennies were only just ceasing their spin, falling onto each other with a clink, and only Scathach seemed with her. As usual mere seconds had passed.

"Well this is fun," the warrior commented dryly, standing and adjusting her sword. "We done? You gonna open the *Lios naTine*? The circle of fire. I'm starved. Do you have anything to eat?"

Holly pinched the wick of one of the candles between her thumb and forefinger just as Mim had shown her, as blowing out the flame was considered an insult to the spirits of fire, she effectively broke the seal of protection.

"No. I wasn't anticipating company. We'll have to go out to eat.

"An inn?"

"Not quite." She considered her visitor's attire and envisioned the stares and comments she'd receive on the streets of New Rathmore's seamy Southside, fearing the warrior's reaction. "But you're going to have to change your clothes first."

The surprised expression on Scathach's face caused a momentary embarrassment but not enough for Holly to back down. She rummaged in her wardrobe, coming up with a pair of army surplus khaki pants, a long sleeved grey tee shirt and a chunky dark blue Arran sweater that would keep the cold at bay.

Scathach stripped without inhibition and drew on the clothing she'd been loaned, all in moody silence but Holly ignored the huff, picking up her bag and checking for cash and keys. "Let's go." She began gathering her weapons.

"No," Holly squeaked. Scathach must have thought she was joking, and she snorted a *Yeah, sure,* ignoring the command.

"I'm not kidding. You take those things out onto the street and we'll *both* be arrested." Holly spent five minutes explaining about cops, weapons in the inner city and modern jails, watching the horrified expression on Scathach's face.

"You won't need them, really," she pleaded.

"But your world's a hundred times more dangerous than mine. Shit, anyone who walks between them knows that."

"You won't need them," Holly repeated, "I promise." She was beginning to consider the responsibility she'd undertaken in agreeing to bring Scathach with her. She had agreed, hadn't she? She hadn't thought it through. The fair folk she'd met so far dealt with the twenty first century by way of an unbroken historical interaction with humanity, but this woman seemed anything *but* a Traveler. How long since she'd been here anyway? *Had* she been here before? Holly determined to spend as much of tonight as she could, learning all about who her companion truly was; to educate her on the state of the world she was in.

Scathach laid her weapons reverently upon Holly's bed, her face animated with trepidation.

"I thought you said you were hungry," Holly urged. "Let's *go.*"

Scathach threw her *brat* over her shoulder in defiance. "Spoken like a true bloody queen," she grinned, following Holly through the door.

"What did you say that for? Is that supposed to be sarcastic?" but Scathach simply smiled a very canine smile and kept quiet.

THE CHINESE FOOD DELIGHTED HER. AFTER an initial hesitation at the unfamiliar smell and flavor she had insisted on tasting Holly's meal, before finishing her own and ordered a second dish, Moo Goo Gai Pan, simply because of the way it sounded when Holly read it aloud from the menu.

After they'd eaten she voiced a desire to get acquainted with the ley of the land and they wandered for half an hour before the warrior appeared disconsolate and edgy. There was, after all, only dirty street after dirty street in a maze of alleys and tenements.

I'll take her to Copperhead, Holly determined. At least it was interesting.

As they wandered Copperhead Lane Scathach's shoulders stiffened as she worked at ignoring the stares of the people they passed despite many of them being unusual themselves.

"You want to get a drink or something before we head home?" Holly asked, worried.

"Uiske beatha?"

Holly recalled the Tuatha Dé Danann on the island calling the golden liquor—whisky—by the same name and she ordered two straight shots from the bar at the small English-style pub on the corner near Dimity's. Scathach picked hers up and smelled the contents before smiling and downing the fiery dram in one gulp. "You have me at a disadvantage," she explained as she replaced the glass on the bar.

"What's wrong now?"

"I haven't any bloody coin."

Holly sensed the unaccustomed vulnerability of the woman who was utterly alone except for her.

"Well I've got enough for us both for a while unless you'd like to go back. And, besides, I owe you, yes?"

"How the fuck do you come to that conclusion?"

"I brought you here."

"There is that," Scathach grinned, exposing sharp white incisors in a smile that could have been threatening.

"And you're here because trouble is coming and then I'll probably owe you again," Holly added.

"So?"

"So I'll buy us a whole bottle of this stuff if you like and we can head back to my place and drink it to celebrate our friendship, what do you think?"

"I think we should get the fuck outa here is what I think," hopping down from the barstool and reaching for the sword at her side that wasn't there.

Holly purchased a bottle of Laphroaig Scotch whiskey, despite the cost, and the two made their way back to Canal Street with Scathach in the lead, uncanny in her unerring ability to recall the route they had come.

Later Holly tried unsuccessfully to get her companion to talk about herself but Scathach explaining that a geas—an obligation similar to a taboo—had been laid upon her by an ancient enemy that disallowed her the reciting of her own glories. She proceeded to become very drunk, asking questions about the Dé Danann that Holly had met on Inishrún and wanting to know as much as she could tell her about her own history. She fell asleep just after 2AM curled up on the floor in front of the little two bar heater that she'd earlier called a "piss-poor excuse for a hearth".

HOLLY SAT ON HER BED WITH ONLY THE bedside lamp for light and powered up her laptop. She logged onto the Internet and entered *"skathak"* into Google, applying different spellings until she hit gold.

CHAPTER EIGHTEEN

STRAUBS WAS ONE OF THE LAST GLORIES of the dying Victorian era, maintaining its *Gentlemen Only* policy in relative anonymity; known of only to its invited members.

Situated in the heart of New Rathmore's central business district it retained its heritage splendor, along with several other gargoyled monuments of a receding age that formed a bastion around the Wallace Hope Plaza. Exclusive restaurants, boutiques, art galleries and antique outlets vied with the bullion repository and a string of jewelry and clock merchants to frame the nineteenth century square where a fountain, statue'd with cavorting Olympian gods and goddesses, took central stage.

There were several small cafes that had permission to serve outdoors like a little piece of Paris or Rome, and where the rich aroma of good coffee vied with those of pastries and exotically-filled baguettes.

The businesses were all closed for the evening as Frank Harvey crossed the plaza, checking his watch to ascertain how late he was for the meeting.

He'd phoned around several of his colleagues for possible contacts who might have an interest in a substantial investment and had been given the names of Felix Tyler and Calvin Riddle, apparently a team. He'd spoken with Tyler earlier on in the day requesting a bit of a chat about what could be a very lucrative undertaking, and the businessman had agreed to meet that same evening.

The two, although still young, were senior partners at Solomon Stone, one of the most affluent and influential law firms on the east coast. And fellow Freemasons.

It was just after 6PM in the evening. He'd taken the train into the inner city to avoid the inevitable peak hour snarls, but it had arrived behind schedule, crammed with commuters, and Frank had had to stand the entire way.

That's okay. They'll still be there. As far as he knew the two went to the club for drinks most nights after leaving work.

Frank was admitted by a doorman known only as Morris (without reference as to whether this was his first or last name) and he walked across the foyer, with its couches and occasional tables, potted palms and newsstand, that was dominated by a wide mahogany staircase, carpeted in thick burgundy, that led to the upper floor that housed the Masonic Temple.

Tyler and Riddle were seated in large wing backed chairs, glasses of golden liquor on a table between them. Both had laptops open and appeared engrossed as Frank approached silently.

Felix glanced up and stood, extending his hand. "Frank. Good to see you man. Pull up a seat. I'll be with you in a second." He sat back down to complete his work on the computer before snapping it closed.

Tyler was a man used to quality. Frank could see it in the cut of his suit, the fitness of the body beneath, without the paunch or stoop one imagines from a person who sits for much of the day. From the brief flash of *Gianni Versace* black dress loafers at his feet when he stood, the classy haircut, the manicured hand he held for Frank to shake, the designer tie nonchalantly loosened, to the hint of expensive cologne. Privilege. All this registered on the dowdy middle aged professor who felt slightly embarrassed by how he envisioned he appeared.

Tyler's colleague, Calvin Riddle was sloppy in a geekish way, although that was either feigned or a lie because sure as anything he was up there with the wealthiest of his kind. He also wore a suit but sported a Black Sabbath tee shirt under the sharply-cut jacket, showed sneakers beneath his trouser legs and wore a Mets cap backwards.

"How are ya?" he greeted, not taking his eyes from the computer screen where the game *Morrowind* had his full attention.

Frank placed his briefcase on the floor explaining he'd be back in just a minute, going to the bar to get a Pale Ale.

Calvin had closed his laptop by the time he returned, and the two men sat patiently waiting for Frank's proposal. Three hours later, the table between them was littered with documents, he sat back, nauseous from hunger but justifiably encouraged that the two were still there.

Both lawyers were in their late thirties or early forties—it was difficult to estimate—and throughout the conversation Frank had needed to constantly pull himself up from being shocked by their boyishness and unexpected behavior. They listened, and had asked pertinent questions at just the right moments, but they also interrupted him with irrelevant commentary on the private lives of several of the other patrons of the club. They were like a pair of seventeen year old *Little rich kids*, Harvey caught himself thinking on more than one occasion, refusing to give up.

Frank concluded his pitch and studiously tidied the data he had spread around for the other men's consideration.

"So what's in it for you?" Tyler queried, his face poker.

The professor cleared his throat: the moment of make or break.

"Well, three things gentlemen. The dig, of course, which would bring acclaim to all of us should it yield artifacts which I'm certain it will. A percentage in any profit from the development of tourist facilities and please—I am not a greedy man—I would abide by whatever you considered appropriate..." he paused, seeking a reaction that wasn't there. *Bloody lawyers* he thought acidly, smiling as he sipped his third glass of ale to mask a throat tasting of ashes.

"And the third thing?" Calvin asked.

"Well the third thing's merely symbolic, as they say." He noted Tyler tapping the arm of his chair, a sign of what? Impatience? Annoyance? What? "You see, the old folk there have themselves this queen."

Calvin barked a short, staccato laugh, leaning towards Frank with avid interest. "Do tell!"

"I don't pretend to understand their superstitious little ways. I'm in archaeology, not anthropology. Some quaint tradition due to isolation perhaps. The point is she was responsible for keeping me, and my students, virtual hostage; for treating us as intruders in some fairy story royal realm ..."

"And you want to see her deposed, is that it?" Tyler's lips quirk as he fought to remain dignified.

"As I said, a symbolic gesture, gentlemen."

Both men assured him that it was an interesting proposition but that they'd need a while to work on the figures, to ascertain its viability, that they'd get back to him in a few days and thank you very much for considering them. Frank stacked the A4 sheets he'd brought with him and handed them to Tyler and all three shook hands.

He left the club, stepping lightly on to the street, before daring to grin with anticipation. They'd bought it. He was certain they'd bought it. It was just a matter of time.

He crossed the plaza into Phillips Street, pausing to purchase two hotdogs with the lot before descending into the subway to wait for the train.

"WHAT DO YOU THINK?" CALVIN ASKED casually as they wandered into the dining area.

"I think the smoked trout and angel hair pasta, Cal, what about you?" He smiled, changing the subject as he studied the menu.

Calvin grinned at his partner. He admired him for very many reasons, cunning being towards the very top of the list.

"Excellent choice."

DAVID RUSHTON HAD SAT AT AN adjacent table, seeming to doze, for the entire conversation. He had the greatest admiration for Wolf Kain who had contacted him three nights prior requesting his aid.

Wealthy beyond words David had bought several of her works over the years and had commissioned several more. He had devoted an entire wing of his home, a palatial estate on eleven acres of prime real estate overlooking Sussex Cove, with its own modern marina, to his love of exotic art. The collection of masks he had acquired from his friend was the pride of the gallery.

He and Wolf had been lovers on and off for many years, the two maintaining respect for each other's desire to live alone, unfettered, and for each other's philosophical and mystical ideals.

David was sixty two years old, handsome, well educated, extensively traveled and Magister of the Senior Lodge here at Wallace Hope. He would do anything for her.

He had to admit that the air of magic that he had sensed hidden between the lines of Harvey's lust was almost tangible and he would have to discuss this with Wolf, but sufficient to say he could sway both those boys, if it came to that, from buying into the disqualified professor's little foray into other people's business. This was out of Frank's league.

Oh, it was all most interesting.

He flipped open his cell phone, accessed Wolf's number and

waited.

"David?"

"My darling, suppose you fill me in on what's really going on with this obscure little island, hmm?"

Wolf paused. "I'm not sure what you mean."

"Is it alright if I pop over?"

"I'd love you to. I'm sitting here *dry* David."

"I can pick us up a nice little Ebenezer on the way then."

"That's my boy, but no, I meant inspiration. It's like my muse has deserted me."

"Well then you should find my visit right up your alley, my love."

"Have you been spying?"

"Oh yes indeedy! Say an hour?"

"Blessings my friend."

He smiled as he clicked off and dialed for Jason to bring the car.

CHAPTER TWENTY

CHARLIE HAD WANTED TO STAY. NEEDED to stay. Saying goodbye to Liath Leannán wasn't easy though and she *did* have to leave. She'd been a Travelers for so long that remaining in one place, despite love, was akin to suffocation.

You're the best of them she said the night before the *Rosie Rua* was due to take the stragglers back to the mainland. *Why won't you come with us?*

He stayed awake with her all night. Talking, making love, talking, making love some more, explaining the abject joy of finally finding treasure only to discover it was a living thing and that the stories were all real and did she know how wonderful that was to someone like him?

She was keeping it all easy, light. Hidden within her was a sense of tragedy that she would not show to Charlie no matter what. That was because she cared for him beyond anyone she'd ever known and to tell him would be to sway him, influence him, and that she would not do. The extent of that love was enough of a bright thing to prevent the sadness from becoming despair for she would not see him grow old and wither; knew it would get harder the longer she was with him. Better this way. This bitter-sweetness.

She saw in him, though, what no one else could see. She guessed it was the intimacy although she wasn't sure that was the reason. Something. Something. The greatness of certain kings who'd once walked the earth. There was no room in him for harm; no room at all.

Liath Leannán was a gifted shape-changer, a potent warrior.

Sometimes these things were not enough. She wished she had the gift of Sight like Selkie Duffy.

She knew she could have asked her, or Mim, to look between the worlds and follow the threads of his destiny but she also knew that to do so could change it. The past was one thing but seeing into the future? Fraught with consequences. No. Leave it. Love him and go.

MIM AND CONNOR HAD TAKEN Charlie in and given him one of the spare rooms at the top of the stairs. Oberon had become his big buddy, joining him on expeditions that had him knowing most of the ley of the island already. He was still not permitted to venture into either the henge or the Barrow ,but he didn't mind. He and Connor had worn each other out being enemies and had found instead that they could spar with each other in different ways: humor and holding the stage in conversation being merely two of them.

The island had transformed the academic into a healthy man who seemed to have grown even taller as his calves and thighs strengthened from the walks he took up mountains and through thick forest, and his upper body spread and thickened with muscle from pole fighting and splitting logs.

He'd also begun fishing with the local men, who could scurry up and down the cliff-faces with frightening ease, to obscure—and to anybody else—dangerous locations. There it was necessary to lash themselves to whatever solid rocky formations they could, to prevent the often mountainous seas from washing them away.

The elder Dé Danann could survive such a thing, could swim back without being crushed upon the rocks—Charlie had seen it himself twice already—but they knew he would not last a second in the icy, kelp-wracked waters and they took special care of him simply because he had the courage to come.

One after the other of the sídhe had him visit for tea, supper, stories. Something about his shine endeared him to them unlike other mortals, and some of them got together to try to fathom why. To no avail. They couldn't pinpoint it. It was just *something*.

Connor and Mim went with him often, along with the Travelers still on the island for the councils, down to the village in the evenings where always there was music and Guinness and whisky in the jar.

Somehow Charlie's mere humanness was seemingly forgotten. It was as though he had always been with them. Mim was the only one who seemed to keep it clearly in mind that he had come without invitation and that the mission of his colleagues heralded exposure and the possible annihilation of their way of life. She had ceased to remind the others: they'd continued to regale her with *Yes, yes, we know,* but she *was* perplexed. It wasn't as though he feigned a glamor—everything about him was honest; guileless. Maybe that was what it was? His father had been the same. Very, very nice men. Was that it? In this day and age the qualities they represented were almost non-existent. Everybody had issues. Everybody had ambitions, fears, a hidden agenda, secrets, guilt. Didn't they? How had all this bypassed Charlie?

There was a mystery here, but she couldn't fathom it. Holly had fought it; had wanted so much to dislike him, when one really couldn't, that she'd fled in self-loathing.

And Mim had been devastated by that. She had such hopes of passing on all she knew to her niece. She wasn't wrong about her; Holly *was* fey, the lineage clear. It hadn't made any sense.

Still, Charlie and Liath Leannán had been good together. It was going to be sad for him when she moved on, but her clan was her family and Mim knew, also, that Charlie was not fey and so would not be invited to the Quickening. Such a shame the rules could not be bent, she caught herself thinking, but she knew better than to question the way of Dé Danann magic.

THE FINAL VOYAGE TOOK PLACE on the third Thursday after Samhain and Charlie had sat on the dock watching the black sails dwindle on a glassy sea until he knew that the thing he thought was the Hooker was just his imagination.

He had an empty place inside him that Liath had filled for the first time in his life and yes, he was sad, but no, he did not regret staying. The idea of being stranded on Inishrún for many weeks over the winter did not bother him in the least. He had his journal half-filled and had bought extra notepads and several pens from the shop on the quay.

Woolly had demanded to see what it was he was writing, and he'd shown him without any rancor. The aged sídhe had sat and read, a pint before him on the bar, and had grinned with respect when he'd finally passed it back.

"It looks like a whole bunch o' fiction the way you've put it down, lad," he admired.

"Is that okay?"

"It's safe, sure. Nowt'd believe a bloody word wert truth, aye?" and he ran his gnarled fingers through his shaggy hair in delight. "What d'you intend t'do w'all?"

"Dunno yet. Just feels right to write it down. No one's gonna believe it, necessarily, but it seems to me that all this magic and stuff ought to at least be there for those who can see through it; who need the faith, so to speak."

"Yeah well 's'long's ye keep changin' th'names an' places to protect th'innocent as they say."

Charlie clinked his glass against the other and quizzed Woolly about the legends of Aengus Óg, the master of love in the old stories.

NEW RATHMORE LAY UNDER A HEAVY, OMINOUS precipitation, the thick, slate grey sky tinged with a sickly yellow, heralding

186

snow, or maybe sleet. The roads were slippery with black ice and a keening wind flicked its lash down alleyways and unsealed buildings and bit into any foolishly exposed piece of skin on anyone who, through necessity, walked the pavements of the eastern seaboard city.

Willie knew he wasn't *supposed* to detest winter, but he couldn't lie to himself. She was a bitch and that was the end of it. He and Black Annis, Matt, Puck, Robin and Alan walked the streets hunched and downcast. Was it just a week ago that he'd boasted to Holly that the cold didn't bother him? He grinned at his own audacity. Now he silently yearned for Meán Samhraidh (Midsummer) and the sluggish warmth of the Great Gathering up on the far north coast, with its palm trees and rainforest and white sandy beaches, its long sultry days and near-naked women. Ahh! This year he'd have Merrin with him and he loved her utterly, but he still liked to look at things of great beauty. Art, he thought dreamily.

The group was all bunched up against the frigid day, greatcoats, duffel coats, scarves, beanies, gloves, several pairs of socks within heavy-duty boots, forming them into a nondescript huddle of slightly odd looking maybe-tramps, maybe-hippies, as they rounded the corner onto Yeats Street and covered the last of the distance to Mary Flannery's Tavern where they sought to organize some gigs for the coming weeks.

The Fíanna were guaranteed work there whenever they came through. They sure did draw a crowd with their foot-stomping, rocked-up Irish tunes. Tom Doddy, the proprietor for the past three years, never asked questions or sought to keep paperwork in relation to this particular band—an old agreement from the days when Mary herself first hired them, paying cash-in-hand from the takings on the door.

Merrin was spending the day with Wolf Kain and some guy that the high priestess knew who'd overheard a whole heap about plans to screw over the island, and they and all of Clan Fíach

Dubh were due to meet up tonight at Flannery's, neutral ground, with a mind to sorting out where everything stood to date.

Merrin wasn't allowed to give much away to Wolf. Hunter and Brighid had said it was best not to until, and if, they found reason to trust and they were, after all, the masters at sniffing out a deceit—a pretense—from a mile away. For the moment the outsiders had been told that old friends, some of the people who lived on Inishrún, had agreed to the Travelers coming each year to have themselves a private festival.

Wolf had assumed that they were all simply generic pagans realigning themselves with the traditional Celtic Wheel of the Year.

It wasn't a lie. It just wasn't the truth.

THE THREATENED SLEET ATTACKED JUST as the group reached the shelter of the pub's entrance. *Thank you!* Willie sent the silent message to the weather gods for having waited.

The tavern was all but empty this early in the day and Wendy Wu was stacking glasses.

"Oh, hi guys," she beamed, recognizing most of the troupe from last year. She had her long black hair tied up in two pigtails causing her to look younger than her years and she wore slightly retro fluro colors in an eye-shattering complexity of stripes, zigzags and peach-blossom bits and pieces under a short-sleeved Manga-design tee shirt. Willie thought he might throw up but he forced himself to smile her way. *Each to their own*, he thought graciously.

Wendy was a long-time friend of Merrin and was aware of her relationship to the cute but incorrigible fiddle player so said nothing when she registered the distaste at her appearance, aware that he probably didn't even realize she could read him so easily. "Doddy's in the cellar. Hang on while I go get him. You want anything while you wait?"

Mumbled *Nah's* and *Thanks love we're fine*, issued from the

188

members of the band as they pulled out the chairs at the table closest to the blazing fire in the oversized hearth that so endeared the patrons to this particular pub.

Tom Doddy joined them five minutes later, desperate. "The band I'd booked for tonight has come down with this damned bug everyone seems to be catching and they've cancelled on me. Don't suppose you'd do tonight?"

"Sure," Annis assured, looking around at the others for objections. There weren't any.

Doddy smiled, relieved. "I'll get a quick cover up and announcement over the other band's name. The word'll spread, you'll see. Nine alright? I'll throw in a meal and yer pints as a bonus. Yer a bloody gift, you lot!"

"No problem, we'll be here," Annis grinned. That was easy. So now what?

Doddy apologized for having to cut the meeting short but he explained that he was up to his eyeballs in a botched delivery down in the docking bay and called for Wendy to fix them up with whatever they might need in the way of fortification before they left.

She provided them with bowls of the tavern's famous seafood chowder, a tray of thick-buttered bread, and coffee all round while the group argued as to which was the sanest alternative to getting back to their winter tuath, other than walking, finally agreeing to run the block and a half to the nearest subway.

At least they'd have the bus tonight, Robin snarled, knowing it was Willie's foolish *Oh to be sure the weather'll hold* comment, that had seemed so certain at the time; that was sure to see them drenched and miserable by the time they got home.

CHAPTER TWENTY

HOLLY DIDN'T REALIZE THAT SCATHACH'S wolfhounds came and went from her apartment as they chose, roaming the streets of New Rathmore fully alert to the little mysteries that inhabited the city: indigenous spirits of the land now buried beneath asphalt and shopping malls, offspring of careless magic, halflings and shiftings from the Dreaming Lands that had come through the veil in answer to the yearnings of the Lost, or by art or poetry or potent story.

The mysteries didn't quite fit: strange mergings of beast and bird, some that looked like bits of forest that walked on two legs or four, others like haunted characters from a child's imagination, twisted from their pattern by neglect, and the harshness of their surroundings, when that child discards them for "real" things

The huge dogs passed them by; could be seen by them—*could* be seen by anyone sensitive to such things—but on nights this bitter the streets were all but deserted by people, and the few homeless, huddled in makeshift shelters, had little time for such hauntings, although many were very aware.

Tonight was different. The hounds ranged farther than at any time since their arrival, following a scent so far unknown to them in the city; curious. It was not a quarry they sought, so much as the source of the lingering musk that announced the presence of the fair folk.

Cullyn was the strongest and most intelligent of the pack, a dark and brindled grey, very ugly and very knowing. He led the hunt into the winding labyrinth of alleyways that were flanked all around by tall eroded walls, the ground littered with discarded junk. They followed the shining trail relentlessly, not stopping except to mark their territory, until arriving at a wide, rusty metal door set into a featureless brick wall where the redolence of comings and goings was strongest.

Cullyn scratched at the door, scoring the dirt and flaking the rust until the claws, in his enormous paws pained him. He gave up, a frustrated whine sneaking from his throat before he could catch himself. Either there was no one home or they couldn't hear him. He sat on his haunches, head cocked to one side, ears alert for any sound from within. Nothing. Damn. He'd been sure that when they found their mark they'd be greeted with pleasure and treated to *an aíocht* as befitted their breed. Better to go get Scathach.

The pack retraced their route unerringly back to the canal and up the single flight of stairs to the apartment where the warrior woman sat cleaning her weapons, feeling somewhat like a square peg in a round hole, and wondering when the action was likely to begin and how long before Holly returned from her class.

Cullyn and the others whuffed outside the closed door and she jumped to open it. The big male brushed against her legs, his tail lashing and his mouth open and grinning.

"What've you found?" She could sense his excitement. Something important had happened. She dug her fingers into his course ruff, loving him, kneeling as the others fawned around her, vying for her affection.

Fuck it, she thought, standing and reaching for the warm woolen brat, *I need some exercise anyway.*

"Show me," she whispered, pulling the door closed behind them.

A blast of damp air slapped her as she stepped out into the street, causing her to laugh aloud at its challenge, the wolfhounds crowding around her in anticipation, eager for her company.

She started out at a walk and slowly built her pace. Before they'd traversed two blocks she was leaning into her accustomed loping run, conserving energy, breathing steadily.

Cullyn led, effortlessly following his own earlier markings, until they arrived at the industrial-style door. Scathach slowed and stopped, the dark-of-the-moon night causing her no difficulty as she studied the heavy lock and bolt securing the entrance.

"So this is important?" she asked.

She had never seen a door like it, full metal as it was, and she was impressed. Shit, she mused, contemplating the problem of access, the whole damned city is impressive: lights that never go out, filling the night with their glare, the constant bloody noise, the danger of traffic, the scream and rumble of what Holly had explained were airplanes, that flew low over the southside on their flight paths to and from the airport, the generally appalling stink.

It was all new and Holly had needed to teach her so much. When her companion had switched on a television in the bedsit for the first time Scathach been horrified at the people trapped within it. That, too, had been explained, although she still couldn't fully comprehend.

Real fear—overwhelming, breathtaking, mind-numbing fear— had almost sent her fleeing back into the Otherworld, despite knowing beyond doubt that it was her geas to fulfill some purpose in this one, with this woman, for whatever reasons. Holly had switched channels to watch the six o'clock news and Scathach had seen images of twenty first century war for the first time and had watched rockets slam into stone cities, learned what tanks were, what men with rifles could do, what a car bomb was.

She had seen vast seas of people and Holly had explained about protests and political rallies and what a Pope was and a President.

Yes, she was impressed. No one could be otherwise confronted with what humanity was doing. She'd caught herself, time and again, grinding her teeth in nervous agitation ever since that first day.

Scathach studied the door. There was no handle, only a bar that reached from one side to the other. She pulled it and jiggled it but nothing moved. Shrugging, undaunted, she leaned her weight against it pushing it down. It gave. Holding it down she pulled and pushed before dragging to the right and hearing the satisfactory scream of metal moving on metal. She kept at it until there was an opening sufficient for her and the hounds to squeeze through.

They entered into a blackness so absolute that it pressed against her like a giant beast, momentarily taking her breath away.

"Cullyn?" she whispered. She could hear the hounds' breathing all around her and felt relief as the huge male shoved his head under her hand, sneezing at the dust that irritated his nose in the wherever-they-were, before taking a step forward, then another, guiding his mistress to a vast well of stairs.

The place smelled peculiar. Not unpleasant, merely like nothing she'd smelled before, even on the streets above them. Her hand found a guard rail as they began their descent, and she was more surefooted because of it.

How far down *was* whatever it was Cullyn wanted her to see? And what *did* he smell that she could not? Was this death, and she hadn't noticed her own passing? Still no light. The only things that she could see were the luminous eyes of the hounds whenever one of them paused to look in her direction.

This is getting crazy, she thought, worried about how long this was taking; worried at not having her weapons; worried that Holly would be home and that *she* would be worrying. *Shut up*, she scolded herself.

How long had they been here anyway? She went to take another step and her leg jarred right to the hip. Flat ground. Every breath and scrape of claw upon the solid blackness rang out with exaggerated loudness that she knew only occurred in enormous, hollow places.

The pack moved slowly, Scathach relying on their superior senses, until Cullyn whined, pressing against her legs, warning her to stop. She heard the others jump down what sounded like several feet.

She dropped to her knees and felt forward with her hands, finding the edge she knew would be there. It was when she lowered herself over the side of the drop, and her boots crunched on the rubble that littered the abandoned rail track, that she heard muffled laughter a slight distance away.

They continued moving, Scathach holding firmly to the pack leader with her right hand, and her left lightly feeling for the edge of the platform that gave onto a wall of what felt like small bricks.

As they rounded a bend a haze of light spilled into the tunnel from an opening on their left, fifty or so feet away, and soft voices ebbed and flowed upon the stillness.

Several of the hounds bounded forward, yipping in delight as though greeting known friends.

Scathach shrugged.

"Hello, the light!" she called, causing a sudden avalanche of tiles from the opposite wall to come crashing to the ground. *Shit* she swore under her breath, leaping away.

A head poked around the corner of the entrance, pale face, black, black hair, as she closed the last of the distance.

"Not a good idea to yell, you know." He whispered, loudly enough for her to hear, and held out a hand with which to pull her up onto the ledge at the entrance to the defunct service bay, seeming delighted.

"Raven?" she uttered, astonished.

It was years beyond counting since the androgynous fairy had had contact with his old teacher but still he thought the shock on her face seriously entertaining as he grabbed her in a deep embrace, momentarily ignoring her confusion.

His old teacher. Well, not so old. She looked as stunning and exotic as ever, reminding him of the time or two they'd shared more than sword-play. How interesting. She was thought lost to time. None of the Tuatha Dé Danann had seen or heard of her for centuries. So many questions, so much to say. So much to *tell*.

"BY THE SEA, I'VE NOT KNOWN there were still fairies in this world," Scathach exclaimed, holding Raven from her, drinking him in.

"We're mostly all still here, *mo fíain chroì*," he assured her as he led her into the heart of the winter hearth-hold where a cut-down forty-four gallon drum exuded light and heat and crackled with the familiar sound of burning wood.

The room was awash in the glow of many candles, and rag-tag furnishings filled most of the space, giving the impression that many dwelt there. Several of the hounds had taken to sniffing at everything carefully, finally coming to the conclusion that a feast was not in the offing on this particular night, and making their way to the source of warmth. Young Cath, no more than a very large pup, stared balefully at Raven, gaining a heartfelt apology and a promise of seeing the situation put to right for the next visit before settling, despondent, beside her dam.

A man and a very pregnant woman sat on a settee close by the fire holding steaming mugs, seemingly unperturbed by the unexpected visitor and her canine companions. Cullyn and his favorite bitch hovered close to her (it was obvious that she could see them) as though greeting an old friend.

"Scathach?" the woman asked, her brow furrowing as though she sought to remember.

"Do I know you?"

Raven, interrupting, asked if his guest would appreciate a dram, and the warrior-woman nodded as she waited for an answer from the stranger.

"No. But I'd know you anywhere. I'm Kathryn," she grinned.

"Well you've got me at a disadvantage Kathryn, because I've no bloody idea who you are."

"When I was a child I traveled the Dreaming Lands. You're a legend there. Songs were sung of you. Descriptive songs. I'd know you anywhere."

"Vincent," her partner offered, holding out a hand in greeting.

"So what's all this then?" Scathach looked around the tuath taking in her surroundings. Raven pulled a bottle of single malt and two glasses from within one of four milk crates supporting a slab of wood that served as a low table, asking her to sit and relax and he'd fill her in on all the news.

It was warm enough to remove her plaid which she draped across the back of her chair. As she did so she noticed two swords, in their scabbards, curved in the way of the warrior-monks from the East, leaning accessibly close to Vincent.

She eyed him, tilting her head in the direction of the weapons. "Those yours?"

He nodded solemnly, taking Kathryn's hand in his own.

"Don't talk much, do you?"

"You have *no* idea," Kathryn chuckled.

She explained that she and Vincent lived two hours out of the city near a village called Falconstowe. She owned a cottage on several rural acres bordering thick forest, and the surrounding area, including the village, was a stronghold for many of the clans that passed through. The two of them had forged a partnership during a spot of trouble that had occurred a while back.

"Long story," she confided, offering to tell the whole of it.

"Maybe later," Scathach shrugged. "Don't know how long I can stay tonight."

Kathryn went on to explain that Brighid was to midwife their first child—due just before the Spring—and they'd come to New Rathmore earlier in the day to check on the baby's progress and catch up with friends.

Raven told Scathach that several of the fair Gentry lived in the derelict Underground's service bay through the winter weeks, hunting up the Lost but that they were all out at a gig (and informing her what that was when she scrunched her brow), and some meeting with a witch about trouble on Inishrún at Samhain.

Scathach's eyes widened as she linked two and two, telling him that she'd come from the Otherworld because she'd met Holly Tremenhere there and her gut had told her it was a good idea to come to this world. *Ah,* he'd replied, briefly filling Kathryn and Vincent in on the connection.

"Well we'll know a whole lot more when the others get here, *mo chroì,*" Raven concluded, bending to the box of timber off cuts beside the fire dropping in several pieces raising a shower of sparks.

He chuckled as he thought of the others' faces when they arrived home. "Yer gonna rock their world to be sure. This all just gets better and better!"

Vincent moved from his seat and over to a makeshift kitchen and set about preparing a meal of vegetables and rice. Whatever was brewing could be taken care of when the moment arrived; it was all Tao, after all.

"And why are you three still here instead of with the music?" Scathach changed the subject.

"Well, I can't bleedin' *abide* crowds," Raven offered, moving to the kitchen to help with the preparations, leaving Kathryn to stretch out fully on the russet-colored sofa.

"And I bleedin' can't abide crowds either," Vincent mimicked, asking if she'd share their meal to which the warrior woman graciously agreed

"And I'm stuck with the both of them for some reason that escapes me for the moment," Kathryn lied, smiling.

She rolled onto her side facing Scathach, plumping a cushion under her belly. "So will you *please* tell me the truth about you and Cú Chullain?"

CHAPTER TWENTY ONE

WOLF HESITATED, HER EYES WIDENING AS SHE glimpsed the large group seated at the long table across the room beside the stage where the band, and that young lad Willie, were busy packing up their instruments.

The magic they exuded was palpable. What were she and David getting into?

She and Merrin and David Rushton maneuvered their way through the sweaty, smiling patrons that were moving off the dance floor, heading back to tables or the bar.

Pity I missed the music, she thought, figuring it must have been a helluva gig. "When are the Fíanna playing again?"

Merrin's eyes were fixed on Willie, the two sending out waves of lust towards each other. "Ah... huh? Oh. Tomorrow night; they're here again tomorrow."

"I'd like to come and hear them. You think you might feel like dancing?" she asked David.

He shook his head. "Sorry, Bella, business and all."

Wolf sighed. *That's okay*, she mused. Life was always interesting when one went places alone anyway.

Her skin prickled as they neared the Travelers' table and her gaze wandered over the people she was to meet.

Her breath stuck in her throat and her eyes felt too small for their sockets as they lit on the big man at the end of the table closest to the exit. He was huge. He had a mass of dreadlocks littered with crow feathers (or maybe raven, she couldn't tell the difference), tied up at the crown of his head with strips of black cloth, his head shaved down either side.

He had skin the color of bronze chocolate, peppered with tattoos, and fathomless black eyes, already fixed on her. He was bundled with clothing, causing him to appear bulky but she knew it wasn't fat. Around him were the half-seen mergings of stag and —what *was* that? Wolf? Bird? Not clear enough. It didn't matter. She knew who he was; knew *what* he was, and she thought her legs would give out under her.

Mother of all living, she breathed, forcing herself to put one foot in front of the other.

"You alright, chook?" David looked at her, worried. He'd never seen her lose her cool before. He searched the table for any hint of danger, sensing none. *Weird folk, sure,* he thought, *but you come to expect that amongst pagans.*

"I'm… I'm fine David." She forced her usual appearance of composure but didn't think she'd ever get it back after tonight. This was her *god.* And he seemed for all the world like a man.

Did Merrin know? Did any of them know whose company they kept?

The three reached the table, and chairs were pulled out to accommodate them. As Wolf sat she turned briefly in Hunter's direction and his eyes twinkled as he grinned, exposing a white, white smile with slightly elongated canines. *Not now,* he seemed to say.

What she could never be bothered to mention to others anymore was that she had the Sight. Always had. It had made her childhood difficult until she'd learned to shut her mouth about such things. But it *had* been a clear road through dark years that she'd always trusted.

She'd taken to the witching as a *natural,* learning what she could from the coven that initiated her and later, from interaction with the witches that she, in turn, initiated into Three White Trees. She'd spoken to them, and sometimes others, about her gift, and so many had responded with, *Yeah, yeah, I know. Me too*, without knowing at all, that she'd stopped mentioning it. Hence the masks.

Show them, she'd decided. None of her artworks were fantasy. Portraits; each one of them was a portrait.

She relegated the shifting images around Hunter to memory. For later, excited at the prospect of returning to her studio and beginning a new work.

But then Brighid came back from wherever she'd been, and Wolf was struck with awe again, not sure just which of the Fair Folk she *was* but knowing, by the brutal power emanating from the...what? Déithe? Sídhe? A bit of both? that she was up there with the big names.

There was no knowing her true age—she looked to be around forty-something, but Wolf figured correctly that it was a glamour. She was small, maybe five-one or five-two, wore her black hair in dozens of neatly woven braids, many of which were tied at the ends with small bronze rings, had ivory skin with totemic tattoos covering her cheeks, chin and brow, and the most unnerving thing—the thing that cemented the knowledge that the age thing was an illusion—were her ancient eyes, so pale a grey they were almost white. She wore a floor-length brown leather coat open over baggy tweed trousers and a hand-knitted green wool jumper that had seen better days. The unmistakable presence of crows or ravens shadowed her in a miasma of companionship that caused Wolf an instant headache.

"Hey witch," Brighid said stonily, ready to provoke; mischief in her eyes. "I'm Brighid, and you're staring like a groupie at a rock concert and I'd appreciate if you wouldn't be so obvious."

Wolf shook herself. "Can I have one of those?" she asked, pointing to the bottle of single malt further down the table, refusing to be intimidated.

Brighid laughed aloud. "So we don't need to explain who we are then."

"What's going on?" David asked, feeling as though he was missing out. The atmosphere was tinged with the sweet feel of magic, and just a touch of acid, but more was unfolding than his psychic gifts allowed.

"Well the most among us are fairies," a young man introducing himself as Robin offered, crowing with delight at the snarls and offended glares that the jibe engendered, pretending offence at the mild slap across the shoulder he received from the fairest, most intimidatingly beautiful creature that Wolf had ever seen.

"M*u*-um!" he complained.

The flitterings around the woman whose name was Puck, whose red-gold hair formed an unruly halo of flyaway curls around a narrow oval face, were the usual kind that occurred around fey people. This was no sprit god; was not one of the fair Folk, either. She was *human*. And from the look that passed between her and Hunter she was beloved of the god.

So was Robin…?

Not five minutes had passed since they'd arrived at Mary Flannery's before Wolf settled into the whole exotic scenario and got down to business. "Brighid? Will you explain all this to David or shall I?"

Brighid's eyes lit with appreciation at how grandly their new acquaintance adjusted. *High priestess,* Merrin had said. *It fits.*

"Don't mind if I do." Brighid gave David her full attention, impressed by the bearing of the older man, so used to human males looking saggy and unkempt by the time they reached what was considered middle aged, and at the intelligence in his eyes. "Are you a Sagittarian?"

"Pardon me?" She had caught him by surprise with the inane question, and he ran one hand through his silver hair, reaching for his glass of ale with the other and attempted to disguise how off-putting this whole thing was for him.

"I'm right, aren't I?" Brighid charmed.

"First of December, ma'am."

Good. Loosen up, ya sweet man.

"We're ordinary folk where we come from, but that doesn't mean we're like you," she continued, being annoyingly evasive.

"Is that disdain in your voice?" David sat back in his chair, undoing the knot in his tie, and wishing he'd dressed down like Merrin had suggested, being prepared, however, to be wide open to whatever Brighid had to say; willing to play.

She snorted, nodding in agreement, causing a ripple of *something* to pass around the table.

"Well your prejudice, dear lady, is unjustified and in extremely bad taste, so save it for somebody else, ah, Brighid, is it?"

There were hoots and howls and oohs from the others and Brighid laughed, delighted, taking David's breath away, her smile transforming her from unpleasant to downright beautiful.

"He got ya there, *mo chroì*," Hunter smiled.

The *Time, Ladies and Gentlemen* alarm went off informing the crowd that it was 10:45 and the last call for the bar. Patrons not up for a final drink chatted and laughed as they donned their coats and headed for the street, but the fairies and their companions sat quietly, unconcerned, while Brighid explained to Wolf and David everything that Merrin had deliberately left out.

TOM DODDY CLOSED THE DOORS HALF an hour later and turned out the majority of the lights, leaving only those of the bar and kitchen where Wendy cleared away the last of the glasses, and Jimmy and Sophie, his kitchen staff, cleaned up out back, and those illuminating the meeting.

"Whoever's last to leave locks up," he called over his shoulder, heading for the stairs that led down to the docking bay, receiving a wave of acknowledgement from the table where the Travelers were gathered. No point worrying about them. They were his luck and he trusted them in a way that he couldn't have explained if asked.

Wolf and David Rushton sat enthralled as the gathering entertained them with stories and anecdotes until well after 2AM when David turned the conversation to the reason for the meeting by bringing up the subject of the island for the first time that night, and holding court for the following hour.

"So their grand plan is like to end in nothing," he concluded. "There are sufficient safeguards set in place at governmental levels nowadays—environmental impact concerns, the protection of national heritage sites, the rights of long term tenants—that they'd be tied up in paperwork for years. What I don't understand is … those boys from Solomon Stone'd know all this, so what are they playing at by telling Harvey they'd "think on it"?"

He turned to Wolf. "I figure I've got a little more snooping to do, my darling, don't you?"

"I should imagine Frank would know it also," she added, "so it gets even more curious. According to Jesse—she's his wife and one of my witches, not that he's aware, mind you—he's turned a bit peculiar since the whole episode began."

She paused long enough to ask if Merrin wouldn't mind rolling her a cigarette, before an idea occurred to her "You don't suppose he's merely out for a bit of revenge do you?"

No one had thought of that.

"It could be that simple," Hunter said, his voice controlled, sending fingers of delight down Wolf's spine. He leaned over to Puck and kissed her gently before scraping back his chair and standing, informing everyone that he had somewhere else to be.

"Can I speak to you for a moment before you leave," Wolf asked self-consciously.

The forest god gestured for her to join him outside and she excused herself from the table, telling David she'd be right back.

THE ALLEY WAS HUSHED AND STILL, SWATHED in a softness of

,unseasonable fog, the cobbled pathway underfoot giving the ambiance of another century.

Wolf stood and looked up at Hunter's face, tears welling annoyingly, taking her by surprise.

"Lady Kain?" he queried gently.

"My lord," she bowed her head, wanting him to know that she was aware of what he was.

Hunter sighed. "I get so busy with the world, the way it is."

"I know. And the Great Mystery? Does she know of us?"

"Promise me something?"

"Anything."

"No matter how unfair it sometimes seems? Don't ever doubt, okay?"

She was about to protest the impossibility of feeling anything other than certain, but he interrupted her. "Some witches are like you—strong, clear, the magic unpolluted, and some are just vague echoes of what they're capable of being. But the differences don't matter to us. We see your dance, you understand. Whether it's you or the others who honor earth's magic. We notice. We know. But it's getting harder to protect the little mysteries."

Wolf's back straightened and her heart felt near to bursting as he took her in a deep embrace and kissed the top of her head.

"Go raibh beannacht na ndéithe agus ár sinsir ar, mo chroi" (May the gods and ancestors blessings be upon you, my love) he whispered, letting go of her.

He moved a simple step away and the night took him from her sight, leaving her with the smell of forest loam and juniper berries and Scotch pine after rain.

Oh Milady, she whispered, knowing the Mystery would understand exactly how she was feeling.

HUNTER SLIPPED INTO THE DREAMING lands, to Forgotten Lake.

"This is getting out of hand."

The Great Mystery wore the garment of one of her much maligned and misrepresented creatures, the form of a Noisy Miner, while still celebrating her splendor with a hint of fire engine red beneath each wing. She darted around Hunter squawking at imagined cats.

He ignored her triviality, gazing instead upon the softness of the distant lake shore, misty in the perpetual gold of an autumn's hazy afternoon. "Too many people know our business. I don't necessarily see it coming to anything, mind you, and I'm pretty certain we can trust our secrets to Wolf Kain and her friend … but those other guys? That Frank Harvey and those two lawyers? What if the press gets involved? There'd be a field day on the island even if development doesn't happen … I'm worried, yeah?"

The goddess landed on a log that had fallen long ago, sensing the newborn fox kits within its hollow as they slept all curled together for warmth, and shuddered into a more-or-less human form, brushing bits of twig and bark from a ground-length brown linen robe (its pockets exposing threads of fire engine red) and spitting feathers from her mouth.

"Yeah well you got permission to interfere, so what's the big deal?" She yawned and stretched before plonking herself, in a gangly tangle of her own limbs, onto the sandy loam beside the rock where Hunter perched.

"So the big deal *is*, for starters, that Charlie's still on the island, having a grand time from what I can glean, and Holly's gone batty."

The Great Mystery barked a laugh, then tsk-tsked him. "What *I* think is that you need a holiday! Find yourself some high, primordial mother forest that the loggers haven't got to yet and disappear until you can get some perspective."

"Well I might just do that, my lady, but not quite yet. And can't you set my mind at ease in the meantime?"

She turned her foxlike face in his direction, suddenly serious. "Charlie's just fine where he is. Oh, and don't write Holly off so soon. It's not over till the fat lady sings, you know."

What fat lady, he thought, sorting through everyone he knew, considering a few buxom possibilities but none relevant to what was currently going on. He'd work that clue out later.

"Oh, and it's not Holly who's batty. Mind the man who plays at being a god. His back's in a corner soon and hell hath no fury. No wait; wrong metaphor…"

"*What* are you *talking* about?"

But she'd already melted into dust motes, caught in the shafts of autumn gold that slanted through the rowan and aspen, oak and alder that bordered the clearing.

Women! Hunter mused, jumping down from his rock and moving between the worlds to Inishrún.

CHAPTER TWENTY TWO

SCATHACH HAD BRIMMED WITH EXUBERANCE when she'd told Holly about finding the sídhe and all Holly had said was *Oh*? She had turned away, gone to the kitchenette and opened a can of baked beans for their meal. She dumped the contents into a pot, lit the gas stove to heat it and pulled sliced bread from its bag, all in silence.

Scathach watched her, confused. "Don't you wanna come meet them with me?"

"Not particularly. You go. Knock yerself out." The bitterness was unmistakable.

The warrior woman sat on the floor by the two bar heater, her legs crossed and her hands idle in her lap, studying the friend whose life she considered so small a thing apart from her ability to travel time's web. Every day, so far, was the same. Get up, get dressed, go the bakery, go to her writing class, take Scathach for a walk like a faithful hound. *Hmph!*

"What do you write about in your school?" she changed the subject.

Holly brought each of them a plate of food, went back for knives and forks, and sat down opposite the warrior woman.

"Set tasks mostly, like how to build a character, plot, that sort of thing."

"Oh. Well, anything else?" She wrinkled her nose slightly as she took a bite of the baked beans.

"My thoughts and feelings. Things that matter to me."

"Kinda cathartic is it?"

This was the first time Scathach had said anything remotely critical of her host, and it slipped out unthought. But Holly *was* getting her down. Moody. Never really smiling. How tragic could her life be, after all?

Holly merely looked at her, a forkful of food halfway to her mouth. "What's that supposed to mean?"

"I'm sorry."

"No. I want to know what you meant."

"I guess I was hoping you'd tell me some of the stories you write about. That *is* the point isn't it? Of what you're training for?"

"Later maybe. Right now it's all just basics."

"Well, if you *were* to write a story…"

Holly laughed, hearing the plea. "If I was to write a story now it'd have to be about this girl who met these mythical people and who ran away, I guess. Nothing before that, nothing after."

Scathach was scheming. Part of it was personal because she was so downright bored. She'd been thinking about it all day while Holly had been gone. If she couldn't get out of this flea-box she was going back to the Dreaming Lands. She'd thought she was needed, the only reason she'd come, but so far she simply felt like an unpaid babysitter for a kid with a giant chip on her shoulder.

At least she could go kick around with the Travelers for a while, but without Holly? She didn't need to feel guilty, obligated, but she did.

"Why do you want to be a writer, Holly?"

A pause. *How do I explain this?* Holly wondered.

"You want a coffee?" she said instead.

"No. I want for you to talk to me, my friend."

"Okay." she rummaged through her excuses for an as-close-to-the-truth answer as she could, because, in all honesty, she didn't *know* what motivated her recently. "Ah, everybody needs to be good at something."

Scathach nodded, waiting for her to continue.

"So my whole life I've never been good at anything. The island changed me in some ways. At least I feel stuff now. And I can work a bit of magic here, like meeting you and journeying between the worlds. But no one sees that. No one knows me in my world. I've *got* to do something to stop being so *invisible*."

"Well," Scathach was careful at how she phrased herself, "it seems to me that for that to happen a person has to live a little more than you do."

Holly tried not to react; sat simply watching the other woman's eyes.

"It's all so tame and safe here. How can you write stories if you don't live them? Seems to me that you're doing all these "tasks", learning all this "form" just to write one story." She picked up the discarded meals and took them to the kitchen, dumping them onto the bench.

Holly stared after her, the realization of what she'd said doing her head in. One story.

"So is that why you want me to come meet your friends?"

Much more selfish than that, Scathach thought. "No. Holly do you want the truth?"

"Of *course*," she replied. *Do I?*

"I'm bored shitless here, and it seems I've got three choices ..."

She's been thinking about this for a while, Holly figured, hearing the resignation.

"I can go back home; I can go hang out with the Dé Danann; or . . . or you and I can do *something* other than stay cooped up in this little prison cell like a pair of docile hermits!" There. It was said. Consequences.

Holly's face crumpled. *How could I have been so stupid?*

"Now I've gone and hurt your feelings," Scathach whispered.

Destiny or the fair folk had set up their meeting, she knew that. But it was wrong, somehow, the way it was going. She also knew that.

"Well what do you want to do?" Holly's voice was crackly with emotion as she fought against tears. *Stop being so damn fragile!*

"I'd like to get out of the city, Holly. And I'd like desperately to get to the sea. And I need to work out. I'm becoming soft already and my sword is becoming dull and pissed off at me. Oh Holly, can't we *do* something?

"The only places I've ever been are here and where I grew up and . . . and down the coast where the ferry goes to Inishrún. But I don't want to go to the island. Can't. Not yet," she pleaded.

"The coast then. Can we go there? Is there life there?"

"Life?"

"Other than people, people and more bloody people."

"It's pretty wild country, I guess." Yes. This was a good idea. They could go down to Weary Bay, get a caravan or something, do some walking. Scathach could workout with her weapons; could even hunt some rabbits. Holly could write a bit. *Cathartic*, she smiled.

She'd see about taking time off from the bakery and the college in the morning. They'd go tomorrow.

"Is tomorrow okay?"

Scathach grabbed her in a fierce embrace. "Yes! Yesyesyesyesyes! Let's go get drunk!"

Why not? I really am so boring.

THEY CAUGHT THE TRAIN TO MIDDLEBOROUGH and linked with the bus to Leachfield after a three hour wait during which time Holly refused to go anywhere away from the terminal. It was Middleborough, after all. There were only taxis out to the remote districts from Leachfield and they reached Weary Bay in the late afternoon.

All eyes were on Scathach, in the pub where Holly organized them a room for the night, except for the bartender, who was also the owner and who introduced himself as Henry Poe.

"How long you ladies plan on stayin'?" he asked cordially.

Holly smiled, telling him they were escapees from the city and could maybe be here for two weeks and did he know of any caravans or cottages they could rent for while?

"You go on and get yourselves settled in upstairs and I'll ask around, orright?"

They both thanked him and went to get their key.

After they'd gone Henry hulloo'd the local patrons asking if anyone knew where the two lovely ladies could stay for a couple of weeks. There were a few snorts of dismay at his compliment and several mumbled *No's* before old Barney Rumford told him they could have the empty croft down on his far pasture, being as how the big girl looked strong enough to wield an axe and that that'd do for payment, plus a bit o' help for Janey in the kitchen o'course, what with his arthritis giving him a hard time and his not having enough wood chopped to see out the winter.

Henry said that sounded fair unless the women were too *city*.

GRAINNE HAD JUMPED AT THE OPPORTUNITY to uproot from New Rathmore.

She and Robbie had talked about how often unsatisfactory things got pushed aside when love was more important and that a silent part of her had never been happy where they'd been. They'd gone to a real estate agency earlier that day to see about selling their house.

Property prices had gone through the roof over the past few years and they'd been gobsmacked at how much they were told their home would probably fetch.

Robbie had phoned *Coombes* in Leachfield, who handled all the sales for the south-east rural region, including Weary Bay, and the Freemans realized that they'd be able to afford to purchase what they wanted outright if their current place took what the agent asked.

The shortage of middle income homes meant that a list of prospective buyers was already available, and contracts were exchanged in a blur of ease within the following fortnight. Within that time they'd taken the truck to Weary Bay and met with the down-to-earth man from *Coombes* who'd showed them over three places, all outside of the town and whose previous inhabitants had done the exact opposite to Robbie and Grainne by heading to the city to work.

The perfect place had been there waiting. A rambling old five bedroom stone farmhouse with gardens gone to seed; two acres set in the lee of grass-covered hills with a spring fed creek running right past the derelict barn on its way to the sea.

There was a ton of work to be done to make the place livable, but they'd purchased it for a song and Grainne had pleaded with Robbie to give her a free hand in the renovating. He'd grinned and shrugged and set about seeing if he could get work on one of the fishing boats, linking up with the crew of *The Watchman*.

THEY'D SAT WITH LIAM MCKENNA—THE bosun aboard *The Watchman*—and his wife Stella, over a meal and a few pints when Holly and Scathach had come in. He'd recognized Mim's niece straight off, recalling how mad she'd been at Charlie from the little he'd seen. He'd tell Grainne all about it later. Better to keep quiet in front of other people, lest they judge out of hand.

HENRY'S WIFE, ALICE, WAS STILL IN THE dining room when Scathach and Holly entered, a few minutes after ten the next morning, desperately hoping they weren't too late for breakfast. She'd clucked her tongue at them and folded her arms across her enormous bosom, defying them to ask for anything she couldn't provide. Both ordered everything: eggs, bacon, sausage, tomato, mushrooms, toast, coffee, and Alice smiled as she piled their table with the food, delighted that city girls had hearty appetites, handing Holly some notes and a map that Henry had jotted down, explaining Barney's deal and giving directions to the farm.

Scathach scanned the map and estimating that the Rumford place was only about four miles away. She was looking forward to the brisk walk, but Holly groaned, asking Alice if there was a taxi or such that could take them. *No, ducks, nowt. It's a good thing it's not rainin' though*, had been the reply.

They'd bolted up the stairs after breakfast and stuffed their few bits and pieces into backpacks. Scathach had her weapons bundled in one of Holly's sheets and tied up with twine. She slung it, and her pack, over her shoulders, badgering Holly to hurry up and stop fiddle-arsing around.

MOST TOURIST SHOPS AND VENUES WERE closed for the winter but there was a *Sizzlers* open just along from the Post Office, next door to the park, where about two dozen of what looked like local youth, attempting to emulate ghetto fashion, sat or stood around, chatting, flirting or performing feats with small stubby bicycles. They spotted the strangers as they approached, gawping at Scathach.

Shit, Holly cursed, saying nothing, hoping the teenagers were *country* enough to be polite.

"'R'you a woman or a bloke?" one of the girls sneered as Scathach and Holly came parallel with the group.

Just keep walking.

"She looks like a spotty version of that Sigourney chick in *Aliens*." Laughter.

"Ya reckon? Betcha she's the alien." More laughter.

Scathach stopped and her unseen hounds, their hackles rising, milled around her.

Shitshitshitshit! Holly thought.

"Hello," Scathach grinned.

"Whyn't you go back to whatever planet ya come from,"

spouted a coltish, rakishly good-looking boy about sixteen years old, with dark auburn hair, and brown eyes that crinkled with glee, who moved to deliberately block her path.

"And you are?" she demanded, unimpressed by the attempted intimidation.

"Who wants to know, Baldy?" He turned from side to side, grinning at his companions who mumbled and nodded, goading him on.

"Name's Scathach, not "Baldy", ya wee, nasty little git." No longer smiling she squatted casually on the cobbled street, laying her bundle on the ground and untying the twine that held it together.

"Scathach, don't," Holly hissed. Trouble with the townsfolk, or the law, was the last thing they wanted. If questioned what could she say to help her friend? Nothing. Why couldn't dealings with the Otherworldly be easy? "Can we just *go*? Please?"

The boys were eyeing the bundle curiously and Scathach's eyes moved between them, her fingers working the knots.

"Yeah, go on Scabby—was that yer name? Bring out yer violin and have a go!" The boy was pushing it; loving the attention. The game with the out-of-towners, usually reserved for the summer tourists, alleviated the crushing, protracted boredom that came with the cold of every winter of their lives. Every one of them had sworn to leave the West Country when they completed the mandatory term at high school. What was here? The stink of fish and an endless life on the boats? Farming? Getting married to someone you knew so well she or he would always be predictable? And all the while *Sea-changers* were buying up their ancestors' land, leasing their own places back to them at hiked rents and demanding they vacate their homes for the summer holidays. No. Fuck 'em. Give as good as you can while yer stuck here.

Scathach opened the sheet just enough to extract her

quarterstaff, and stood, leaning on its smooth knobby strength, with one foot on the opposite knee.

"I asked who y'are y'disrespectful little shit, so tell me your name? It's only fair I know yours, when you know mine, before I beat the crap outa ya."

The others backed away, unsure that the fun was still fun, and a few of the local folk came out of their street-front houses to see what the fuss was about.

Barney Rumford rounded the corner at the same time, coming into town on his tractor on the way to the general store. He recognized the two women who were to stay at his croft and slowed the old Massey-Ferguson to an idle, pushing his glasses up his nose before extracting a pipe from inside his jacket, tamping it with tobacco and lighting it, obscuring his vision momentarily with plumes of blue smoke. He was curious.

The teenager stood his ground, glaring at Scathach, defying her to strike out. Holly jumped between them just as the warrior raised her staff.

"Stop it. Both of you," she hissed. "Look you..." She faced the young man whose mouth twisted in a smirk. "She's a black belt, or something, in an ancient form of Celtic martial art. How about you back down?"

She whirled on Scathach glaring. "And *you*. You ought to know better."

"Orlando."

"What?" Holly spun back to the boy.

"Orlando Flynn. That's my name."

Scathach grinned from behind Holly's shoulder. "Yeah, like that's a local name."

He appeared to go back on the defensive at the taunt, but the warrior woman stepped around her companion and held out a hand for him to shake.

A kid, maybe ten years old, pushed forward, looking so like Orlando it was obvious they were brother and sister. "I'm Pen," she grinned, her front teeth missing. "What are the blue spots for?"

The tension dissolved as Orlando registered the small girl and her gesture of friendship, and he walked the two steps needed to take Scathach's outstretched hand before the other boys and girls clustered around asking a thousand questions and offering to help carry the bags. Holly let out the breath she hadn't realized she was holding, dumbfounded at the rapid change of the group mood.

A short, stubby, freckled boy said, *Hi, I'm Jonesy,* and grabbed for the sheet containing the bow and sword, and Scathach lunged, grabbing for the bundle before he took hold. *Not this,* she stated, dropping to her knees, and retying the twine possessively.

"Are they weapons?" Orlando crouched down beside her, transformed from antagonist to ally.

"Yes."

"I din't *never* hear o' women that can fight."

"Din't you?" Her lips quirked, playing with him. His admiration grew.

"Can you give me a demo maybe sometime?"

"You organize yourself a pole like mine, a bit taller'n yourself, and come over to where we're stayin' sometime later this afternoon."

"Where's that then?"

"Wi' us." Barney had wandered across to meet his guests, amused by his grandson's spunk.

"'Lando and young Pen are our lot," he added, tipping his cap to the two women. "M'son's dead to th'sea and his wife pissed off leavin' me 'n' Janey wi' their bairns. You wanna dump yer stuff in the tractor? I'll take y' to the croft in a wee while," and Orlando, Pen and two other youths hefted the women's bags into to the tray, Scathach and Holly climbing up after.

THE SMALL CROWD WALKED BESIDE THE vehicle all the way to the store, chatting and asking questions when Barney went inside to purchase the supplies he needed. They were about to leave when a fair haired girl, maybe fifteen years old, who would have been considered beautiful had acne not scarred her face badly, pushed her way to the front of the cluster, reaching up to grab Scathach's arm.

"What about me?" she asked, the question obscure, a challenge in her eyes.

"What *about* you?" The warrior sensed a keenness to her assailant; a fire, a rage.

"Will you show me like you're gonna show Orlando?"

"I'll train whoever turns up. And you are?"

"Mercy. Mercy Reilly."

"Ask Orlando what to bring, Mercy," she yelled over the top of the tractor engine as Barney cranked it into gear, turning it back the way he'd come.

The kids followed—except for Mercy, whom Scathach watched wander off in the direction of the sea—until they'd passed *Sizzlers,* where the majority branched off into the park, chattering like sparrows. *Something in that girl's eyes,* Scathach mused, half-remembering where she'd seen the look before, shrugging when the knowledge eluded her.

THE TRACTOR RATTLED ITS WAY ALONG HEDGE-LINED, badly rutted lanes where black faced sheep wandered at leisure, impeding the already slow journey. Scathach looked out over barren, windswept grassland, dotted with clusters of lichen-covered boulders, the wildness broken only by the occasional cottage. They traveled north along the coast road, a great bone of ridge to their left and barren hills—stark and ancient—ahead and to their right, forming the horizons. She breathed the sense of *this* beauty, feeling the tension, that had bunched the muscles around her shoulders and neck since arriving in Holly's world, slowly let go.

The raucous calls of plover and curlew and gull sounded all

around them as they chugged off the narrow road and down a dirt track heading for a saddle of land in the shelter of two high hills.

"What are you then?" Holly startled Scathach out of her reverie, her friend's brow furrowing as she registered the question.

"What?"

"You some kinda Pied Piper? What was all that about back in the village?"

"I don't know what Piper you're meanin', but I can smell the Great Mystery in all this, *mo creidhe*, is what it's about," Scathach replied, her eyes clear for the first time since they'd left the city.

Holly chuckled, telling the story of the unpaid ratter over the remainder of the bumpy ride.

BARNEY SWITCHED OFF THE MASSY AND climbed down gracelessly, wincing with pain. "Bit of a stop t'meet the missus," he scowled, "and for me t'show y'round the chores, orright?"

Smells of baking and woodsmoke wafted on the early afternoon air as Barney led them across a clearing—where chickens bokked and scratched at the near-frozen dirt—and through the back door of a rundown drystone farmhouse, into a warm, clean kitchen.

Barney and his wife Janey both looked to be in their early fifties and hardship had damaged their bodies, but not, it seemed, their spirits.

Like honored guests, Barney introduced Holly and Scathach to Janey, who beamed with delight and ushered them to a table laden with tea things, bowls of thickened cream, preserves, honey, butter and a plate piled high with golden scones, fresh from the oven.

"We don't get guests much," Barney whispered to Holly out of the corner of his mouth.

"Tuck in," Janey scolded, pouring tea.

"This is grand!" Scathach pulled out a chair and reached for a scone with no further prompting.

The Rumfords chatted about this and that—the workings of the farm which consisted of dairy cows and a modest barley crop, Janey's garden produce that she sold at the spring and summer markets, and the baking that she'd won prizes for—before asking the girls a bit about themselves. Holly kept it simple, telling them about her work at the bakery and the writing course she attended in the evenings, adding nothing else, but Scathach remained quiet, continuing to eat until she needed to undo the top button of her jeans.

"Wha' bout you lass? Yer a weird one t' look upon is sure. Where'd you come from?" Janey didn't believe in mincing her words, endearing her to the warrior the more so.

"Ah... Scotland."

"Ye don't sound Scottish, lass," said Barney.

"Traveled a lot."

"Oh."

A strained silence followed.

"So the tattoos are...?" Janey wasn't about to be sidetracked.

"My people are the Painted People. Picts, we get called sometimes. Priteni."

"I thought they all died out long ago," Barney added, knowing a bit about history.

"You wanna pinch me? See if I'm alive?" Scathach retained her calm despite the nerve Barney had struck in awakening memories of genocide that had once almost broken her spirit all those centuries gone.

Janey flushed with embarrassment and Barney cleared his throat, aware of having put his foot in it.

Scathach broke the tension with her unfailing grin, suggesting that Barney show her the axe.

"Just brief, mind," he smiled back, glad to be on familiar ground. "Ye'd best settle in today, if y'agree to th'old house."

The two scraped back their chairs and Barney led his charge out the door, leaving Holly and Janey to clear up after them.

HALF AN HOUR LATER AND THE TRACTOR took all four across a fallow field and over one of the hills that sheltered the farm from the salt laden wind blowing constantly in off the western ocean.

The raw force of the winter blast was checked by the curve of an inlet where a weathered stone cottage sat hunched and deserted just above the high tide line. Several slate shingles were obviously missing from the low roof and Barney apologized, mentioning that he hadn't been near the place for years; fearing that he'd invited them into an uninhabitable mess.

As they chugged closer Janey told them that their son and his wife, a girl he'd met off at college who'd thought she could cope with the quiet and who'd ended up a misery, though bearing him two babies, had lived here until he'd drowned off one of the fishing boats nine years gone. The wife had packed up and left the night before the funeral, leaving the children sleeping. Orlando had been five years old at the time and Barney said the hurt had never left him so that, despite all the love they'd been able to give, both his grandparents feared he'd turn *bad*.

The wolfhounds bounded ahead onto the flat stony beach where bright blue soldier crabs swarmed in vast orchestrated swathes around the low tide mark, their movement fracturing into discord as they sensed the hunters.

Scathach watched them cavort and yip, Cullyn whuffing like a pup at the smells and movements, his guard down for the first time since they'd all arrived. The Massey-Ferguson grunted to a stop where two wide planks, set there as a narrow bridge, forded a spring that cut across ground at the back of the cottage on its journey from its source, high in the rocky escarpment that rose to the right of the cottage, to the sea.

Scathach jumped down from the tractor, gathering her possessions, her eyes alight with pleasure.

"Bright the day!" she exclaimed, sucking in a deep breath

before loping across the bridge ahead of the others.

The house was one large room. The door and windows had been shut tight when the Rumfords had deserted it, and the slates that had come away were closest to the hearth so there wasn't too much in the way of damage from the elements, but there were owls in the rafters of the low roof, and compact pellets of regurgitated bone, fur, hair and feathers littered the floor, and a thick layer of dust mantled the bed linen that had been hastily thrown over Spartan furnishings.

"Oh me," Janey whispered, leaning into her husband's body in despair.

He stiffened; emotion hidden behind a resolute *Hmph.* "A bleedin' mess we've led y'to. I've made a mistake and I'm sorry. Best be takin' y'back t'town now."

"No!" Scathach straightened. "Holly? What do you think?"

Holly was caught between the sadness of the whole thing and the desire to remain. She'd brought Scathach into her world and so far she'd done a lousy job of making her welcome and she dread the thought of losing her one friend, willing to do whatever was necessary to see her happy, noting the pleading in her eyes.

"I think," she said, "that if Barney wouldn't mind finding us a ladder so's we can get to the roof... Is there's likely to be a broom here somewhere?"

The warrior sighed with relief as Janey pushed Barney out the door with orders to also bring back enough tea things and other supplies to see the girls comfortable until tomorrow, before setting-to opening windows and getting the other women to help her to carefully remove the dusty covers.

SCATHACH WAS COMPLETING THE LAST OF THE make-shift roof repair—Janey yelling from below to hurry up as they were ready to light the fire—when the first of the village youth breached the hill overlooking the croft. She counted eleven of them, the tallest by far, Orlando, trilling a hello and waving like a fury, bounding down the slope ahead of the others, followed at a distance by the distinctive pale, pale hair of Mercy Reilly who appeared to be purposely remaining detached from the group.

Scathach whooped with delight, any thought of further domesticity driven from her by the task ahead. She'd trained the best amongst warriors. Always had done. And every one of the approaching teenagers bore a staff in hand.

Her intention, however, was far deeper than any of the youngsters knew. Scathach had walked the streets of their world and she had watched; she had listened. The people had no pride. At first it made no sense and she had pondered the problem, of what she was intuiting, asking Holly question upon question about history; about what had happened to the clans and the magic over time.

The people had no pride.

Well, she would teach these few more than how to fight. She would teach them of the ancient gods, of the Great Mystery and all her little mysteries. She would tell them of their ancestors before the Romans came and took away their *Celtic* soul.

Yes. It was going to be an interesting couple of weeks.

She never once asked herself *why* she needed to do this. It was irrelevant. Scathach felt a deeper power press itself upon her resolve.

CHAPTER TWENTY THREE

THREE DAYS AFTER THEIR ARRIVAL AT Weary Bay a change had been wrought in both women.

Janey had asked around her acquaintances and there was now more than adequate furniture and supplies. And should they, as she had subtly hinted, decide they wanted to stay longer than a couple of weeks, they would be welcome.

Scathach was in her element training her enthusiastic young students, and even though there were only a few hours of daylight in which to do so, school holidays were due to begin the following week, and all had asked permission to bring tents and other camping equipment with the intention of gaining as much from the warrior as could be had in the time remaining.

Holly had dreamed the same vivid dream two nights running. A dangerous dream. As though she watched herself from a distance. The boar that had seemed to threaten her in the Otherworld stalked her other self like a predator, closing in on its prey in short, silent bursts.

Her *other* self was sitting, deep in concentration, beside what Holly knew to be a sacred pool, unaware of danger.

She'd called out to her to run, but her *other* self could not hear. She'd tried to move, to get to her, but her *other* self would not obey.

The great boar had charged, its tusk boring into her *other* self's exposed back, and she'd woken screaming, the pain from her *other* self, lancing between her shoulder blades.

Scathach was already awake and away somewhere so she'd made herself a pot of coffee and gone to the farmhouse to help Janey with the morning chores.

The two had sat in the kitchen before they began, oatcakes and honey and a cup of tea between them, and Holly discussed the disturbing dream with the older woman.

Janey had turned her cup in its saucer, thinking.

"It could be the place," she said, before shaking her head. "Don't understand what the boar means though, love."

Holly didn't want to mention the Otherworld, but it took an effort to maintain the secret. She shrugged.

"Ye know about the boar, do ye?" Janey offered.

"What about it?"

"Poor, much maligned creature that it is. Only gets its reputation for bein' a bad bugger coz o' how it fights when it's cornered ye know." She turned her empty teacup upside down on its saucer, spinning it three times sunwise. Holly watched the strange ritual, perplexed, but Janey did nothing else.

"Once upon a time it were a grand symbol o' kings or chieftains or the like," she continued, "afore the Romans came, mind."

She paused again, watching the other's response. *What do you want me to say?* Holly thought. *What's that got to do with my dream?*

"Not that it's got anythin' t'do wi' yer nightmare I suppose," Janey added, as though in answer to the unspoken question, before turning over her cup and peering within, her face a study of concentration.

Realizing that she was scrying the tealeaves Holly went to interrupt only to be shushed.

"That's peculiar." She sat back in her chair, pushed her glasses up her nose and peered at the cup at arm's distance.

"What? Can you see something?"

"Looks like a pack o' dogs chasin' a flock o' ravens."

She turned the cup and pointed to what Holly saw only as a cluster of tealeaves down one side. "See that?"

"No…"

"And there, look, a crown beneath it all."

Holly's dream was forgotten as she looked. She *did* see the shape of a crown.

"What does it mean?" she asked.

Janey growled in her throat, standing and starting to stack the breakfast things, including the cup that was the source of her vision. "Trouble is, I'm not me mother. I can see, but I don't mostly get what the seeing means. I'm no clearer today I'm afraid."

Holly began helping with the ritual of morning chores, beginning with washing dishes. The two worked in uncomfortable silence until Janey blurted out that Holly must think her a superstitious idiot.

"*Why?*" She was stunned as Janey's face reddened and tears welled. "Oh no, Janey, no, don't be upset. I think what you said is really important."

She dried her hands on the tea towel and took Janey in her arms, confused at such a huge reaction to such a silly thing. She led her into the sitting room, feeling oddly more like the hostess than the guest, and the two sat side by side on the sofa before the smoldering fire.

Janey took a hankie from her pocket and blew her nose, avoiding eye contact with Holly. "If I could know what I was seein' when I look int' the cup I coulda maybe warned Paul not t'go t'sea on the day he died."

It was the first time either she or Barney had said their son's name and it took Holly a moment to realize who she was talking about.

"Because I *did* see it. But I didn't know what it meant," and her face crumpled again. All Holly could do was offer soothing shushing sounds, but the sense of the burden this must have weighed on the sweet, dear woman twisted her gut.

Eventually Janey cried herself out, having apologized several times throughout.

"Can I share something with you?" Holly was disturbed that she was going to talk about the Otherworld and the sídhe—the Fíach Dubh in particular.

Janey listened without once interrupting, nodding occasionally, her eyes owly behind her glasses.

"So I don't think I want to discount what you saw," Holly confided. 'And I think we ought to take your 'seeing' seriously and keep our eyes and ears open."

"And your dream…" Janey added. "I don't think we should chuck *it* away as meaningless either."

The two promised to keep each other's secrets that morning, bonding them in a conspiracy of omens. Janey had desperately needed the company of another woman to discuss the things that she could not with Barney. He was always uncomfortable with strong emotion; he'd never liked her mother's strange ways and would have been disgusted to know that Janey had continued with what he called pagan nonsense. Without any remorse she hoped her new ally would never leave.

PART THREE

The Darkest Hour

CHAPTER TWENTY FOUR

WHAT'S THE FUN IN SCORING A SAPPY LITTLE island in some bleak part of the sea away from anything anyway?" Calvin Riddle was already bored with Felix's current 'great plan'.

There'd been hundreds of them over the years but the most enduring was their so-called *magickal* order.

Both had been offered places with Solomon Stone back in the '80s when they'd passed their Bar exams (with a whole lot of help from large family donations to the university) and they were nominated and accepted into the Masonic Lodge almost as a prerequisite. Privately they chuckled over the whole secret mystical brotherhood thing, declaring it an antiquated bore that gave good ol' boys a chance to dress up and pretend meaning where there was none.

The two had a taste for luxury, great sex and good drugs, and Felix had artfully crafted his 'great plan' as a backlash to the Lodge's drab rituals and, based on some B Grade version of what diabolic occult pleasure was all about, he'd dubbed his creation *The Temple of Earthly Graces.*

Somewhere between a Dennis Wheatley novel and Anton Le Vey's Church of Satan, Felix mapped out a format for the order based on the O.T.O. charge of "Do as thou wilt", inviting good looking chicks to act as priestesses and do the sex-on-the-altar thing, and as many of their buddies who could keep their mouths shut and their money flowing.

He had taken on the title of Grand Ipsissimus, with Calvin as his right hand man.

Over the years it had been Felix, ever the Capricorn, who had perfected the flagrant rituals, assigned grade advancements, proclaimed Chiefs, Magisters, High Priestesses and specialist training regimes. When his father had died, and his mother had become an incompetent Prozac-popping infirm he had sued for control of his family's estate and won. He was worth millions in liquid assets alone. The sky was the limit; New Rathmore, his playground.

"Because I want to own an island," he replied smugly, gazing out over the city lights from the balcony of his penthouse apartment.

He'd bought the building several years ago and transformed some of it. The fourteenth and fifteenth floors were lavishly decorated with the spoils of his travels, from China to Africa, Amazon to Bali. His forays into the arcane of other cultures had only whetted his appetite for the unusual, bizarre and sometimes cruel forms of ceremony and sex.

Thirteen floors were empty, abandoned, but the basement accommodated both the Temple's elaborate rituals and the occasional Rave party, open to the initiates and all their friends, with abundant designer drugs and top shelf booze.

Both men knew that their "alternative lifestyle" would never be made public as too many city officials, dignitaries, high-ranking members of the press and the Bar, let alone pollies on their way to the top, were sworn initiates of the order—the only place where their deepest (and often most debauched) fantasies could be realized.

FELIX KNEW HE COULD SIMPLY BUY THE island. He knew all the right people to bypass protocol. It would be fun!

"Suit yourself," Calvin considered, wondering just how much work this was going to take, "but what about all those old folks?"

"You think I give a rat's fart?"

Calvin shrugged. His friend had to be the coldest bastard on the planet which made him the best ally he could have. Better to bask in the reflected glow.

"And the professor?"

"Just keep him on a leash until I've got it all set up. I don't want him stirring the pot with outsiders."

"Sure but—"

"Think," Felix suggested, turning around and leaning his elbows on the stone railing, a glass of Chardonnay dangling from a well-manicured hand. "I want him on side for the moment, okay? The alternative's to get rid of him but I don't want to do that yet. I want what's in his head."

"So?"

"So, have him watched. And that includes his little wife."

"Can I put Duffy on to it?"

Felix chuckled. Ron Duffy was New Rathmore's Chief of Police and a long-term member of the order.

"I take that as a yes," Calvin mumbled to himself, snorting an indulgent line of coke through a slim silver tube made especially for the purpose. It was one thing to have started this charade in the first place, and maintained it all these years to the point where it seemed very real and a bit too much like hard slog. But it was something else to hold covert *summer camp* ritual expeditions and to be stuck with their bunch of whackos for an extended period of time. His friend was taking this whole "sacred site" bullshit far too seriously.

Calvin would rather be off snow-boarding all day, somewhere expensive, with the predictable bevy of winter resort babes for *afters*.

"In the meantime," Felix moved to his desk and flipped through his diary, "let's go check the place out for ourselves, this Friday?"

"I thought Harvey said it was impossible to access until the spring?"

Felix held out his upturned palm for the silver tube, mumbling

Oh ye of little faith, before snorting a liberal line and suggesting they get a couple of girls in for the evening.

THE SLEEK SEVENTY FOUR FOOT FAIRLINE *SQUADRON*, cut effortlessly through the roiling turbulence of the winter sea, sighting Inishrún only briefly, almost like an optical illusion, through sheet after sheet of driving rain. The craft's state-of-the-art guidance system guaranteed a safe crossing, and she accessed the relatively calm harbor of Seal Bay at just after one in the afternoon.

Surprisingly, docking proved the most difficult part of the undertaking, with the boat coming perilously close to smashing against the wharf at the first two attempts, but all four men aboard were so coked-up, and intoxicated by the wild ride, that nothing could dull their good humor.

Tyler had decided, at the last minute, to enlist the *heavies* they employed to guard the Rave parties, on the off chance of a scenario developing like that experienced by the archaeological expedition. There was no way he intended to suffer the same humiliating outcome. Both men were elegant, efficient and reliable. And both owed him.

The quay was deserted as they passed the shuttered general store and leapt the padlocked turnstile onto the empty street of the tiny village.

When they passed into the bleak, unwelcoming countryside Felix paused to consult the step-by-step directions that the professor had included in his portfolio, and Calvin Riddle adjusted his grip on his baby, a *Sauer 202 LAW* hunting rifle, enjoying its heavy weight in the bag that slapped against his thigh.

The rain abated to a misty drizzle as all four moved swiftly overland, stopping only once or twice to check their coordinates.

Calvin was unnerved by so much open space, but he attempted to suggest that perhaps Harvey had been canny after all because you sure as hell could get a *bit* of development done here without screwing with the touristy-wilderness-thingy, before Felix hissed at him to shut up 'cause sound can travel in weird ways in the outdoors and the last thing they wanted was company.

They passed down the track that led towards Mim's cottage and turned off in the direction of the forest keeping to cover as much as possible. The woods looked eerie and daunting in the half-light; ancient and skeletal with winter barrenness, and a low keening of frigid wind haunted them with its alien song. The feeling of being watched was overwhelming and Calvin, nervous and intimidated by this much nature, pulled the rifle from his carryall, comforted by its accessibility.

A hundred yards further on and Felix's eyes widened as he took in the expanse of high, ragged cliffs, the megalithic henge at their base and, where meadow met fen, the enormous, stone-encircled burial mound with its crown of sacred trees.

"*Damn*, that's impressive!" he hissed, whispering for Calvin to get the images on his camera

; considering that the professor had grossly understated his description of the site.

Frank Harvey had been adamant that there was no access into the tumulus from either above or around the perimeter. Felix extracted a pair of binoculars from their case, scanning the surrounding scrubland for clues to a remote entrance.

His sights fell on a large, mostly spherical boulder that, with the strong magnification of the glass, displayed the faded delineation of a carved pictograph of a simple triple spiral motif. He smiled, tilting his head in the direction of the find.

"I'll bet my balls that's the way in," he whispered, chuckling deep in his throat.

Calvin merely feigned interest. He was cold and was becoming more and more freaked out as the drug-induced confidence wore off, to the point where he just wanted to get to shelter no matter what the ramifications. He distracted himself with thoughts of the deposition he had yet to prepare, that would take him most of the weekend—it had to be on Jake Solomon's desk first thing Monday—and with the memory of the newly pirated, and as yet untried, computer game that awaited him in his cozy apartment.

"This is a stupid idea, man," he complained softly.

Felix whirled on him, his eyes steely and flat in the half light.

"We *stay*," he hissed, "I *will* see this! Now get the fuck with the program!"

He and the body guards broke cover, bent low, heading directly towards the stone in the field. Calvin let out a high-pitched whine of frustration and ran to catch up.

INSIDE MIM'S COTTAGE OBERON AND HARRY awoke from where they'd been sleeping by the fire and scrabbled to their feet, their hackles raised and their ears flat against their heads, frenzied barking startling the small, dark woman from her book.

What on earth....?

She hastily threw on her thick sheepskin coat and wool beanie, and ran for the door, struggling with the enormous, frantic dogs in an effort to open the latch. It crossed her mind that this might not be a very smart thing to do, what with Connor and Charlie off somewhere, high up in the Mothers where they'd ridden, at the Scotsman's suggestion, in an effort to defuse the Dé Danann's growing agitation at the incessant confinement, but there was something very wrong. Now. And she had to trust the dogs to take care of her.

Oberon shot across the fallow garden and out into the meadow with Harry on his heels and Mim running after them as fast as she could.

Halfway across the open expanse, the grass still flattened from the recent gathering, she half stumbled, horror and fear assaulting her senses, as she saw the unmistakable outline of four men disappearing into the tunnel leading to the Barrow.

CHAPTER TWENTY FIVE

FRANK HARVEY THOUGHT HE WOULD GO LOOPY if he had to wait much longer for word from Tyler and Riddle. He had nothing to occupy himself anymore, and he'd spent the first several days after their face-to-face meeting making phone calls to one government agency after another, seeking information on the protocol necessary for the private acquisition of Crown land. He'd been juggled from department to department, petty official after petty official, and had received a constant stock-standard, bureaucratic hyperbole about the "rights" of everything—long-term tenants; possible indigenous claims; the environmental impacts of development. And always in such generalized terminology that he might as well have been listening to pre-recorded blah-blah.

No one he'd spoken to had even *heard* of Inishrún and even trying to establish the shire to which it was allocated he'd been given the runaround.

The exercise in self-education was a monumental failure and he turned, instead, to the Internet. The results were the same. He came to the ultimate conclusion that his project could take years, and that even then, with property such as this, it was standard practice to open prospective bidding to the wider public. His fellows could quite possibly be out-maneuvered by corporate enterprise from virtually anywhere in the country.

All he could do was trust the wheels he'd set in motion thus far.

What an idiot, a small voice heckled constantly in the back of his mind like a warning.

What? he'd challenged. *What am I missing?*

His nights were spent at Straubs in the hope that his associates would happen by and that he could corral them into updating him on their progress. They never showed.

Instead he found himself befriended by retired Q.C. and current chief of the Wallace Hope Lodge of Freemasonry, David Rushton.

To Frank's delight David admitted to an avid amateur interest in archeology with a sideline passion for mythology and folk-lore. He'd listened ardently as Frank regaled him with anecdotes on everything from *Lindow Man*, the mummified body of a first millennium priest or king found buried in the bog at Lindow Moss, in 1984, and thought by some archeologists to have been ritually sacrificed in a desperate attempt to halt the Roman occupation of their lands, to the *Ice Maiden*, a "shaman priestess" whose body had been discovered in 1993, perfectly preserved in the frozen tundra of the Altai Mountains, raising debate as to just how much influence women had actually wielded in earlier history.

Their discussions ranged from pagan sacrificial traditions to ritual tattooing, with Rushton's foremost knowledge centering on Neolithic, Bronze and Iron Age Britain and Ireland. Frank was stunned by his companion's acumen.

When the subjects of archeology and mythology overlapped, however, the professor took a back seat and listened, fascinated, as David merged traditional legend into a contemporary historical framework, speaking of gods, nobles, heroes as though they lived on some twenty first century street, wearing twenty first century clothing. It was eerie, mesmerizing.

He spoke with such intimacy that Frank's curiosity was aroused. At the end of each evening he went home, locked himself into his study and logged onto the internet, keying in as many of the names and stories as he could recall.

He'd located thousands of entries on each, written in jargon ranging from the academic, eco-environmentalist and Celtic Revivalist to the sensationalist and downright silly. A great many of the sites he accessed, however, were connected to witchcraft, druidism, and of all things, fairy lore as it is understood by the Scots and the Irish. In difference to what had been invented in Victorian England The legends of these spirits of the landscape and the weather are anything but sweet and benevolent. Contrary to what he would have believed in the past, most sites were highly informative, well sourced and disturbing, to say the least.

Frank compiled a database at a 90° variant to everything he had ever considered valid, and printed out the accrued texts for bedtime reading.

After many evenings in each other's company the two men found themselves engrossed in topics as diverse as therianthropy, or shape-shifting, whether the ancient Britons used hallucinogenics in their rituals, whether language defines a culture, to speculating on how different Celtic lands and culture *might* have been had the indigenous magical and spiritual systems not been marginalized and demoralized by both the persistent succession of invasions over the past two millennia and, of course, by Christianity.

AS THE WEEKS PASSED, HIS ENFORCED retirement and late nights brought about a change in his daily routine, and he began taking long walks, no matter what the weather, all the way across town to St Brendan's Park, several acres of well-maintained botanical garden, hosting a tame forest at its heart, surrounded by high stone walls punctuated occasionally by heavy wrought-iron gates kept locked between sunset and sunrise. The events of the past month, and the direction of his newly-recognized freedom, caused Frank unprecedented emotions that were only relieved by the hypnotic metronome of his shoes upon the pavement and by the majesty of the silent little wood.

He felt that, for the first time he could remember, he had found a true friend in the aristocratic Q.C. An intellectual equal. And his dawning interest in things never before considered pertinent sparked a growing awareness that the mystery that baffled him— the sense of Inishrún's sacredness—might be more than a product of a post-traumatic imagination.

His health improved with the fresh air and physical exertion and, he thought wryly, it might be time to invest in some new clothing, a size smaller, as his weight dropped effortlessly with his emerging wellbeing.

As for David—he kept Wolf Kain updated on the meetings, even suggesting that the old bastard wasn't, perhaps, as much of a liability as was first surmised.

THIS IS ABSURD, FRANK CHASTISED HIMSELF as he placed his toiletries on the top of the other luggage and zipped his old leather suitcase closed. He'd argued with himself all day about the irrational desire to get back to Inishrún despite the season.

Irrationality had won.

He'd walked down the driveway to his car and dumped his case on the ground, fumbling the key into the lock, his hands shaking just as Jesse arrived home with her artist friend, Wolf.

The two women approached him with Jesse in the lead looking confused. "What are you doing Francis?"

"I'll be gone for a few days, Jesse. I'll be fine." He refused to look at her, afraid she'd see the madness in his eyes, and he opened the car door, stowing his belongings in the passenger seat.

"Where are you going?"

"Doesn't matter. I'll be back soon."

"Where are you *going*?"

Eventually he lifted his face to hers, an intensity burning in his eyes that she did not recognize.

"Fucking Inishrún," he hissed, slamming the door and thrusting the key into the ignition.

As the motor revved to life his face changed. As he drove past Jesse he was smiling like she hadn't seen for years.

Irrationality won out completely. The peculiar thought crossed his mind that he was going home. It settled inside him like a warm thing.

CHAPTER TWENTY SIX

THE DÉ DANANN'S KEEN VISION PICKED up the big dog streaking flat out across the open expanse of the low mountain summit, a bolt of pale fur against the gloom, and he scrambled to his feet as the animal staggered and fell, sending up a shower of small stones.

He ran like a demon to where Harry lay drenched with sweat; foam white at the corners of his mouth, trying valiantly to stand.

Fear crawled over Connor's skin like a million spiders as he hefted the animal into his arms, using all his strength, and screamed for Charlie to get the horses.

He hurried to the banked-up fire burning fiercely against the coming night under an outcropping of rock they had set up as a shelter, and laid his burden on a pile of bedding, pouring water into a pot and positioning it close, just as Charlie reentered the camp pulling two horses by their halters.

Connor took a moment to stroke the dog's damp fur, desperation making his hand shake. "I'll be back for ya, *mo chroì*. Let's *go*," he growled at Charlie, vaulting onto Cloud's back.

No saddles. No time. Just ride.

Connor's heart pounded faster than the thunder of the grey mare's hooves as, heedless of the treacherous descent, they galloped flat out; near-reckless.

They soon outdistanced Charlie on Durrum, the smaller dun unable to match the pace; spooked by the rough terrain.

She's had an accident, Connor repeated over and over in his head. *She's had an accident*, because any other thing was impossible to consider. *She's hurt. She's had an accident.*

In the depths of him was a foreboding like no other he had ever felt and as they gained the flat land, and hammered across the fen, tears stung his vision before the wind whipped them away.

As they passed the boulder that marked the Barrow's entrance Cloud shied, issuing a high-pitched scream.

Connor had been fixated on the light streaming from the wide open door of the cottage up ahead and he fell, tumbling, jarring his shoulder as it broke his fall on the frozen ground.

Oberon lay on his side, unmoving, not three feet away, and Connor scrambled to him across the ice, placing his hand gently on the dog's thigh. It came away sticky with blood.

"M*IIII*M!" HIS SCREAM CUT THE NIGHT AIR like a razor and he doubled over, clutching his gut, vomiting.

Stop, he demanded of himself, working to clear his head and gain some control. He carefully lifted himself from the ground, his shoulder hurting with the movement, until he sat upright. He ran his hand the length of the dog's body. Oberon was still alive, attested to by the shallow rise and fall of his ribs and Connor sucked in his breath and held it, listening.

Everything was unnaturally silent. No rustling of creatures in the grass. No plovers cac-cacking their usual warnings. The sound of his own blood pulsed in his ears, and he could hear Cloud's labored breathing, but otherwise there was nothing.

With absolute dread Connor stood and walked the few steps necessary to enter the tunnel, his eyes adjusting to the wall of sheer blackness.

MIM'S BODY LAY SPRAWLED ACROSS THE dirt at an unnatural angle and the fairy man, like a marionette, forced himself forward, the light dying inside him.

For all the longevity bestowed by the brew of the Quicken Tree, a thousand and one things—like a bullet—could still kill.

Connor knelt helplessly. *Mim?* He whispered to the dark. He turned her over from where she lay face down, her staring, angry eyes sightlessly accused the empty air, and he took her in his arms with all the reverence he was capable of.

And he began to keen.

THE EERIE, AWFUL SOUND PENETRATED THE tunnel and entered the Barrow, unheard-of for a thousand years. It knifed into the Otherworld and the Dreaming Lands disturbing all who dwelt there.

It fled out onto the wind of Inishrún and across the land, into the ears of every sídhe, and out over the waters in all directions.

. . .

THE GREAT MYSTERY AWOKE FROM HER winter slumber and roared. And Hunter and Brighid looked wildly around themselves at Vincent and Kathryn and the Dé Danann of the winter tuath in New Rathmore.

. . .

SCATHACH, RACING ACROSS THE MOOR, LOVING her time alone, stopped dead in her tracks as though struck by an unseen fist.

. . .

WOLF KAIN'S HAND SLIPPED, THE KNIFE SHE USED to cut the leather for her newest mask embedding itself in the workbench; a jolt of sheer desolation washing through her.

That morning she'd gone with Jesse to check up on her husband's computer files—the other witch assuring her that lately he was never home during the day—to find him packed and ready for a journey. She'd sensed trouble when he'd informed them he was going back to Inishrún.

She wondered now whether he'd managed to get there

somehow. Her intuition was sure that her sorrow was connected to that place.

She'd phoned the Q.C. from the professor's house but got the answering machine. She tried him again now.

...

LIATH LEANNÁN'S ENTIRE CLAN ACTED WITHOUT hesitation and, like a well-oiled machine, packed up their camp and headed for the coast within the hour

...

THE OLD PRIEST AT ST MARY DE LA MER HAD FALLEN into a gin-induced stupor hours earlier, in his armchair by the slow-burning fire. He awoke, disoriented, to the tail end of the eerie sound, an icy fist clutching painfully at his heart.

He sighed, reaching for the bottle on the table beside him.

His god had deserted him long ago and he wanted nothing finer anymore, than to die drunk.

...

WOOLLY FLEW TOWARDS THE BARROW LIKE THE very wind itself, in the guise of a swan, knowing in his heart that he was too late and that she was dead. He arrived at the same time as Charlie, changing back to a man in a sickening blur. The two entered the Barrow together.

...

HOLLY WAS WITH JANEY, WHO DROPPED HER PAINTBRUSH into the newly laid carpet.

"What just happened?" she whispered, the look on the other

woman's face giving her the creeps.

Without replying, Holly Tremenhere bolted for the door, ramming full on into Orlando who'd come from the camp looking for their instructor. She clutched his arms for a second, the wild look in her eyes frightening him.

"Find her!"

He turned, alarmed, and raced back to get the others.

Holly scrambled to the top of the hill behind the house and screamed *Scathach!!* to the encroaching night.

And the warrior heard.

...

FELIX, HIS TEETH CLENCHED IMPOSSIBLY, HELPED the two guards as they struggled with the moorings holding the *Squadron* securely against the jetty.

Calvin stood by, useless; in shock. What had he *done*?

The huge ugly dog had roared into the tunnel, teeth bared, his deep, rumbling growl echoing from the enormous stones that lined the passage, and Lee Parker had drawn his pistol, shooting wildly with no time to aim. The beast had landed with a thud. Calvin had raised the rifle instinctively, his entire body shaking with fear.

When the crazy-eyed woman had come at them through the beam of the others' flashlights he'd fired in sheer panic.

She'd dropped in mid-run.

What had he done?

The other three men had stared at him in disbelief; in horror, their eyes accusing.

"Fuck!" Felix swore, startled into action. He moved to the woman lying face down on the ground and knelt, feeling for a pulse.

"Fuck!" he repeated. "Fuckfuckfuckfuckfuck!"

"What do we do?" Lee asked, replacing the gun in its holster under his jacket.

"We get the fuck outa here is what. *Move!*"

The bodyguards needed no prompting, but Calvin had stood transfixed by the body, and Felix had to drag him away.

"You do *anything*, until we get away from here—*anything*—and I'll kill you myself," he hissed in the dazed man's ear. "You're a fucking moron!"

...

LIAM MCKENNA, THE BOSUN ABOARD *The Watchman*, was on lookout on the bridge.

"Off t'starboard, Skipper." He handed the glass to Stan Rumford, Barney's brother, who ground his teeth in frustration.

Jaysus, Mary and Joseph, silly buggers never learn, he swore. *Four eejits adrift in a bloody fancy dinghy.* They'd a good catch and the pub was waiting and the last thing he felt like doing was rescuing stupid tourists risking the open seas this time of year.

"Haul her about," he ordered.

ROBBIE FREEMAN PAUSED FROM WHERE HE and the other fishermen had been stowing the nets, as the boat turned. He could see the tiny figures aboard the sleek craft and couldn't help but wonder two things: how a boat like that could possibly break down, and whether it'd been out to Inishrún.

CHAPTER TWENTY SEVEN

MERCY. SILENT AND BROODING. SHE'D TAKEN the lightweight longbow that Scathach held out to her, an unreadable flintiness in her eyes.

The warrior explained stance, sighting and draw before passing the pale girl the first arrow. She nocked as she'd been shown, sucked in her breath, drew the string back to her lip, and released.

Their target was an old canvas laundry bag, stuffed with rag, upon which Holly had drawn a fair sized smiley-face instead of the predictable three rings and a bull's eye, and it hung suspended by a rope from the lowest branch of a winter-denuded oak.

Mercy's first arrow struck just left of center, between the two dots that represented eyes.

"Fluke," Orlando had said flatly, standing with hands on hips awaiting his turn.

In silence Mercy held out her hand for another arrow, sucked in her breath, took aim and fired.

"No bleedin' way!" Orlando had barked. Everyone stared at the second arrow protruding from the bag mere millimeters from the first.

Scathach handed her a third, her lips twitching...

OUT OF THE FIVE KIDS CAMPED ON THE sparse-grassed dunes beneath the cliff that broke the wind's persistence, Mercy was the only girl.

Eleven of the town's youth had originally come "for summat to do", but most had become disenchanted with the dawn to dusk hard slog that Scathach demanded of them.

What's the point of sticks 'n' shite, they'd agreed, *when coppers've got guns an' th' army has enough shite t'blow th' universe t'smithereens?*

The remaining teenagers hadn't cared and had stayed.

Scathach was their treasure.

She'd organized strident runs overland to strengthen their legs and their lungs that, day after day, involved longer distances and more difficult terrain. The tasks she set them were complex, everything from a tactical understanding of the ley of the land to the use of trenches and pikes as disincentives to an enemy charge.

One aspect of their training included expeditions into the deep forests where, amidst sleeping deciduous giants, they'd found ancient yews that yielded the best wood for the making of their own bows, and plentiful ash for arrows.

Down along the marshy, northern reaches where the springs that originated from the Mothers' summits pooled before forming streams that made their way, eventually, to the sea they found sufficient flax to create bowstrings, and Janey took Holly to Maisie Raith's farm to beg for enough goose quills to fletch six practice arrows apiece.

Only Orlando, Jimmy Wallace and Mercy Reilly made adequate bows, that shot cleanly, but all five chose perfect branches, from a variety of different trees, which they stripped of bark and hardened through fires to make both staff and spear.

Scathach had been careful to show each person the correct way to honor the taking of wood with gifts of manure, vegetable matter or beer (which even the hard-drinking warrior would not touch if it had been allocated as an offering), telling them *No, it isn't stupid, it's appropriate* or, *Don't take my word for it, just see what ills befall ye should y'be neglectful!*

Holly joined them for the most part, especially in the night when, after gathering dead wood and building the almost ritualistic fire, Scathach filled their heads with heroes and legends and, even more to the point, what their ancestors had been like before their grandeur was crushed beneath the armies and dogma of the usurpers.

None of them doubted her. Something in the blood rang with the truth of what she said.

How she knew what she did was another matter, and one she would not divulge. Who knew?

Maybe she was some rare genius who'd studied it all and then dropped out, preferring *weird* to some kind of predictable *normal*.

They'd asked about the tattooing too, and that had led to even more tales of "painted people" and clan status and animal totems. And throughout, Mercy said nothing.

Holly side-tracked her on the way to the bathroom one evening, asking whether she wanted to talk about what was making her so sad, because it was obvious that those were the emotions haunting her, but Mercy had simply shrugged and pushed past.

Mercy wasn't sad. She'd met the De Dánann before. They had saved her when she was truly lost. She'd known abuse and brutality as a child, had escaped and been found by Black Annis two years before this. She had been told to say nothing and she intended to stay silent for her entire life if it came to that. It was for her protection from her abusers, the institution that had raised her. Once fostered with a resident of Weary Bay that the Travelers knew to trust she had attended school. Once gain she knew cruelty. This time to teenage girls' taunts.

She had the blood of the ancient fairies flowing as strong as salmon muscle. But as far as she was concerned she was a child of no one. The truth might as well be on the other side of space.

Mercy didn't know who or what she was. She didn't realize that they would come for her again one day. Would take her with them on their travels if she chose to go, but right then, with these women, she felt different and she felt special. And one of the reasons she stayed at the camp was because neither Holly nor Scathach looked at her with the word 'ugly' in their eyes.

When she'd first held the bow she'd known in her gut that she could use it proficiently, and, in her gut, she knew she could use it to kill.

In two weeks she developed a consummate and uncanny skill, and Orlando looked at her through new, and interested, eyes.

THE FIVE OF THEM RACED OUT INTO THE GLOAMING in the direction Scathach took each time she left them to claim her solitude.

They saw her, pale against the almost-night, up on the high cliff, the insubstantial shapes of the wolfhounds that accompanied her obvious only to Mercy.

Scathach stood very still, staring out to sea, and the young people followed the direction of her gaze.

The lights of *The Watchman* could be glimpsed occasionally, appearing and disappearing within the huge swell, and in her wake was another craft, white and sleek, almost as long as the fishing boat.

"Scathach…" Orlando's heart was pounding as he reached her, not from the run which his training had made effortless, but from the odd, dangerous look on the warrior's face.

"Scathach," he repeated.

She turned, slowly, looking upon her students, eyeing them each in turn.

"Did you hear it?" she asked quietly, their confused looks causing her to sigh.

"And that…" her arm shot out in the direction of the boats headed for Seal Bay. "Can you smell that?"

"It's *The Watchman* comin' in t'port wi'a tow behind," Jimmy confirmed, squirming.

"I smell fear," Scathach breathed the night wind off the sea.

"Prob'ly some eejits got theyself in trouble an' the boat rescued 'em?"

"Nah, me friend, that'd be *relief*, wouldn't it?"

The six of them ran back to the camp with the warrior continuing ahead going directly to the cottage. She told them to bring their weapons.

CHAPTER TWENTY EIGHT

WHILE THE REMAINDER OF CLAN FÍACH DUBH hurried to the bus and drove, well beyond the speed limit, shielded from detection by a powerful glamour invoked by all except Rowan who sat at the steering wheel, Hunter and Brighid passed into the Otherworld he, in frightening silence and she, screaming like a beansídhe in anger and outrage.

They tore through the veil between the worlds, and into the dimly lit cavern of the Barrow where only a single candle, kept burning from Samhain to Imbolg, cast their shadows onto ancient stone.

Both smelled blood.

They raced along the passage, their skin prickling in horror as they moved through the miasma of earlier emotion and out into the icy night.

Woolly/Aengus cradled Connor in his arms; Connor held Mim's lifeless body, repeating *bring her back bring her back* in a rapid whisper to the Great Mystery whose presence was all around them, unable to interfere.

Charlie laid the length of Oberon, shielding his body from the ceaseless wind, one hand clamped firmly over the gunshot wound halting the loss of blood.

The dog's rapid breathing informed Brighid how dangerously

close to death he was, and it was to him she ran. This she could fix; this she could heal. She had to pry Charlie's hand from the wound before sensing for the bullet. She touched the spot above the gaping hole, sending calm and warmth into the shattered nervous system, and gently probing beneath the flesh until her fingers found metal. Oberon whimpered at the pain but knew this touch, this power, and so did not move.

The bullet was lodged deep in the muscle but had missed both bone and artery, and Brighid carefully maneuvered the foreign object to between her delving fingers before pulling it to the surface, the flesh closing behind.

"Get him to the house, m'bonny," she whispered to Charlie, who fought to his knees, his arms still protectively around the great ugly dog's body. He staggered to his feet with his burden, walking to Mim's cottage as fast as he could.

He never uttered a word.

MIM'S SPIRIT HAD NOT FLED TO THE OTHERWORLD. She had waited. Hunter could see her iridescent form shimmering around Connor, encircling him with her arms, her mouth kissing his face and lips, trying with all her love to get him to realize she had not gone.

But he couldn't see. Despair raged through him like poison, changing him, aging him before the others' eyes.

"Open your eyes, *mo chroì*," Hunter demanded carefully, kneeling before the cruel tableau.

"Open your eyes now! Connor, open your eyes."

The war that confronted the forest god from the heart of Connor's red-rimmed gaze struck him like a physical blow of hatred, love, despair, desolation and worst of all, helplessness.

He regained his calm, ignoring both Aengus and Brighid, and took his wild brother's face in his hands as Mim's ghost moved to one side, in hope.

"Now is it me that's got to comfort you, mo chroì, or you that's got to comfort her?"

Connor added confusion to the list of raging emotions, screwing up his as yet unlined brow trying to make sense of what Hunter said.

"Let her in, man! She's desperate for you to see her."

Still cradling his friend, Aengus began to softly sing a love song in a language so old that no one in the world, except the sídhe and the gods and the púca of the land, understood it anymore.

Connor did. And it tore him to pieces because, despite everything, this was all he truly felt and, fight as he might, tears scalded his cheeks, and a maw of emptiness beckoned that living without her assured.

Then he felt it. An insubstantial softness touching his eyes, his cheeks, his forehead, his mouth.

"Oh, please," he moaned, recognizing her; knowing she hadn't left him yet despite the stiffening body in his arms.

Hunter gestured to Aengus to leave them; to come back with him and Brighid to the cottage.

"But...." The guise of Woolly superimposed itself over the bright Dé Danann lord, enclosing him in a seeming shell of aged, grizzled mortality as he stumbled to his feet.

HUNTER'S JAW CLENCHED AND UNCLENCHED again and again, in nervous anticipation, as the three walked swiftly back to the house.

"Don't you lose the plot," Brighid warned, knowing that look; fearing the havoc that could follow.

CHAPTER TWENTY NINE

ERASE THE FILES," WOLF FUMED INTO her cell phone.

"But—"

"Erase the fucking files, Jesse! Do it now."

"Frank'll kill me if I touch his stuff, you've no idea." But the line was dead.

Jesse sat in her bedroom looking at the earpiece in her hand with distaste. What was that all about? She'd never heard Wolf angry before but there was no way she was going to jeopardize the goal of all the years she'd put into this lousy marriage by doing it. He'd know it was her. Unless… Maybe she could stage a burglary? Then she laughed at herself. How melodramatic.

Shit. But what if she didn't do what Wolf asked? She could be out of the coven so fast…

She groaned. She hated being put in situations. This was not fair! She picked up the pack of cigarettes on her bedside table, pulling one out and lighting it, pondering the rock and hard place she seemed stuck between.

Why had she mentioned the stupid little island to her husband? Guilt nagged her. Sheer smart-assedness had been why. And now everything had got crazy.

What was the point anyway? The university was sure to have the details wouldn't they? Just because the press hadn't covered more than the accident didn't mean that the university wasn't acting on it, although it was probably only Frank who'd so far thought of the development lark.

She'd just decided to get herself a beer from the fridge before breaking into Frank's study when she heard car doors slamming out front of her house.

She raced to the window and looked down at the drive as Wolf Kain and her friend David walked up the path leading to the front door.

Jesse was momentarily incensed. How dare they come to her home and take over? She ground out her cigarette and headed for the stairs, considering which bridge was better burned: a hubby-dear or a high priestess.

She smiled as she opened the door for her guests, having no idea how close she was to the loss of one desire and the fulfillment of the other.

...

RAURIE MÓR HAD BEEN ENJOYING A MILDER CLIMATE at the very tip of the continental edge. He'd decided to stay on the mainland this winter, rather than sailing to the more temperate Pacific, because Gemma O'Maile refused to cross the open sea for anyone, even him.

Now the *Rosie Rua* tacked the high winds, following the sea lanes back towards Inishrún in a death-defying race with the elements.

He'd been summoned. He was needed, as sure as the day was grey. The Great Mystery guided his craft from the air and Manannan Mac Lír, from below.

If the feeling he felt was not so resolute and focused he would have been exhilarated by the wild ride.

He'd savor the sensation another day.

...

"WILL HE COME IN?" CHARLIE asked.

The mind-numbing, bone-shattering shaking had finally passed, and he sat on a blanket beside Mim's big stove with Oberon's sleeping head in his lap.

Hunter shrugged. "Not yet. He'll stay with her till the Otherworld takes her."

"What if…?"

"Mim's no fool, me ol' son," Brighid added. She poured another cup of strong black tea from the yellow teapot, adding spoons of sugar and tapping the edge of the cup idly with the spoon. "She'll go; she understands the pattern of things."

Hunter was itching to leave; to find her killers, to see justice done. It was Brighid who held him.

These men are important right now, she'd said. *Deserting them would be wrong and you know it.* He'd wanted to argue that Aengus was here—the others were here—but he knew that a bond had been forged between the three; Mim, Connor and Charlie becoming like a private clan of their own over the last three months. Her loss would devastate both men.

"Right then," Charlie shifted, carefully removing Oberon's head before standing.

"What're ya doin', Sunshine?" Hunter asked. The big Scot pulled his jacket from the back of the chair without reply, moving to the door.

Oberon stirred, fighting hard to stand in order to go with him, halting the man in mid-stride. "No mate," Charlie begged, looking to Brighid for help.

The little dark sídhe knelt beside the wolfhound, stilling him with soothing sounds, looking from him to the ginger haired Highland fey and registering the similarity of their eyes, something twigging in her.

CHARLIE WENT OUT INTO THE DEEP AND SILENT night. The incessant wind had stilled and the stars in the velvet black sky

263

shone like jewels of ice. It was all so stunningly beautiful. He thought that if he never had to leave the island again he would be a happy man. Except for Holly.

Bitch, he thought with sadness. He'd loved her from the very first. It made no sense. She hated him for her own reasons. He'd come to accept that early on in the piece and so had pushed his feelings aside.

Liath Leannán had soothed his soul, given him great joy, a ton of fun, but he'd known she wouldn't stay. And even though she was unique and precious, and he'd loved her in so many ways, she wasn't Holly.

He sighed. Forget it. Everything would change with Mim gone. Fucking mainlanders.

He shoved his hands deep into the pockets of his big coat, scrunching his shoulders against the cold. His boots crunched on the frost-covered grass as he crossed the meadow heading for the entrance to the Barrow.

He looked ahead to where Connor had sat with Mim, but they weren't there. His night vision had become stronger for every day he spent away from the city and it didn't occur to him how unusual it was to see that far in the blackness.

Where were they? In the Barrow? No. Until someone with the skill to do so came to rid it of the taint of what had occurred, no one would enter. He'd learned about the place from Mim, along with everything else important.

He followed his instincts and changed direction, heading instead towards the tumulus.

He clambered up onto the grassy slope and made his way to the summit, heedless of the many warnings he'd received against doing so, and passed within the ring of sacred trees.

Connor had laid Mim's body on the altar and he knelt on one knee before it. One hand was upon the ground and the other was caught in hers, his head tipped to one side as though listening.

Charlie knelt beside him, taking up the vigil.

However long it took he would stay, to be there for his friend; to honor the island's queen.

CONNOR'S SPIRIT WAS BOTH CONSCIOUS OF BEING atop the sacred hill and also of standing with Mim on the border between this world and the Otherworld, where she fought desperately against the tide that pulled her.

He sensed Charlie beside him, a deep respect for his friend's silence warming him, but he would not return until she'd finally gone.

Mim had initially thought the despair would kill Connor and that they would take this journey together, then the Great Mystery had whispered the truth to her that she had to do everything in her power to prevent that from happening, hinting that it would be an unforgivable mistake, because for a fairy to die that way...

Would have what? Sent him elsewhere? The realization struck her. He wouldn't *go* anywhere! He would... cease. The horror fueled her massive will, forcing her spirit to materialize sufficiently to prevent that from occurring.

That had been hours ago. Strands of silver now shot through his rich black hair, but the change had been halted. She'd told him— no, demanded—that he stopped wallowing, because otherwise he *would* be lost to her. She'd explained what she knew, and begged him to get his act together, and somehow learn how to come to her alive. *Surely you can learn in time*, she'd said. *Hunter does it. Brighid does it and she's Dé Danann also.*

She faded as the Veil thickened. She couldn't stay any longer and Connor knew it. He watched her leave, a twinkle in her eye to the very last.

And he resolved to find a way, but not yet.

First her dead body must be honored as befits a queen.

Then she was to be revenged.

DOWN IN THE VILLAGE THE ELDER SÍDHE waited, their seers attuned to Connor's return.

Aengus had summoned the horses, all of which were bedecked with saddles and panniers on which silver, gold and bronze adornments glinted in the light of a hundred burning brands, their bridles tinkling with small bright bells.

The Tuatha Dé Danann had shed the glamour of domesticity and fragility and, although grey and lined they stood upright and imposing, dressed in finery that they had hidden away for years beyond recall.

Caitlin Bres was the first to stir from the vision of the man upon the mound, whispering *It's time* to the others nearby.

The ripple of acknowledgement washed over Aengus Óg who stepped lightly into the stirrup of a snow-colored lead horse as he reached down to Hewie Dowd for the first of the pennants—a blood-red rose on a background of summer-green, representing the lineage of the queens of Inishrún—swinging into the saddle and lifting it. It fluttered lazily six feet above him on the end of a slender hazel spear.

Hewie Dowd ran the length of the hundred riders, handing up pennants, one for each of the clans, to those not carrying torches, before taking the rearmost mount for himself and raising the final banner, for Clan anFaoileán, proud of himself to have done his job without misgiving.

The musicians amongst them remained on foot, their instruments ready, and the grand procession moved out of the village, forsaking the road, up over the hill, to the sound of the pipers and whistlers and harpers and drummers, playing an air in honor of the memory of the brightness of Mim's *shine*.

BECAUSE OF TRADITION THEY'D NEEDED TO PASS by the henge known as the Sea Gate that stood brooding, surrounded by the grave stones of the few priests buried there, a little to the left of the church and refectory of St Mary de la Mer.

Their passing stirred Father Joseph Dougherty from his troubled sleep and he awoke, disoriented. He wasn't dead then after all. Or was he? The music that had roused him was unlike any earthly sound. Or was it?

Confused and slightly disoriented he shoved his feet into his slippers and bundled himself into his dressing gown, throwing his overcoat over the top. His hand reached out to pour himself another tot of gin but, just this once, he thought better of it.

He stumbled through the dark room, wincing as his shin collided with something sharp, holding his hands out before himself in case of any other unseen obstacle that could hurt him.

He made the front door and pulled it open to a sight both terrifying and wonderful. Suddenly he was thrust back in time to when his Gran had whispered of legends and enchantments, and tales of the Gentry, before his family sent him away to boarding school where the Brothers had filled his head with another kind of story.

As a young priest he'd been shunted from one boring parish to another until his growing disillusionment could no longer be dulled without drinking. Until it became a necessary start to his day and, eventually, an embarrassment to the church governing body.

The archbishop's solution was peace and quiet and so he'd been sent here over two decades ago, where no one except the occasional visiting tourist came to confession or mass during the summer months.

Joseph was a lonely man.

He followed the procession, feeling very old and very tired and surprisingly unafraid.

...

ALL ALONG THE ROUTE TO THE BARROW THE TROUPING Tuatha Dé Danann picked up rocks, stowing them in pouches hung about their shoulders or else reaching up to deposit them into panniers that were slung across the horses' backs for just such a purpose, while within the depths of the Barrow, Hunter and Brighid prepared themselves in ritual finery not worn since the death of Nuala Tremenhere, six hundred and forty seven years before.

Hunter was the only one strong enough to move the King Stone and muscle and sinew heaved and strained against the enormous block of granite that moved inch by inch until the stairway beneath was revealed and accessible. The two passed down into the island's secret heart—a chamber hewn from the earth herself when the dreaming lands were still young, and the otherworld was this world.

Inside was the accumulated treasure of an immeasurably ancient race, the turned-to-earth-and-water ancestors of the long-lived fairy folk, scattered amidst the long-dead roots of an enormous rowan tree, that had once graced the summit of the Barrow, cut down by the vassals of a bitter chieftain, in betrayal of immemorial agreements between the race of humans and the elder race of the fairies: the legendary Quicken Tree.

From within a trunk of ornately carved oak Hunter first withdrew a cloak of ravens' feathers, their quills stitched together, layer upon layer, black within the blackness of the chamber, that Brighid donned, that covered her from head to toe, and secondly his own, made from the pelts of countless long-dead animals that had once roamed his domain—forest, fen and all the wild places—which he draped over his enormous, now-naked frame.

They exited the chamber and Hunter pushed the stone back into place while Brighid lit a waiting brand from the perpetual flame, nurturing it to brightness. The two made their way out into the night surrounded by the movements and flitterings of their anamchara—ravens, wolves and deer—walking unhurriedly towards the henge.

CONNOR, HUNTER SENT. *IT'S TIME. BRING HER NOW*, AS, stepping light for all his size, he entered the ancient site, whispering *Are you here, Milady?* Before sensing her all around him, empowering the menhirs and dolmens with a pale luminescence, filling the air with the scents of hyacinths and jonquils and other promises of springtime.

Brighid touched the firebrand to the pre-laid cauldron at the base of a wide, flat stone measuring twice the length and breadth of a man and half again his height. And they waited.

Connor lifted Mim's body into his arms and left the grove atop the Barrow, making his way down its slope and leaping effortlessly from its lip to the ground below. He was followed by Charlie.

They crossed the distance towards the henge as the procession of Dé Danann passed Mim's house to an outraged howling from within.

"Get that, will ya?" Aengus asked Pete Neath who walked beside his horse.

The accordion player broke away from the group and hurried through the turned-earth garden, opening the kitchen door.

Oberon rushed past him on three legs, scenting for Charlie and Mim and ignoring everyone else. Charlie registered his presence as the dog brushed against him before catching up with Connor who was laying his dead friend on the big wide stone.

Oberon lay down—a good boy.

Connor removed the queen's garments one by one until she was naked. He folded her hands upon her breast and kissed her on her icy lips before kneeling at the head of the bier while Brighid took Mim's measure with red thread.

The Dé Danann arrived and those on horseback dismounted. One by one they entered the henge to lay their stones, firstly around the body of the queen, then higher and higher, covering her entirely in a rounded cairn, where she would be left to the elements until only the bones remained. All but the skull would then be bound with the thread and consigned to the Samhain fires, adding her essence to air and earth.

The skull would then be placed alongside the ancestors, in its own niche, deep within the Barrow where the mementos of those who'd loved her would also lie.

THE MOONLESS NIGHT WAS AT ITS BLACKEST BY the time the ritual was complete, and the lament was played giving sorrow its rightful place. Hunter and Charlie helped Connor to his feet as everyone began to depart, heading for the village for the wake. He was okay; he'd had his time with her ghost. He knew she wasn't really dead. He passed a look to Hunter that the forest god understood, the latter nodding at the wild feral light in his friend's eyes.

"Raurie's on his way, *mo chroì*," Hunter assured him.

"You comin' with me?" the Sídhe croaked, turning to Charlie.

"I am that," the ginger haired Scot assured.

OBERON DIDN'T LEAVE; HE WAITED. HE'D BEHAVED himself long enough and when the air and land again were silent of the two-leggeds he raised his enormous wiry snout to the night and howled and howled.

Harry heard him. Scathach and her seven hounds heard him. So did every dog on Inishrún and across the water at Weary Bay.

The night filled with the unnerving sound.

Someone just died. Grainne clutched her throat at the instinctive thought and reached to turn off the television, as did everyone else in the village who heard the eerie cacophony; memory and superstition running deep. Those few with a loved one not with them were afraid.

JOSEPH DOUGHERTY HAD HIDDEN THROUGHOUT, LYING amongst the gorse and bracken. He was startled from his hiding place by a voice behind him.

"You gonna just lie there till you freeze?"

He sat up, visibly shaken and pale, as a young girl with ice-white hair and seal-black eyes, dressed in what he thought was a ridiculous concoction of clothing, plonked down beside him.

"Who... what are you?"

"Doesn't matter, me ol' son," she grinned. "But suppose you stop being stupid and catch up with the agenda."

He didn't understand and she laughed.

"They're havin' a big wake down in the Community Centre. Better food 'n' booze than *you're* used to."

"They won't let me have anything to do with it."

She flicked a stray lock of hair off her face, showering the priest with tiny icicles and he thought his heart would stop.

"Oh come *on*! You're talkin' yerself to death, you know that, don't you." It was not a question. "Of *course* they'll let you; it's a wake, duh."

"You think?"

"Trust me. I'm never wrong," and she mouthed a kiss before bouncing to her feet and skipping away in the direction of the Barrow, disappearing into the darkest hour.

The old man creaked as the stood. His slippers and dressing gown were drenched with dew that froze the garments to stiffness. The thought crossed his mind that he could get pneumonia and he snorted at himself as he began the long walk to town.

CHAPTER THIRTY

FELIX HAD ORDERED CALVIN AND THE TWO GUARDS, Lee Parker and Skeet Sheehan, to say nothing about anything to either those aboard the trawler or, later, to those on shore. If asked, they were only to say that he'd just purchased the *Squadron* out of Port Waldon and had taken her out on her first long cruise to see how she handled even in bad weather.

They were winched aboard *The Watchman* and hurried below decks to the galley while their craft was secured aft.

They'd spent hours adrift and their distress seemed real even though it was feigned by all except Tyler who hadn't stopped shivering since leaving the scene of the killing.

Liam McKenna was left at the helm to guide the boat to shore while Stan Rumford sat with the rest of his crew, including Robbie, quizzing the castaways, who were huddled over mugs of steaming tea.

Felix was calm, smiling, grateful for their safety as he explained who they were and their situation, expressing dismay at how a craft that had set him back a shitload of money, and that had such an amazing reputation, could simply die like that. He exhibited sufficiently justifiable outrage, he was certain, to convince the sailors of his credibility, assuring them that the manufacturers of the luxury craft would "hear from his firm" and compensate him accordingly.

What none of them realized, and what Felix had forgotten from

Frank's notes, was that Inishrún had a radio transmitter. Woolly had contacted the pub in Weary Bay after having worked his spell to flood the *Squadron*'s motor, a half hour before the procession, letting Henry Poe know what had happened and to not call in the cops from over at Leachfield; that the Travelers would be back and that it was their business to be sure, and asking that any boats to sea keep a lookout for strangers coming to port.

Henry had radioed *The Watchman* and every one of her crew knew what had been done on Inishrún.

…

"HEY RYAN, IT'S ME…"

The trawler was close enough to Weary Bay for Tyler to get reception to his cell phone and he needed to organize their return to New Rathmore in a hurry. Ryan was his manservant—a do-anything, fix-everything aide de camp.

"Oh, hi Mr. Tyler, how'd it go?"

"Shut up and listen."

He had the use of Solomon Stone's *Bell 206B3* charter helicopter along with every other partner in the firm. It seated six people easily and could be here in less than two hours as long as the Friday night traffic didn't catch his man on the freeway into the city. Ryan couldn't fly the thing but Mick Rice, one of *Earthly Graces'* dedicated party-boys, could. "Get onto him right now and call me straight back so I know it's been set up."

"You want us down there tonight?"

"I want you down here five minutes ago," and Tyler hung up.

How long would it take them to get here? Anywhere between an hour and a half and three hours depending on a multitude of things. No problem. Just as long as there was no contact from the island.

Fuckit, he fumed, his jaw working overtime. There was nothing to tie them to what had happened. Everything they'd told the

274

skipper apart from their visit to the island was true: Port Waldon; first day out; blah blah.

He was lawyer-enough to know that merely being in the vicinity of a crime was circumstantial.

Nothing.

He relaxed, his confidence asserting itself. Everything was covered.

. . .

THE *ROSIE RUA* ARRIVED AT SEAL BAY without incident.

Hunter, Brighid, Conner, Charlie and Woolly were already at the wharf and they boarded the Hooker before she even tied off.

They'd been at sea not ten minutes when the night seemed to fuzz with a wraithlike mist. In the following quarter hour it gathered in on itself like an old woman's memories, slowly blotting out vision, graying to whiteness.

Don't you bloody quit on me, Raurie challenged, as the breeze dropped to a whisper the closer they came to their destination. But that wasn't the Great Mystery's plan and the three black sails continued full.

. . .

FRANK HARVEY'S CAR CRAWLED INTO THE VILLAGE AT 10:40 PM, the headlights flinging their beam back onto the windshield as they struck the wall of fog; the washed-out yellow glow from many windows attesting to the *awakeness* of the town. What had he expected? That a tiny obscure place like Weary Bay should close up early?

Well that was all well and good because he was hungry.

He parked the car in the laneway down the side of the pub, noticing a light on behind the ripple-glass door upon which he could just make out a *Reception* sign.

Alice Poe was in the kitchen tidying up after the last of the meals, preparing a big tub of spaghetti bolognaise for the crew of *The Watchman*, when the bell rang.

She rinsed her hands and was still drying them on her apron as she pulled open the door, stepping back in surprise at the sight of the professor.

"Welcome back," she lied. He was the *last* person she'd expected to see today.

"I'm sorry to bother you this late."

"No bother." Alice opened the door wide enough for Frank to pass through with his overstuffed suitcase, eyeing it with trepidation. "You run away from home or summat?"

Frank chuckled. That *was* what he was doing, after all. "Is there a room?"

"Never been so popular this time o' year," Alice mumbled as she led Frank to the desk to sign in.

"Top o' th'stairs. Room four. Rest're empty, mind, but it's got a nice view o' th'harbour."

"Ah, would there be the slightest chance of a meal?"

"There'll be a spag bol ready in a wee while but that's all I'm afraid."

"And is the bar?"

"Yep," she finished for him, assuming he'd like a drink.

He took the key, smiling and saying thank you, and headed up the stairs.

Alice's brow scrunched as she made her way back to the kitchen wondering what were the odds of him turning up the same night as the castaways who she and Henry were sure had killed that lovely little woman from the island?

Alice didn't believe in coincidences.

. . .

JUST BEFORE ELEVEN THE FOG HAD INTENSIFIED AND visibility was no more than an arm-length ahead.

The pub had officially closed but was unlocked, and Scathach, flanked by Holly, Janey and the five youth, entered quietly, leaving the wolfhounds to watch the door.

"I'm closed..." Henry took in the sticks and bows that all but Janey carried. "What's all this then?"

"We're here for the visitors," she said, being the only local and feeling it her right to play spokesperson.

"You know?"

"Yeah, we know," Scathach replied, her face unreadable.

"Well ya can't stay here," Henry huffed. This all looked like more trouble than he wanted in his establishment and he was not about to have a shit-fight wreck his place when nothing was sure or proven. That Janey and the kids were with the outsiders was curious enough but that they carried weapons was something else again.

When none appeared about to leave he sighed. "You kids can't be in here; you're all under age and I'll not take on trouble, mind. So off y'all choof."

Janey was about to say that they weren't there to cause any trouble' but she caught herself. They were, weren't they?

"Sorry

Henry." She turned to the others, raising her eyebrows, and shooed them back out into the night.

"Plan B," she said softly to Scathach.

CHAPTER THIRTY ONE

RYAN CALLED TYLER BACK, ASSURING HIM that he'd organized the 'copter but the lawyer's phone battery had been about to give out, so he'd hung up. Fifteen minutes later when Mick Rice had called Tyler's man telling him all air traffic was grounded until the fog lifted Ryan had been unable to relay the bad news to his boss.

Felix and the others were unaware that the four of them were stranded in Weary Bay.

They and the crew of *The Watchman* entered the warmth of Henry's pub at 11:15pm, Felix checking his watch and Calvin clutching his carryall to himself, not willing to part with it for a second in case anyone was tempted to look within and saw the *Sauer*.

The cozy atmosphere from the open fire was offset by the icy attitude of the publican who took the men's orders for drinks, and wrote down how many of them were for a meal, refusing to meet the eyes of the strangers.

Then Frank Harvey entered the room.

A MILLION THINGS PASSED THROUGH MY mind, the professor was to recall later, *but the first was that they shouldn't be there. Why were they there? What were they doing with the fishermen? Why hadn't they answered my phone messages, or kept me informed of what they were doing?*

That only took a second, mind you. The looks on their faces when they saw me, well, that said it all as far as I was concerned. Betrayal; somehow it came down to that.

My second thought was how peculiar the fates are; at the overwhelming urge that had brought me here in time for this. I know now but I didn't then.

TYLER AND RIDDLE REGISTERED THE PROFESSOR'S entrance simultaneously. Rats in a trap. Felix would have dealt with him back in New Rathmore—the only person outside his cabal that could link them, beyond doubt, to Inishrún. He would have been erased.

But now? Here?

Calvin jerked from his seat and headed to the men's room, one hand over his mouth, willing himself not to vomit before he got there, the other on the strap of his belongings. *We're screwed*, his mind screamed.

Felix eyed the professor with an unveiled threat, followed by a conspiratorially raised eyebrow. *It's not over till the fat lady sings,* he thought to himself. *Just play it by ear. Maybe he'll get the message to just shut the fuck up.* Harvey, he knew, was implicated in this mess. Had, in a way, instigated the whole thing. He wondered if he realized.

Frank wasn't. And he didn't. He stormed across the room, his face red with rage.

"Why are you two here?" he demanded over the skipper's head.

"We..." Tyler began.

"There's been a murder," said Henry Poe, coming out from behind the bar, arms crossed over his chest.

Felix turned to him, confusion at how he knew battling the need to appear bewildered, unaware that the look he presented was that of an arrogance he had not intend to convey. "I'm sorry. I don't know what you're talking about."

"They're here because there's been a murder on Inishrún," the skipper repeated, ignoring Felix, directing his attention to the man he recognized from the ferry incident. "You know this lot I gather."

Frank stared from Rumford to Tyler and back again, momentarily stunned by what had been said.

"I'm, ah, I'm not sure I understand. What murder?"

"Mim Tremenhere. You would have met her. You were there."

The professor's mouth fell open and he reached out a hand to the nearest chair for support. What was going on? Had Tyler and Riddle...?

"What have you done?" he hissed, oblivious to the cajoling look from the Solomon Stone lawyer.

"*Nothing,*" Tyler fumed. "*I* don't know what these men are on about. I bought a new boat and my friends, and I had her out for the day; you just watch what you say here Harvey."

A sacred place, Frank heard again, from deep within.

Too much had changed over the past few weeks for him to disregard the mysterious small mantra that had accompanied him since his near-death experience. Listen, Frank, listen.

He sat down on the chair he had been unaware of holding, white-knuckled, and asked Henry if he might possibly have a Guinness; composing his thoughts while the publican grudgingly complied.

Listen.

For a mere moment no one spoke, and in the silence Robbie Freeman heard the distant sound of running. He headed for the men's room.

CALVIN DIDN'T KNOW WHERE HE WAS GOING. AFTER THROWING up until his throat was raw and all that was left was bile, he'd rinsed his face under the frigid cold tap before looking around. Part of his mind retained a clear understanding that he and Felix were probably still in control of the situation and that he'd be home in his nice, cushy city apartment in no time, but it was overridden by the knowledge of what he had done and the image of that woman's body jerking into the air as his bullet had torn into her.

Calvin was no longer rational. All these people were strangers. He was undone. *Sweet Jesus what have I done?* Over and over and over.

He was suffocating. He was not waiting. Nothing could have

induced him to go back into that room with those men, and now the professor. He was undone.

He carefully slid open the bathroom window and lowered his carryall to the ground before scrambling over the sill as quietly as he could, and on to the street, just as Holly and Janey emerged from the fog making for the pub door.

He panicked. He picked up his bag and bolted.

ROBBIE FREEMAN AND STAN RUMFORD HEADED for the door, almost knocking the two women over as they pushed past them, running in the direction of the footsteps.

Tyler thought quickly, years of strategy and professional acumen rising to the challenge.

"This entire situation is getting out of control," he said with authority. "Your threatening behavior has obviously compelled my partner to go looking for the police. I hope you realize that I can make you pay—"

"You fucking *liar,*" Frank screamed, scraping back his chair and heading for the larger table, rage in his eyes, yelling, *"I want none of this; I want none of it do you hear me?"*

And Skeet Sheehan stood and drew the Beretta from its holster under his jacket, pointing it wordlessly in the old man's direction, causing him to stop dead.

"Gentlemen," Felix said, "ladies," nodding to Janey and Holly, "my boat has broken down; we have spent hours freezing on the high seas; we are way past a scheduled return; my friend has disappeared; you have all but accused us of involvement in a crime to which we have had no part whatsoever, and my helicopter is due to land. Now this obviously deranged old man threatens to attack me and none of you intervene."

He was utterly composed as he and Lee Parker stood from the table, picking up their belongings and shouldering their packs, while Skeet continued to arc his gun across the company.

"These men are private security and are licensed to carry

firearms. They attend me on many occasions as a matter of professional protection.

"We thank you for your assistance." He looked from one to the other of the fishermen," but this situation is becoming a little too much like *Deliverance* for my liking." He actually chuckled, almost believing himself as he turned and walked towards the door, stopping in front of Holly and Janey.

"Could either of you ladies direct me to the town's park please? Our transportation is due to meet us there."

Holly smiled disconcertingly, seeming, he thought, impressed by his clear delivery.

"Two blocks up the road. Right next to the *Sizzlers*. You can't miss it."

He thanked her and the three walked out, pulling the door closed behind them, almost casually.

Janey and Holly looked at each other like butter wouldn't melt in their mouths as they approached the others.

HOLLY HAD REGISTERED CHARLIE'S EXPEDITION LEADER the moment she'd entered the room, deliberately maintaining a non-accusatory stance for the time being while putting two and two together and knowing both in her gut and by the looks that passed between him and the strangers, that he was somehow behind the night's events.

And knowing beyond all doubt that she was now responsible for the wellbeing of Inishrún.

Hadn't the Dé Danann asked her to intervene on the mainland on their behalf if the need arose? Hadn't she agreed—her and Charlie?

No more crap, she told herself. *You either live up to your commitments willingly or you slit your wrists.*

If the situation hadn't been so downright tragic and dangerous she could almost have laughed. Holly felt truly alive. More focused than she'd ever been.

283

She fingered the talisman beneath her layers of clothing as she and Janey sat at the table with Henry and the fishermen, ignoring Frank Harvey deliberately, knowing he would not, could not, get away. He would pay for her aunt's death. For what he had unleashed.

She didn't know how bright was her *shine*, nor how strongly the line of ancient queens fired her next decision.

"Janey," she asked, "will you fill them in? I have to get back."

"No," Janey stammered, unnerved by the look in her friend's odd eyes.

"Don't let him out of your sight." She glared in Frank's direction.

"Wait," The professor begged. "None of this was meant to happen."

"Then why did it?" Holly asked calmly.

The look in Frank's eyes, however, was not what she expected to see. It was oddly beautiful; filled with *something*.

"I fucked up before I understood," he said quietly.

She stared at him. He was pathetic. She didn't have time for this.

She kissed Janey on the cheek and went back out into the night in search of Scathach. He would wait, but the others had to be prevented from leaving.

THE HOWLING OF THE DOGS BEGAN AGAIN, RAISING THE HAIRS on Holly's neck as she ran quickly and silently through the dense fog in the direction of the park, just as the *Rosie Rua* dropped anchor.

CHAPTER THIRTY TWO

GO AFTER HER, FRANK.
What?
Go after her.
I'm going mad, and he smiled at the idea.
Frank!
Damn!

Frank lied to the men at the table, saying he was going to bed; *Ah, nah yer not,* they'd replied, right before the crack of gunfire broke the silence outside, scattering everyone into a panic.

Within seconds the pub was empty, except for him.

Fraank!

Yes, yes, I'm going, and he ran warily outside, unable to see further than a foot in front of himself.

Can't see a bleedin' thing.

Cross over the road. You're close.

Are you a figment . . .?

Not now Frank. Go save Holly.

I can't see.

Hey, I'm working on it. Cut me some slack.

He almost stumbled. *That* had not come from his mind.

Haunted, he thought, just as he had back in the days of his illness.

The sound of distant thunder rumbled out over the sea and the wind picked up, disturbing the fog into kaleidoscopic patterns.

Frank thought he heard the sound of a child, chortling with mischief, from somewhere in the murk, but that made no sense, like nothing made sense anymore.

WOOLLY, CHARLIE AND CONNOR FOLLOWED HUNTER AND Brighid unerringly through the dense, white night, catching up with Robbie and Stan at the entrance to the park. The skipper, broad as he was short, looked up at the five big men and then at the small, strange woman accompanying them, uneasy with it all. He'd never been comfortable with the Travelers, they were just too *other* for an ordinary man like him.

"I'll leave ya to it then," he growled. All except the grizzled old islander were younger than he was, and he felt superfluous; better off with his missus who was sure to be worried by now.

"Thanks a mill for everything," said Charlie, half an eye on Connor who appeared wild and distracted.

"Yeah, we'll sort it Stan, thank you," added Robbie. Why was he not surprised that Charlie was here?

A SOFT WHIZZ, FOLLOWED BY A SCREAM, CUT THROUGH their hurried goodbyes, and all except Stan Rumford—who didn't turn for home; didn't dare move—ran towards the sound, as the wind raced in from the sea and thunder cracked directly overhead.

Charlie fell over the body of an unknown man, pierced through the throat by an arrow, his gun still clutched in his stiffening grip.

"His name's Skeet-something," Rob offered, recognizing him. The Scotsman was even paler than usual, the freckles on his face standing out livid against the pastiness. He'd never seen a dead body, not in his whole life. "And who on earth's shootin' bleedin' arrows?"

Back in New Rathmore Raven had told the forest god of Scathach's visit, and Hunter figured the traditional goose-feather fletches kind of gave it away. But what was she doing here?

The rain began falling by the bucket load, tattering the fog into ribbons before dispersing it completely. The weather didn't make sense. Thunderstorms were unheard of this time of year and the flicker of ball lightening, lending a lurid strobe across the landscape, only highlighted the anomaly.

Suddenly Connor jerked to his feet from beside the body, his nostrils flaring, his teeth bared. Hunter and Woolly sniffed at the air, smelling it also. Mim; Mim's blood. Her killer was close.

In between the lurid flashes the night was utter blackness and Calvin Riddle was hunkered down, hiding behind the granite War Memorial that stood proudly beneath a fifteen hundred year old oak. At the very edge of the park. In the corner between the grassy area with its swings and slides and the stone wall that kept the high tide at bay. He squatted, shaking uncontrollably, the butt of his hunting rifle jammed against his shoulder, with the crazed idea that if he couldn't see them, his pursuers couldn't see him. He kept mumbling *It was an accident, it was an accident. I didn't mean it. It was an accident*, like a litany of guilt.

Brighid morphed. In the shape of a glossy black raven she lifted from the ground in the pouring rain and flew to the granite stone honoring the massacred, and landed bedraggled and ragged, peering down on the enemy.

Ark, ark, she stacattoed loudly.

Calvin panicked, nearly jumping out his skin as he corkscrewed around and looked up.

Brighid's head cocked to one side, fixing him with one white eye before ruffling her feathers to dislodge the wetness.

Hunter changed his shape to wolf; Connor to that of a hound, whilst Woolly stayed as a man. Charlie stood rooted to the spot in disbelief, while Robbie merely shrugged, unfazed. He'd believed the Dé Danann when they'd talked about shape-shifting back on the island all those weeks ago. The revenge, however, was not his concern and he stayed beside Charlie as the sídhe, joined by the seven ephemeral forms of Scathach's pack, encircled the killer of the woman whose blood they could smell where it had splashed onto the sweatshirt he wore hidden beneath his thick jacket.

Under cover of the icy, pelting rain and raging wind, with thunder still rumbling even as it abated, the three Dé Danann and seven hounds rushed Calvin Riddle before he could pull the trigger. They tore him to pieces, while Brighid bore witness.

The townsfolk heard but none dared venture from their homes. Some recalled the legends of the Wild Hunt when Gwyn ap Nudd wrought havoc through the winter nights, but most were simply afraid and that was enough to keep them behind locked doors. No one thought to pick up the phone to call the police; the Great Mystery made sure of that, sending out confusion: each person certain that someone else had done it already.

BARNEY RUMFORD WAS OBLIVIOUS TO IT ALL, MILES away in the comfort of his sitting room. All he knew was that he'd gone too long without his dinner. Where *was* Janey? Bloody woman. Bloody weather. Bloody visitors keepin' her away all the time. Still, the two weeks had come and gone; they'd leave soon, and things'd get back to normal. He lectured himself pointlessly from his chair in front of the telly before finally giving up and going to the kitchen to fry up some sausages. *I can make my own bleedin' dinner,* he huffed resentfully.

SCATHACH, ORLANDO, MERCY AND THE OTHERS HAD also marked the man cowering behind the War Memorial, but the warrior woman held them back when she'd sighted the Dé Danann with her hounds. She was still impressed at how calmly Mercy had taken out the fellow with the hand gun. The pale girl was shining with no hint of remorse. It was as though she'd banished a ghost.

Scathach wondered, fleetingly, where Holly and Janey were but things were too pressing. There were others responsible for Mim's premature death and they were yet to be brought to justice.

CHAPTER THIRTY THREE

THE RAIN CEASED ALTOGETHER, ALTHOUGH THE CLOUD remained low, blotting out the sky. The night was almost, but not quite, warm.

When Holly left the pub she thought she'd heard whispered voices and instead of making her way to the park where the citified stranger had told her he and his friends were going to wait for their helicopter she'd gone across the road to where the ancient stone wall guarded the town: a bastion against the sometimes-raging high tides that would have flooded in otherwise.

Not so tonight. The tide was way out, and distinct, faint whispers came from below on the pebble and shingle shore.

She felt along the wall until her hand had encountered a stile with steps leading down and she'd scrambled over the edge, more by feel than anything, and inched her way carefully down the moss-slippery stair.

She had no idea what had taken place in the park. Driven single-mindedly, towards the muted conversation—voices she could hear talking urgently—taking place in the lee of the jetty where Tyler and one of his friends crouched behind its relative protection just out of sight.

Holly made her way closer, as silently as she could.

"Man, this has to be the insanest situation ever!"

"Yeah, well we've still got to find Riddle. And we can't leave Sheehan behind."

"We could wait here till we hear the chopper coming."

"You don't think those crazy bastards are looking for us? Jesus, man, they'll be everywhere."

"Why'd your mate have to *shoot* her anyway? Man, he's *got* to be off his rocker! We gotta find him before he maybe lets loose on these folk."

"No way would he do that. He was just freaked the way she came at us."

"But a *woman*? And no weapon? Jesus."

"There's a bunch of loonies out there in the bushes with bows and arrows. Skeet's dead, and we have no idea where Calvin is, and a mob of pissed off local yobbos'll be lookin' for him *and* us."

"Try my phone again."

Pause.

"Still no reception."

Holly was freezing, her wet clothes turning to ice on her thin frame, her hands and feet numb. *I gotta get out of here; tell the others*, she thought as she moved sideways along the adjacent wall, needing to be somewhere warm really soon. But her foot slipped on the shingle and she just managed to stop herself from falling but not before the two men heard her.

Tyler and his buddy (holding his handgun out before him) scrambled around the corner and Felix grabbed Holly by the sleeve.

"Oh, it's you. You okay? Did you fall?" His tone was caring, conciliatory. Holly needed to be careful.

"Thanks. No, I'm fine."

"Hi, then. I'm Felix, and you are—?"

"Holly."

"You live here Holly?"

"No. Just visiting my aunt. That lady I was with in the pub," she lied, through chattering teeth.

"Oh. So what're you doing down here on the beach? Were you looking for us Holly?"

"No," she lied, scared.

"Shit, girl, you're drenched."

"Mr. Tyler…" His friend was still holding the gun, barrel down, by his side.

"What?"

"She'll let the others know we're here."

"No I won't, I promise." Holly pulled to move away, her body starting to shake from more than the cold, her lips chattering uncontrollably.

"Tsk," Felix clicked. "What a mess. Look, Holly, you've got to understand, we're not responsible for anything those people accused us of, okay? But we're in *Crazyville* and one of our friends is dead for no reason and the other one could very well be, we don't know. So we're not about to just walk out into the open and have some nutter take us out. We have to stay put until our transport arrives."

Holly couldn't speak she was shaking so hard. Maybe these two *were* innocent of the shootings. But they'd been with whichever of the others had killed her aunt and they still weren't owning up to that fact, so they weren't *that* innocent. "I've… got… to… go…" she stammered, fighting to loosen Tyler's grip on her arm.

"Sorry," he said, pulling her back towards the covey where they'd been sheltering. "Not till the chopper comes," and he pushed her down onto the stony wet ground fatalistically.

Holly didn't have the energy to fight; didn't know what to do. Tired. So cold.

I WAS SITTING BY THE FOREST POOL. THE AFTERNOON was soft, and a multitude of greens shimmered in their new foliage. I lived close

*by in a cottage with my family—had for all my life—being taught
the ways of earth and sea and sky for as far back as anyone knew.*

*But something was wrong; something had threatened. We'd
been hearing chainsaws for days and my father and brothers went
to find out what was happening and didn't come back.*

*I'd slipped out at dawn to come here and scry them in the
sacred pool.*

Oh, what I saw.

*Outsiders, taking down the forest. Big trucks; fifty or sixty men.
Cutting it away from the outside in.*

*My father and Jake and Thomas had demanded they stop. Tried
to tell them it was our home, that they had no right.*

They were attacked and it ended in their death.

*I was beside myself with the horror of it and didn't hear or
sense danger approaching; didn't know that one of the loggers
had followed the track all the way into the forest and was
watching me, leering, thinking of the sport.*

*The boar smelled the threat to one of the children of his
territory and ploughed through the undergrowth to warn me; to
stop the intruder.*

*I'd spun as he'd charged between me and the guy, squealing
his rage, his huge bulk heading straight for the stranger who
pulled a long, wicked-looking hunting knife to defend himself... he
threw it, toppling the boar, the weapon plunged deeply into its
shoulder.*

*I screamed and the outsider turned and ran back down the
path, and I went to where the enormous animal lay bleeding and
in pain.*

*I wasn't afraid of him; I knew what he was: a sacred thing; an
ancestral guardian of the forest.*

*As I knelt to remove the dagger a wicked pain shot through my
hands and feet; agony that made no sense.*

Holly came to consciousness cocooned in blankets, on a makeshift stretcher in the main room of the pub, with Charlie beside

her, holding her hands, the pins-and-needles in her extremities the remnant of the excruciating pain she'd felt in the dream.

"Holly? Wait; don't try to sit up yet." He stroked her face as her tears fell.

"Charlie?"

"Shh."

Her throat constricted at the unexpected emotion that flooded her seeing him here.

Stop it, she scolded herself.

Shut up, you, replied her inner demon. Or was it?

"Oh Charlie, I'm *so* sorry!" she choked. He bundled her into his arms, pressing his face against her hair, whispering soft soothing sounds.

Brighid, Janey and Scathach saw that she was awake and jostled each other to get to her, the small, dark Dé Danann growling at them to get out of her way.

"Let me check her first," she demanded. She crossed the floor and attempted to move Charlie who lashed out with one arm, telling her to wait.

Brighid *hmphed*, placing her hands on her hips and cocking her head to one side in feigned offence.

"I'm alright," Holly mumbled into Charlie's neck. "What happened?"

...

FRANK HARVEY PICKED UP THE NEAREST THING to hand—a weathered length of 4×2 that lay discarded amidst a pile of rubble and old crates, his only thought outside of the protracted two-way conversation with the ghost to save the queen of Inishrún. Somewhere within him a rational little voice explained that she'd been murdered already but that's not what his Mystery said, and *her* voice was more insistent than anything he could argue against.

Age and a lack of fitness were not a consideration as he leaped the wall, down the ten foot drop, onto the shingled beach below. His knees protested, despite his having bent them when he landed but that didn't matter. No thought entered his mind other than to help her, and he charged the corner, roaring with feral rage swinging his stick. Then he registered the woman he was committed to defend. Unnaturally still. Possibly dead.

His swing connected with the side of Lee Parker's head but not before the bodyguard fired off a single shot that took the old man in the shoulder. Tyler ran, sprinting along the high tide mark beside lines of stranded bull kelp, desperate to get away.

Frank knelt and took the unconscious woman in his arms. He was too old and out of shape to lift her and he howled with grief, thinking he had failed, oblivious to the blood that pumped from the bullet wound.

The whole town had heard his earlier roar—followed by the sound of a gunshot—and no one but Brighid, Mercy and three other of Scathach's warriors (for none could call them otherwise) were left within the park to watch over the bodies.

Charlie Freeman and his dad arrived at the quay ahead of anyone else and Charlie pulled Holly from the professor's grip, struggling to lift her. Carrying her to the pub's warmth as quickly as he could.

ROB, TORCH IN HAND, HAD KNELT BY THE OLD MAN whose jacket was crimson with his own blood.

"Shite. Hang on mate, there's others coming. You'll be okay." The look on Frank's face was one of abject sorrow.

"I lost her," he said softly. His jaw quivered and tears spilled over his cheeks. Frank didn't care who saw; what they thought.

"I think she's still alive," Robbie offered, not at all sure, as the others arrived.

They helped the wounded man to his feet but Hunter and Woolly needed to carry him for most of the way to the pub.

"Bring him too," Hunter had ordered Robbie and Orlando,

indicating Lee Parker who had been stunned, but not killed, by Frank's blow.

FELIX TYLER WALKED ALONG THE BEACH THAT extended well past the village until it ended at a promontory and up onto a track that forked left to the cemetery high up on the headland and onto the northbound road. He was determined to walk, if need be, all the way to the next town.

The night was clear, but the cloud cover caused a blackness almost as blinding as the fog had been. It took intense concentration to see the asphalt beneath his feet.

Keep going, keep going, he demanded of himself.

Terror had been an alien emotion to the lawyer, but he knew it now.

What he did *not* know was that Connor stalked him, silent; that he wasn't going anywhere; that the sídhe had lost the most important thing that had ever happened for him. No matter who had pulled the trigger, all those in collusion would pay the Piper.

Tyler was beyond the town. Ahead of him was deliverance from this nightmare and he began to jog. Connor didn't care. At this point he needed the hunt even more than he needed the outcome. He could drag this out for hours.

Then lights crested the rise ahead; four vehicles in a convoy towards Weary Bay.

Tyler didn't know what to do. Flag them down? Were they going straight through? Surely they were going straight through. Would they be stopped in the town? Shit, a vehicle was a way out of this wasn't it? Worth the risk. There mightn't be any other traffic through this fuckin' arse-end of the world until daylight. Even then it'd more than likely be a local.

He stood waving, caught in headlights like a rabbit. An old double-decker bus that looked as though it shouldn't be allowed on the road, not that it mattered under the circumstances, pulled over onto the verge, its motor idling as a side door concertina's open for him.

He stepped in, relieved by the pleasant-looking man behind the wheel.

"Break down somewhere?" the driver asked, smiling.

Tyler summoned his most charming face as he pulled himself up the step. "Sure did. Exploring side roads. Silly. How far...?" He froze as he sensed someone at his back. He turned to see a tall, wild eyed, hippy-looking man, with black hair streaked with silver hung in two long plaits over his chest, with dark circles under hostile eyes.

"Evenin' Rowan," Connor said, pushing the lawyer into the cab of the bus.

"Evenin' Connor," the driver replied, closing the door with the controls on the console and grinding the bus into first gear.

"Come on in, me ol' son!" someone called from the dim interior, where the faint glow of a tiny lamp showed the faces of a ragtag band, none of whom looked the slightest bit welcoming.

"Sit down," hissed Connor.

CHAPTER THIRTY FOUR

IT'S YOUR CALL," HUNTER said.

Connor considered what to do. He wanted justice; wanted the bastards dead. But they were unarmed, and neither had been personally responsible for shooting Mim or wounding Oberon.

He had to respond like a Dé Danann. Mim had taught him that; had been proud of him.

Felix Tyler and Lee Parker were seated on two chairs, side by side, watched by several of the Travelers, while others in the crowd made themselves at home.

All of Fíach Dubv and their companions, had been aboard the bus, and Liath Leannán's clan had caught up with them, in the other three vehicles, for the last leg of the journey. Scathach, Janey and the young people who trained with the warrior were present as were the crew of *The Watchman*, Raurie Mór, Hunter, Woolly, Henry and Alice Poe, and Robbie and Grainne Freeman. Warmly dressed, Holly was cared for by Charlie Freeman, while Brighid, at the back of the room, worked fruitlessly to save Frank Harvey who, although conscious, kept slipping into a seemingly delirious discussion with some invisible presence. He had told the whole story, implicating himself.

Connor badly wanted the old man here along with the others responsible. But he'd have to wait. And he'd have to think again because the professor *had* saved Holly's life and all was not as it seemed, because her recurring dream had ended with the astounding revelation that Harvey had been assigned as her guardian; that he was the boar and had not been her enemy after all.

"I've thought it through," Connor began, unsteady on his feet through grief, supported on one side by Willie the Red, the fiddler from Fíach Dubv, on the other by Liath Leannán who had already asked if he would travel with her and her clan for a while, to which he'd agreed.

"And I'm callin' up the ancient curse o' exile: banishment beyond the seventh wave."

He moved in close to Felix Tyler, pointing his index finger at the man's heart.

"And I lay a geas upon you and yer man both…" he looked with loathing from the lawyer to Lee Parker and back, "that should you survive—make it to land—you take this whole thing no further, and you make up a reason that yer friends died, tyin' nothin' of us to you. You and no one you know are to come near us ever after, nor mention us, or the events, to anyone at all.

"If you break this geas—I curse you now—the sea'll rise up to drown you, the earth'll open up to swallow you and the sky will fall to crush you."

An Tribhis Mór—the Great Triskel—had not been invoked since before Christendom and the Troubles, and the fairies were exceedingly impressed that he remembered the binding after all this time.

Connor stumbled away from the living men who had taken away his love and reached for the glass of whisky on the table beside him, taking a hard mouthful before leaving the room with Liath Leannán.

Hunter sighed, fearing how the wild sídhe would fare, knowing he could do nothing.

"Okay, get them to their craft. Stan, would you and your men do the honors and tow them out beyond the seventh wave?"

"How far's that, lad?" the skipper asked him, before shrugging, embarrassed. "Sorry, o' *course* I know how far."

FRANK HARVEY'S HEART GAVE OUT JUST AFTER DAWN despite everything Brighid had done to save his life.

He sat up and started his conversation with the unseen entity, seeming to argue in good humour. He died with a smile on his face; an inexplicable flurry of icicles falling from his hand that had been closed since the shooting.

Brighid was singing his spirit to Tir na n'Óg when the whole crew returned from setting Mim's murderers adrift.

Connor took up a shot glass and downed the dram of whisky in one gulp.

"You gonna take to the road with us?" asked Willy, pulling up a chair in front of his friend. Afraid. Knowing that now he had time to dwell on Mim, that he could likes as not get old and die of sadness.

"Conner?"

The others formed a protective circle around him that included Charlie and his dad.

"I s'pose so," Connor mused, lost.

"Ow!" Holly clutched at her chest. "Ouch!"

Hunter stood and walked towards the door.

"What?" Brighid demanded, confused.

"Holly?" the big man said softly. He knew. She looked at him while pulling the talisman from beneath her sweater.

"It's burning," she replied in wonder.

"Did Mim teach you?" And he opened the door onto the deep night.

"They're going to betray us, aren't they?"

"Bastards!" Connor was set to kill. He'd swim to the launch if he had to.

Holly leaned into Charlie and kissed him. "I have a duty," was all she needed to say.

"Can you do it?" Hunter said gently.

In response Holly folded herself back into her warm jacket and passed Hunter out into the calm black, followed by the scraping of chairs and the stomp of boots as the others followed her.

SHE STOOD AT THE EDGE OF THE WATER LOOKING OUT over the gentle breakers as though to pick up the minds of her aunt's killers. Realizing she was queen. Feeling nothing of the latter and everything for the former. She was going to kill tonight. She had a choice, and this was it. She knew, with every fiber of her being, that she *was* the island as much as every rock and stone.

"You don't have to do this," Charlie whispered into her ear, his lips a caress.

Brighid's grip on his arm just then was painful. "Now's when you better love her enough," she said softly.

"I'm not *sure*," Holly moaned to Hunter.

"*Think*," hissed Brighid.

"Shut up, woman," Hunter responded. "Give her time. She taught you, didn't she Holly?"

All was silent but for the susurration of the water on the shore. Connor stood behind Holly and gently placed his hands on her shoulders. Charlie took her hand, loving her enough to trust that what she did was right.

Holly's breathing was deep and ragged. She closed her eyes.

One by one, then by the dozen seals poked their heads above water, darker than the night, their presence the power of the wild things to listen. To back her.

HOLLY OPENED HER EYES AND LOOKED OUT over the vast ink of ocean under a leaden indigo sky. An acceptance overtook her. She *was* queen of Inishrún and protecting it was the same as being its mother.

The ancient Irish curse began haltingly.

"Le carraig, abhainn... Le carraig, abhainn agus báisteach...

Hunter?"

"It's right, *a cara*. Only you can do this. It has to be the queen of the island. It's the way of things."

"Le carraig, abhainn agus báisteach. Le farraige, spear agus grian." She had it.

The wind stirred and Connor squeezed her shoulders gently.

"Le uisce, gaoth agus ton. Le talamh, gealach agus réalta. Le tinteán, baile agus treibh. Le breith, beatha agus grá. Le misneach, cear agus draíocht Le onóraigh, fírinne agus ansinseara. Le ríocht, ceart agus le banríon Inishrún…"

She yelled as the wind rose to a shriek like metal on metal and the seals vanished beneath the rising waves.

"AnÉagóir Leasaigh. Ansídhe Cosain. AnRúndiamhair Mór díoltas. Tiarna Inishrún." The massive mountain of storm hit with a power beyond anything she had ever experienced. Holly's face was ethereal, Connor pensive, Brighid and Willie visibly shocked.

"All hail the bloody queen," Hunter sighed under his breath as he led them all, like savage heroes, back into the warmth of the pub.

Far out to sea the Squadron sank with all aboard her.

CHAPTER THIRTY FIVE

One White Stone

"The small white stone held the soul of Inishrún within it so that the sweet song of the island could guide her back when she was ready."

WOOLLY HELPED CHARLIE BUILD the shed out in the orchard.

Its four corners were of mortared island stone into which great beams of recycled timber had been fitted to form the struts and lintels supporting wide sliding glass doors instead of walls, and they'd even had a double-glazed skylight worked into the thatch of the roof.

Just one room, a desk, a generator-fed computer, a couple of old sofas and a half a dozen plump colorful cushions, scattered willy-nilly across rugs that covered the rammed-earth floor.

The walnut tree was garmented in little buddy pale green leaf shoots, and the ancient pear, apple and quince trees were awash with blossom. The air sang with the sound of bees and the scent of hyacinths and jonquils drifted through the open door on the buttery sunlight.

Another Samhain gathering and another wild winter had come and gone and Inishrún was still a secret. Holly was big with hers and Charlie's baby and she could no longer sit on the floor, as she would have preferred, amidst the notebooks and bits of paper full of ideas that the two had worked on for over a year.

They'd spent the cold season getting ready; mulling over just how to start the book they'd agreed to, and Charlie was as patient as a man could be knowing that sooner or later Holls would write what he couldn't—he was an academic, after all.

Clan Fíach Dubv was camped out near the Barrow; had been for weeks, mainly 'cause Brighid needed to be close, what with her being midwife, along with everything else—organizing life the way she did—and Robbie and Grainne, Wolf Kain, David Rushton, Scathach and Janey Rumford would all be sailing over from the mainland this Friday for the countdown: the week the baby was due.

"Just go make tea," Holly ordered with a huff and a grin. "I can't think with you hangin' around so much."

"Sure, but have you got all those notes I wrote on Tir na n'Óg?"

"No. Okay, so let's find them, *then* go make tea."

Charlie grinned. He'd gotten *really* proficient at distracting her over the past few weeks. She'd mellowed, maybe.

HOLLY DIDN'T REALLY NEED ANY MORE OF HIS NOTES. SINCE just past a year ago when the fairies had come by the boatload at Imbolg, and the rituals, feasts and ceremonies proclaimed her as the rightful heir to the line of legendary queens, *and* she'd announced Charlie as her consort (they'd been lovers for weeks and weeks already), Inishrún had become an epiphany of 'rightness': rocks and forest, sea and sky, everything that swam or walked, or called from the treetops; that spoke to her of being home.

Oberon and Harry hadn't left her side since she'd returned, and she'd learned to ride Cloud like she'd been born to it, making early morning forays—alone, mostly—to deepen her understanding of, and communion with, the mysteries and spirits and soul of the land.

The 'dark' days of her past, the murder of her aunt and the threat from those who had no right to threaten, had only, after all, forged her will and awoken her clear-mindedness. She felt no guilt. What she had done she had done for love. She had claimed her birthright and knew that as long as she lived she would protect this family.

She was carrying a daughter.

BETWEEN THE WORLDS, DOWN BY THE FORGOTTEN LAKE, THE goddess dressed down: a tiny thing of a tartan skirt over yellow and white striped stockings with the feet cut out so she could feel the sand squish between her toes, a black tee shirt with an anarchy symbol proudly proclaiming itself on both back and front, her bare arms reflecting the gold of the perpetual autumnal sunset, and her short red hair (this time), spiked up every which way.

Walking beside her, peaceful, ever-so pleased to be there, was an enormous boar, and the two chatted about nothing in particular, content with each other's company.

Joseph Doherty still said mass and heard confessions in the summer, for the tourists, but the rest of the time he hung out with the other old guys on the island, swapping the bottomless gin bottle for a pint or two at the pub each evening, talking about the weather or the day's catch, getting invited to any of the do's they had and coming to understand his God in a whole new light.

EPILOGUE

Some time way into the future

NEW RATHMORE WAS ONLY ONE OF UNCOUNTABLE cities in upheaval and devastation. There were mass protests on the ruined streets as people sought justice and, let's face it, food to eat. The internet was down for most people. Since the banks and large financial institutions of the so-called free world had closed their doors to the lower classes no one was safe. No one knew where their next meal was coming from and martial law had been in force for three years.

Connor, his hair now streaked with silver, still appeared as though he was in his thirties. He had been on the road with the whole of the clan of Fíach Dubh, including Scathach and her hounds.

Their lives had not been affected by the massive collapse as they were at home taking a living from the land.

Connor had left them to take a solitary road, but Scathach and her hounds had followed him in search of action, leaving Mercy behind to learn from Brighid. To grow up enough for Raven to love her.

Connor had promised to catch up with them, for Samhain on the island, but something had drawn him to the city. At the wrong time of the year. Into this mess.

He and Scathach had joined this latest protest over even tougher food stamp injunctions. These were people who had a right to justice. They had not brought this down on themselves. There had been no safety net and yet the wealthy did not suffer.

Revolution was as inevitable as Connor's empathy.

They and her wolfhounds were close to the front of the protest line when the troops in tanks or on the ground, dressed in black armor, their visors hiding their identities, their shields bullet-proof, had opened fired on the protestors with both rubber bullets and live ammunition, creating chaos and screaming.

The dead lay where they were but some dragged wounded into alleys or the relative shelter of abandoned department stores, already looted but temporarily safe.

Connor was grabbed by the sleeve by a strong, wiry arm attached to the skeletal frame of a young man who looked like something out of Dickens. The look he passed the fair man gained his immediate trust and, crouched low, he led the way deeply into a warren of alleyways that wound their way through the old part of the city—one that Connor had travelled many, many decades ago—and onto the familiarity of where the old shunting yard met Wharf Road. Connor ran by his side as they turned the corner into Copperhead Lane, the part of town still more alive than any other. The docklands had always been the forgotten part of the city, attracting artists and misfits, the fey and those hardened by neglect. They were still there in the shops abandoned a century ago when the money had run out and the power gone off.

They finally filed into a narrow passage between two boarded up shops, around a corner and into what was once a pretty warehouse garden, long since gone to ruin. Something very familiar stirred in Connor's blood but it was so obscure it slipped like mercury from his senses.

The young man slid to the ground, his back against a wall and Connor joined him. Scathach stayed standing, the wolfhounds close.

"Jack Doff," he grinned, a gold front tooth glinting, wiping sweat from his eyes with the back of his cutoff, gloved hand.

He wore a battered and filthy cap, a vest and jacket over an old sweater, wore ex-army camouflage trousers and thick, steel-capped boots. Around his hips was a wide mesh belt sporting all manner of things from a wickedly long hunting knife in its sheath, binoculars and a crowbar to handmade, leather medicine pouches, beaded and stitched with colored thread.

"Connor. You're name supposed to be funny?" And the two men shook hands in a warrior grip. "My friend here's Scathach."

Jack nodded at her.

"Where we going?"

"You two look like you know how to fight but there's nothing to be achieved by marching."

Connor pulled his old tobacco pouch from his coat pocket and rolled himself a thin cigarette. "You know a better way, I suppose?"

"We know a better way."

"Who's "we"?"

Jack stands and wipes the grime from the seat of his pants.

"C'mon, we're almost there."

They walked the remainder of the twists and turns until arriving at a blank sheet of a warehouse, its concrete façade pock-marked with rust. To the ordinary mortal this was a long abandoned building but Connor and Scathach could sense the hidden eyes. Dozens of hidden eyes, and the hounds' hackles rose as they walked in stiff-legged wariness.

Jack knocked on a narrow steel door in a series of almost-silent, ratatat-tat-tattoos and it was opened immediately by a dark islander man, even bigger than Hunter, with a face marked by intentional scarifications. One white eye attested to blindness and he was covered in well-crafted ink.

"C'mon in," Jack beamed, "and meet the queen."

"Your... Your *what*?" Connor stopped in his tracks, the unfamiliar term accompanying a wave of isolation.

Jack merely grabbed him by the arm and pulled him inside.

"The hounds okay?" Scathach asked the guard, who smiled and nodded in such asway as to suggest anything she wanted was okay.

"I'll be here until nightfall and I'd love some company when you settle in," he said, his voice gentle in a mockery of his appearance.

He was exactly what she needed, and she assured him she'd be back before following Jack and Connor into the building, ghosted by the hounds.

Inside is vast. Furnished. Livable. Hundreds of people sit around talking, reading or working on weapons of which there were abundance.

The entire back wall had been graffitied into a cornucopia of delight: gardens and food and market stalls with happy people sharing laughter and their bounty. In the center was a slogan that said *The People for Self Determination.*

In a half-shadowed corner was a table littered with used coffee cups, books and scattered with maps and journals.

She wore baggy khaki trousers and a sleeveless t-shirt, her long, black dreadlocks wound into a bun and piled on the top of her head. It was Mim. Writing in furious concentration. Ignoring jack and Connor as a distraction she could ill afford.

"Miriam?"

"Go away, Jack."

"Miriam, we got new people if you're okay with it."

She slammed the pencil down and looked up, from Jack to Connor, back to Jack. Her face giving nothing.

"You brought them here why, Jack?" Her voice was ice. But it was her voice. Connor was giddy, disoriented. His heart pounded, sweat ran down his back. His hands shook.

"We was getting shot at. They was using live ammo. You want I should take 'em back?"

She looked across at Scathach who was deep in conversation with the guard on the door, and back at Connor, getting lost, for just a moment, in the blackness and depths of his eyes before remembering her authority.

"What the fuck am I going to do with you?" she said, flatly.

He just stood there mute.

"Come and sit and tell me who you are. But forgive me if I don't trust you.

"Miriam."

"Sit."

"Miriam, I'd forgive the world for you."

Olympic Games 2000, Australia
Opening Ceremony

ABORIGINAL DANCER AND SONGMAN DJAKAPURRA Munyarryun represented the ancient spirit of this land. A young white girl approached him, and he guided her through a journey of Australia's history to the beat of sticks and song, awakening the ancient past and the spirits that represent it.

The girl was shown a representation of ancient Australia—a continent with a culture over 40,000 years in the making, and over 600 indigenous nations. Members of over 250 groups came forward and called the Dreamtime spirits—asking visitors to listen for the sounds of the earth.

What followed was something that has never happened before. Members of different ancient nations from all over the continent came together and presented their contributions to the journey. Starting with over 300 women from central Australia, dancing *The 7 Sisters*, they embraced the past for the young aboriginals of today. They prepared a welcome for the 'rebirthing' as one mob—the youth of today and the ancient culture. The Flag Song was performed by the people of Arnhem land, known to have traded with Asia over 4,000 years ago.

The Rhythm Dance was next, a gift from the Torres Strait Islanders, celebrating the energy of northern Queensland, before the Dungdung (red kangaroo, represented by the sound made by the large animal as it bounds across the land) welcomed the members of the western New South Wales nations.

With most of the representatives now gathered, the Smoking Ceremony commenced to cleanse the air; to cleanse the meeting place: Stadium Australia. Once that happened all the spirits were awakened, called by Djakapurra, and from the Western Australian region came the long leggeds, who called upon the great spirit from the Kimberley region of northern

Western Australia, one of the oldest lands on earth, to join the gathering and help guide the future. It rose slowly, with eyes and nose, but no mouth with which to pass judgment.

The girl's journey then took on a totally different air. From the harmony and spirituality of the original inhabitants, the beauty and glory that arose from the ferocious forces of nature, to the arrival of European settlers.

As the forms that created the kaleidoscope of color representing the Australian native flora and fauna scattered, a large caricature, representing Captain Cook and European settlement arrived center stage, carrying with it an interesting representative cargo— a rabbit.

But then a steel horse, representing the new 'technology' arrived in the arena, surrounded by other Australian icons, such as galvanized iron water tanks, and corrugated sheets of iron representing the wheels of agricultural machinery making their mark on the landscape.

With the spread of agriculture into the rich and fertile country west of the Great Dividing Range, came an increasing dependence on wool, cattle and wheat. The big properties—some covering thousands of acres (and it was illegal until the 1950s, mind you, to leave any trees standing on these big properties) and into the arena came the musterers, their dogs and the shearers who would travel from shed to shed. Rural Australia had arrived.

From here sprung the 'great Australian dream' to own your own 'block' be it a few hundred thousand acres in the outback, or a simple quarter acre in suburbia, Australians all wanted their piece. And with that quarter acre came the *Victa* lawnmower. And I watched, stunned, as packs of lawnmower-wielding performers marched proudly into the spotlight, wondering how this was supposed to fill me with national pride.

The girl watched this scene unfold—this part of Australia's

history—and walked out to meet the monolithic monster representing the arrival of the 'technical' age. It lowered its huge steaming head, dwarfing her. And she offered it an apple.

I was horrified. Who had we become?

In an era of reality TV and puerile sitcoms, when the nightly news is all quite tragic and the terms 'economic growth', 'consumer spending', 'yearly net profits of . . .' are the current barometer of the supposed health or illness of our civilization, and where war and terrorism are the headlines lauded by every tabloid, and where the words competition and development are repeated so often they threaten to anaesthetize us, where are we?

The cultures of both east and west are in danger of the broad-sweep loss of uniqueness and identity. What, of any depths, will we leave our children? They, their children?

Without roots we are lost. Without community we are devoid of solace and true belonging. Without a creative understanding magic becomes marginalized to a "thing done" by kooks and whackos.

Back in 2002, a workshop, one of the people present asked me to explain just what magic is. I laughed. I asked him if he could spare me the next year or two of his life, then I added "Nah. Let's not bother!"

One cannot define magic, just like one cannot define things like wonder, life, love. You know them when you experience them. They're something that doesn't make sense to everything we are taught to consider rational.

When you experience magic it's like what I imagine Dian Fossey felt when the young male gorilla she'd named *Peanuts* touched her hand, accepting her without saying "...and what do *you* do?" Without asking her to give a reason why he should. Magic is about connection; belonging to the whole of everything makes sense.

Around two thousand years ago the Roman Empire invaded Celtic lands. There've been umpteen invasions since then and slowly but surely the indigenous ways of an entire culture have been blanketed, marginalized, condemned or trivialized to the point that we forget deep roots, and many people do not even realize that the 'West' *has* a spirituality; its own unique sacredness.

Only recently have these suppressed cultures begun to reclaim themselves, mainly through the revival of their ancestral languages, because, in many ways, it is language that could be said to define culture.

But so many of the stories are relegated to the past!

Most texts I have read use the words *was, then, were, once,* as though the people, gods and goddesses, spirits, faith, knowledge of how to live presented to us through allegory, celebrations of the sacred, are not still here, yelling at us, through everything from our unease to the freaky weather, to pay attention.

Facts, text books, can only do so much.

Without art, story, song, dance, music and poetry they are dull; presentations of one-dimensional opinion or theory; limiting.

Well, anyway, you tell me.

What happens for many of you when you hear bagpipes?

This story is going to end up on the fiction shelves in the bookstore where you buy it, but the Tuatha Dé Danann aren't fiction; the sídhe aren't a fiction and neither are fairies as this story portrays them, the seasonal festivals aren't a fiction, and neither is the Otherworld. That everywhere, still, there are sacred sites, and traditional ways of living that don't fit into the ideal of uniformity, isn't fiction.

The misappropriation of indigenous lands certainly is not fictitious. Holly's feelings? Well, we've all been there to some degree or other. People like Felix and Calvin? We all know of people (corporations or governments) like that.

We are educating the future generations in all kinds of ways, I know, but I ask myself: with how much joy?

United Nations Declaration of Human Rights

Article 1

All human beings are born free and equal in dignity and rights. They are endowed with reason and conscience and should act towards one another in a spirit of brotherhood.

Article 2

Everyone is entitled to all the rights and freedoms set forth in this Declaration, without distinction of any kind, such as race, colour, sex, language, religion, political or other opinion, national or social origin, property, birth or other status. Furthermore, no distinction shall be made on the basis of the political, jurisdictional or international status of the country or territory to which a person belongs, whether it be independent, trust, non-self-governing or under any other limitation of sovereignty.

Article 3

Everyone has the right to life, liberty and security of person.

Article 4

No one shall be held in slavery or servitude; slavery and the slave trade shall be prohibited in all their forms.

Article 5

No one shall be subjected to torture or to cruel, inhuman or degrading treatment or punishment.

Article 6

Everyone has the right to recognition everywhere as a person before the law.

Article 7

All are equal before the law and are entitled without any discrimination to equal protection of the law. All are entitled to equal protection against any discrimination in violation of this Declaration and against any incitement to such discrimination.

Article 8

Everyone has the right to an effective remedy by the competent national tribunals for acts violating the fundamental rights granted him by the constitution or by law.

Article 9

No one shall be subjected to arbitrary arrest, detention or exile.

Article 10

Everyone is entitled in full equality to a fair and public hearing by an independent and impartial tribunal, in the determination of his rights and obligations and of any criminal charge against him.

Article 11

(1) Everyone charged with a penal offence has the right to be presumed innocent until proved guilty according to law in a public trial at which he has had all the guarantees necessary for his defense.

(2) No one shall be held guilty of any penal offence on account of any act or omission which did not constitute a penal offence, under national or international law, at the time when it was committed. Nor shall a heavier penalty be imposed than the one that was applicable at the time the penal offence was committed.

Article 12

No one shall be subjected to arbitrary interference with his privacy, family, home or correspondence, nor to attacks upon his honor and reputation. Everyone has the right to the protection of the law against such interference or attacks.

Article 13

(1) Everyone has the right to freedom of movement and residence within the borders of each state.

(2) Everyone has the right to leave any country, including his own, and to return to his country.

Article 14

(1) Everyone has the right to seek and to enjoy in other countries asylum from persecution.

(2) This right may not be invoked in the case of prosecutions genuinely arising from non-political crimes or from acts contrary to the purposes and principles of the United Nations.

Article 15

(1) Everyone has the right to a nationality.

(2) No one shall be arbitrarily deprived of his nationality nor denied the right to change his nationality.

Article 16

(1) Men and women of full age, without any limitation due to race, nationality or religion, have the right to marry and to found a family. They are entitled to equal rights as to marriage, during marriage and at its dissolution.

(2) Marriage shall be entered into only with the free and full consent of the intending spouses.

(3) The family is the natural and fundamental group unit of society and is entitled to protection by society and the State.

Article 17

(1) Everyone has the right to own property alone as well as in association with others.

(2) No one shall be arbitrarily deprived of his property.

Article 18

Everyone has the right to freedom of thought, conscience and religion; this right includes freedom to change his religion or belief, and freedom, either alone or in community with others and in public or private, to manifest his religion or belief in teaching, practice, worship and observance.

Article 19

Everyone has the right to freedom of opinion and expression; this right includes freedom to hold opinions without interference and to seek, receive and impart information and ideas through any media and regardless of frontiers.

Article 20

(1) Everyone has the right to freedom of peaceful assembly and association.

(2) No one may be compelled to belong to an association.

Article 21

(1) Everyone has the right to take part in the government of his country, directly or through freely chosen representatives.

(2) Everyone has the right of equal access to public service in his country.

(3) The will of the people shall be the basis of the authority of government; this shall be expressed in periodic and genuine elections which shall be by universal and equal suffrage and shall be held by secret vote or by equivalent free voting procedures.

Article 22

Everyone, as a member of society, has the right to social security and is entitled to realization, through national effort and international co-operation and in accordance with the organization and resources of each State, of the economic, social and cultural rights indispensable for his dignity and the free development of his personality.

Article 23

(1) Everyone has the right to work, to free choice of employment, to just and favorable conditions of work and to protection against unemployment.

(2) Everyone, without any discrimination, has the right to equal pay for equal work.

(3) Everyone who works has the right to just and favorable remuneration ensuring for himself and his family an existence worthy of human dignity, and supplemented, if necessary, by other means of social protection.

(4) Everyone has the right to form and to join trade unions for the protection of his interests.

Article 24

Everyone has the right to rest and leisure, including reasonable limitation of working hours and periodic holidays with pay.

Article 25

(1) Everyone has the right to a standard of living adequate for the health and well-being of himself and of his family, including food, clothing, housing and medical care and necessary social services, and the right to security in the event of unemployment, sickness, disability, widowhood, old age or other lack of livelihood in circumstances beyond his control.

(2) Motherhood and childhood are entitled to special care and assistance. All children, whether born in or out of wedlock, shall enjoy the same social protection.

Article 26

(1) Everyone has the right to education. Education shall be free, at least in the elementary and fundamental stages. Elementary education shall be compulsory. Technical and professional education shall be made generally available and higher education shall be equally accessible to all on the basis of merit.

(2) Education shall be directed to the full development of the human personality and to the strengthening of respect for human rights and fundamental freedoms. It shall promote understanding, tolerance and friendship among all nations, racial or religious groups, and shall further the activities of the United Nations for the maintenance of peace.

(3) Parents have a prior right to choose the kind of education that shall be given to their children.

Article 27

(1) Everyone has the right freely to participate in the cultural life of the community, to enjoy the arts and to share in scientific advancement and its benefits.

(2) Everyone has the right to the protection of the moral and material interests resulting from any scientific, literary or artistic production of which he is the author.

Article 28

Everyone is entitled to a social and international order in which the rights and freedoms set forth in this Declaration can be fully realized.

Article 29

(1) Everyone has duties to the community in which alone the free and full development of his personality is possible.

(2) In the exercise of his rights and freedoms, everyone shall be subject only to such limitations as are determined by law solely for the purpose of securing due recognition and respect for the

rights and freedoms of others and of meeting the just requirements of morality, public order and the general welfare in a democratic society.

(3) These rights and freedoms may in no case be exercised contrary to the purposes and principles of the United Nations.

Article 30

Nothing in this Declaration may be interpreted as implying for any State, group or person any right to engage in any activity or to perform any act aimed at the destruction of any of the rights and freedoms set forth herein.

Who were the key contributors to the drafting of the Universal Declaration of Human Rights?

Eleanor Roosevelt (United States of America), Renй Cassin (France), Charles Malik (Lebanon), Peng Chun Chang (China), Hernan Santa Cruz (Chile), Alexandre Bogomolov/Alexei Pavlov, (Soviet Union), Lord Dukeston/Geoffrey Wilson (United Kingdom) William Hodgson (Australia), and John Humphrey (Canada).

Signatory countries of the UNDHR –

Afghanistan, Argentina, Australia, Belgium, Burma, Bolivia, Brazil, Chile, China, Columbia, Costa Rica, Cuba, Denmark, Dominican Republic, Ecuador, Egypt, El Salvador, Ethiopia, France, Greece, Guatemala, Haiti, Iceland, India, Iraq, Iran, Lebanon, Liberia, Luxembourg, Mexico, The Netherlands, New Zealand, Nicaragua, Norway, Pakistan, Panama, Paraguay, Peru, Philippines, Siam, Sweden, Syria, Turkey, United Kingdom, United States of America, Uruguay and Venezuela.

GLOSSARY OF UNUSUAL TERMS

Ard-filíocht—high poet

Anamachara—(lit: "soul friend"). In the context of the story the anamachara (also simply known as anam) are the totemic allies of the sídhe and the fey. The anamachara are 'spirit friends', often genus loci

Banríon— High queen

Barm brach— Traditional Irish spiced fruit bread

Béansídhe—A woman sídhe

Billy—A metal tin with a handle used in the bush to boil water for tea

Bodhràns—Traditional Irish drum

Brat— A form of cloak. The brat would usually be fringed and trimmed with fancy stitching and was almost always woven in colorful patterns of some sort, either variegated with stripes or plaid patterns, or of solid colors edged with other bright colors.

Brándubh—Traditional Irish board game

Breacan feile—A belted plaid

Canopic jar—Used by the ancient Egyptians, in the mummification process, to store the vital organs

Curragh—Small Irish boat made of leather

Docker—Slang for a dock worker

Dumnonach—The pre-Roman name for the tribal people inhabiting the lands in the (current) Cornwall area of ancient Britain

Empathy—An individual with the psychic talent to pick up on emotions of people, other species and often objects and places

Faídh—Fey, or cannie

Fairies—*fae or Good Folk,* the name of the spirits of place, in later years denigrated to an illusion for children

Fíach Dubh—Raven (lit: dark hunting), the name of a clan of Tuatha Dé Danann

Geas—Magical obligation (similar to a taboo but individual rather than cultural)

Guesting law (*an* aíocht)—An obligation to feed and host any guests as honored visitors

Henge—Henges are circular enclosures (most often stone) marked out by an earth bank and an inner ditch. They often have one or two entrances. Sometimes internal pits or circles of post-holes can be seen. They are often found associated with a range of other monuments including barrows and processional avenues. They date to the Bronze Age (2500BC to 800BC) and were used for religious or ceremonial purposes.

Hooker—Three-sailed sailing boat, native to Galway, Ireland

Imbolg— (pronounced *imelick,* lit: *in the belly*) The ancient Fire Festival that heralds the reemergence of spring on the Celtic Wheel of the Year. Also called The Feast of Bride, Oimelc and, since the advent of Christianity: Candlemas

*Imramma*Literally *wonder voyage* it is considered the journey of the soul through all the worlds and all of 'time'

Inishrún—Isle of Secrets

Keen—Gaelic: Caoine (pronounced *keena,* the anglicized word became keening). This is a great lamentation, traditionally interspersed by periods of praise for the dead.

Lios naTine—Circle of fire

Mo cridhe—my heart (Scots Gaelic)

Mo chroí—my heart (Irish Gaelic)

Mór banríon—Great queen

Oíche Shamhna—Samhain

Priteni—*painted people, or tattooed people*

Proddy—Slang for Protestant

Samhain—Traditionally October 31st in the Northern hemisphere, this sacred day of the ancient Celtic people is also known as New Year to many pagan people, including witches and druids.

Scéala—stories

Seannachai—storyteller (considered a sacred art)

Selkie—The seal-people. They are known to shed their seal-skins to walk on land as hum

Seventh wave—In the Celtic tradition to go "beyond the seventh wave" was to disappear entirely; to be banished beyond the seventh wave was to be cursed with permanent exile.

Tai-bo—A form of cardio-vascular exercise combining martial arts movements

Teamhair— (pronounced *tahra*) ancient place of the high kings of Ireland. The most important socio-political sacred site of pre-Christian Ireland to both human and Tuatha Dé Danann

The Folk—Descendants of the Tuatha Dé Danann

The Lost—Humans who are naturally draíochta (magical)

Tuath—Both the clan and the territory within which the clan dwell

Tuatha Dé Danann—A race of people with magical abilities. They inhabited Ireland prior to the Milesians. No one knows what became of them, but legends abound.

Uillean Pipes—Irish pipes that use bellows and chanters

Uiske beatha—Whisky, literally *water of life*

REFERENCES

The Galway Hookers, by Richard J Scott, 3rd Edition, 1996.
http://www.galwayonline.ie/history/history2/hookers.htm

A Short History of Crofting in Skye, by Jonathan MacDonald
(curator, Skye Museum of Island Life)
http://pages.eidosnet.co.uk/~skye/crofting.html

Fishing Boats—crew
A typical trawler crew would consist of the Skipper, Mate, Bosun
(Boatswain), Chief Engineer, Second Engineer, 2 Firemen, 1
Radio Operator, 1 Cook and 5 or 6 Deckhands (Deckies).
http://www.nettingthebay.org.uk/explore/deepsea/fishermen.htm

The International Foundation for Human Rights and Tolerance—
United Nations Universal Declaration of Human Rights
http://www.humanrightsandtolerance.org/udhr.html

CPSIA information can be obtained
at www.ICGtesting.com
Printed in the USA
LVHW022140170720
660993LV00009B/266